Bonita's Quest

SEQUEL TO BONITA (1)

Carl R. Brush

Inks and Bindings
888-290-5218
www.inksandbindings.com
orders@inksandbindings.com

Contents

Chapter One

Blockade

"You live an unsavory life, Bonita Kelly. Your parents were horse thieves. Your business partner, that disgusting Sylvia Gonsalves, is a prostitute. You live in a hotel instead of a proper house. You are unfit to enter my home, let alone associate with my daughter. Miguel and I won't allow it any longer."

Flora Torres and I faced one another in the library of the San Francisco hillside mansion built by her dead father, Benito Alvarez. The place reeked of the same fusty odors of old leather and stale cigar smoke he left behind. She gestured to the maid who had escorted me into the library. "Laura will show you out." Her lips squeezed together like pincers. Her husband, Miguel, was away on business, as he so often was, leaving her to manage. And she was managing with even more than her usual ferocity.

Her arms folded like scissor blades across her chest, and she stood so straight and stiff I wanted to cut her corset strings, fancying she'd go all wobbly like a marionette. The image amused me, but I couldn't indulge in humor now, not with her stern dark eyes locked so intently on mine. I held my gaze as steady and fierce as hers.

"Two years I've been calling on Margarita," I said, using the name Flora had given my daughter, instead of 'Bonita', the name I had bestowed but had yet to broach with her. "Piano lessons, games, stories.

We have delightful visits. You know she calls me Tía, her make-believe aunt, and she relishes our relationship. Why issue this decree now?"

"I should never have let things go this far, but now it's over. From this day forward, you will not cross our doorstep. Now, if you please. . ." She pointed toward the door, but I stepped toward her instead of away.

A gray cat suddenly scampered across the room toward me. I knelt and invited Chuckles into my arms. She cuddled there, meowed, then purred. I looked up at Flora, whose hands were fisted in irritation. I smiled and got to my feet. She knew me and my determined personality, so I was puzzled that she thought she could get away with this.

Flora's father had stolen my Bonita from me at birth in 1847. Benito Alvarez probably considered his action as merciful, or at least presented it that way to his childless daughter. The infant was a child of rape, after all, the progeny of an attack on me by several members of a gang calling themselves the Bear Republic who had occupied Maríano Vallejo's rancho during the swarm of conflicts that led to the Mexican-American war. I was not only a young woman with no husband. My Bonita's father was unknown. Unknowable.

For years I had searched for her. Then the miracle. She returned to San Francisco as a six-year-old, the adopted daughter of the Torres family who assumed control of Alvarez's affairs after his death. I knew her at first sight, because looking at her was like looking in a mirror. The Torres family knew nothing of me, though. Not then. But they certainly did now.

Rather than declare the truth to Bonita and attempt to tear her away from the woman she had always called Mother, I had befriended her and the family, assumed the role of an imaginary aunt in order to have at least some contact with her. The whole time I was waiting for an opportunity to take things further, but nothing had yet presented itself. Now, eight years after the original kidnapping, Flora was attempting to repeat her father's crime. This time, I wouldn't allow it.

"Since you choose to avoid my question," I declared, "I'll answer it myself. With Chuckles' help, of course." I held the animal up and rubbed noses with her. "You are issuing your proclamation now because Margarita is beginning to suspect the truth, beginning to wonder if I am not her pretend aunt, but her mother. You've been doing a pretty comical Mexican Hat Dance trying to avoid some of her questions.

"And I admit I have, too. Logical questions about the similarity in our looks and the dissimilarity between hers and the rest of the Torres family. It's obvious how comparatively pale and blond we are, for example. The more questions she asks, the harder it is to come up with answers, and the longer it goes on the more likely you are to trip over your own fancy stepping and land flat on your duplicitous nose."

She drew herself to an even sterner height. "Inventing answers to Margarita's queries is a burden you'll no longer have to bear, since you will have no more conversations with her."

I stepped closer. We were inches apart now. I smiled.

"You know, Flora. I thank you."

She started back, a question in her eyes.

"I've avoided revealing all this to Bonita because I thought it would pain her too much to find out you were her pretend mother instead of her real one. But now, I will hold nothing back." I went right on without waiting for a response.

"Let's start with these accusations against me. You brought up Sylvia Gonsalves." I started circling her.

It felt good to be on the offense. It was as if a boil had been lanced, the pressure relieved as the infection poured out. I felt like dancing my way around her, but I only sidled slowly as I spoke. Her head wagged back and forth in confusion, trying to keep track of me.

"Yes, Sylvia owned a brothel. But now she and I own and run successful businesses. Real estate, a drayage company, and more. And well you know it. Many of the businesses are managed by the very women Sylvia once employed in the brothel. She rescued them from perdition, Flora, and her spirit is as pure as any nun's. So Bonita can be proud of who I have become, not ashamed."

"Once a whore, forever stained," Flora said.

"Oh, there's one for the ages," I said. "Very Christian."

I reversed direction as I continued to wind my way around her. She had quit trying to follow my movements and now stood solid as a maypole in the center of my circle.

"As for my parents, I wish I'd begun earlier to clear their names. I delayed because I must leave this city to do it, and I didn't want to give up time with my daughter. But I will go after that proof now, proof to erase the so-called stains on my character and establish legal verification of my motherhood. On that day, my Bonita and I, as daughter and mother, will together dance an Irish jig out your front door, and neither you nor any judge will deny us. Look forward to that day, Flora. It is sure to come. And soon."

Chuckles squirmed her way out of my arms and bounded from the room, doubtless to join the girls in their play. The proof of motherhood I'd mentioned to Flora was the testimony of the midwife attending Bonita's birth. She'd agreed to take the stand if necessary, but I hoped never to bring the matter to court because she was a member of a prominent family and would undergo considerable embarrassment should she appear. Not to mention the hurt the revelations would inflict on Bonita herself.

I left Flora, my heart pained at parting from my daughter, but my feet as light as if I floated down a path toward redemption.

Chapter Two

The Quest Begins

A torrent from above and a muddy stew below. Those are what I remember about that July day in 1855 when my friend and protector, Luis, and I entered New Orleans. We rode a pair of exhausted horses and led a faltering pack mule. That poor animal, Romero we called him, was all that was left of the three-mule train that had accompanied us when we left San Francisco. The bodice and skirts I wore were mucked and muddy and sagging, and I felt as if I were about to sink into the swamp.

My gorge rose and I swallowed hard to remember watching one mule, Camille, tumble and roll down a cliff in the Tehachapi Mountain wilderness, scattering provisions and garments across the landscape as she smashed our trunks and her poor body among the boulders. I'd wanted to climb down and try to recover some of the cargo, but Luis, ever the wiser one, stayed me.

Our mouths were dry, our tongues swollen with thirst when I'd been forced to lay a pistol to the head of the mule, Mateo, who had split his hoof and laid himself down on the trail under the blazing heat of the Texas desert. Luis had offered to perform the execution, but this quest was mine. I was determined not to play the squeamish lady every time we faced a painful necessity. I pointed the pistol barrel, turned my head, and pulled the trigger. And on we went, our physical burden lighter, our spiritual one a bit heavier.

Now, we had finally reached our destination. However bleak it appeared in the moment, I was sure better times awaited. I crossed myself and whispered another *Padre Nuestro*, an offering of sorrow for the trunks we'd had to leave behind and for the sacrificial mules who had died in our cause. Finally, I sent out an offering of thanks for our safety after our grueling two-month journey.

"We are here at last, Bonita." Luis gestured like a master of ceremonies as we approached what appeared to be a lake, but which I knew was a river whose dimensions my San Francisco senses could not comprehend as a stream. And hard though it rained, the air was still warm. Another anomaly. Likewise the swirling odors of rot and decay that rose from the swampy earth.

The torrent washed away some of the optimism I'd expected to feel at this moment of arrival at the place where I'd hoped to prove my parents' innocence and return home to claim my daughter as my own. At that moment, the so-called charming metropolis they'd nicknamed the Crescent City, after the sharp bend in the Mississippi beside which they'd built the main part of it, appeared that day to be no more than a cluster of hovels.

"We should never have come here, Luis," I said.

He laughed. "If it were not for your stubbornness, Bonita, we would still be in San Francisco fighting the Torres family on our home ground."

"Yes, yes, Luis, I know. It has always been like this. I ask. You refuse. I insist. You relent. You have always been the adult to my child. You are ten years older, after all, yet you can never tell me 'no' and mean it. Now look at us."

He smiled, his white teeth shining even in the gloom. Water poured from the wide, flat brim of his *vaquero* hat, which still somehow managed to look fresh with its white horsehair band. I should have been wearing one of those instead of the oilskin hood that dripped water down my nose and chin and into the neck of my bodice.

"Tell you 'no?' I do not have that power any more than I can turn the tide or stop the wind from blowing. I could not when you were twelve. Now you are a woman grown and I had no hope to persuade you away from this expedition."

"I do give you credit for trying."

"But you are displeased that I failed. Perhaps I should leave."

I knew he didn't mean it, but I shivered at the thought of life without Luis. He was head *vaquero* on Rancho Sausalito, where I grew up. He'd been like a big brother to me. Somehow, his feigned threat dissolved my anguish and fed my courage. I smiled back at him.

"It was my fear speaking, *amigo.* If I cannot prove myself worthy of my daughter, I have no future in this world. If I am to succeed, we must begin here. And how, I ask you, could I manage without my knight?" I gestured toward him, palm up and open.

"Or I without my Monita."

"Monita" was Spanish for "little monkey", an endearment he'd used for me since I was a child. In this context, it was an uncharacteristically sentimental comment for Luis, and I sensed his discomfort. He backed off it quickly, for which I was grateful. "But for now," he said, "we must stop babbling and find our boarding house or we will drown before we can begin our work."

The stinking mire—mud mixed with manure and slops and garbage—sucked at our mounts' hooves. We passed the great Saint Louis Cathedral, which I hadn't been able to spy in the mists from farther out. Along the way we shouted requests to passersby for directions and listened to replies we could scarcely understand, so thick were the accents, even when they were shouted in English instead of French. At last, we managed to find our way to the house on Conde Street, owned by one Angelique Chevalier, a former madam and close friend of the Sylvia Gonsalves Flora despised so much.

I had known Angelique a little in San Francisco, but it was during the days when I had been but fourteen years old, disguised as a boy and playing piano in Sylvia's brothel, El Marinero Feliz, The Happy Sailor. Years later, Sylvia closed her establishment and she and I set ourselves up as entrepreneurs in gold rush San Francisco. Angelique was unlikely to remember me, but I trusted Sylvia's letter had reached her.

Luis hurried up the steps and knocked, which brought forth a woman I assumed to be Angelique herself, accompanied by three servants. They were all three of them Negro—a somewhat rare sight compared to San Francisco where Mexicans and Indians did most of the menial work. The three worked as a team, sporting large umbrellas to help us up the steps to the wide veranda.

"Bring the baggage inside, Michael," Angelique called.

"These two trunks is all, sir?" the man named Michael called to Luis.

"Yes, Michael," Luis said.

"For all that way?"

"Unfortunately, yes," Luis said.

I explained, "We began our journey with much more, but Providence intervened. We thank Heaven that we have arrived with our lives and our health."

Angelique smiled and laid a sympathetic hand on my shoulder. "An arrival both *triste et huereuse*, sad and happy, then. We will hear more of your adventures later. For now, we must see to your comfort, *c'est vrai?*"

"Thank you, Angelique," I said.

"You are a godsend," Luis added.

While the servants readied our rooms, Angelique ushered us into the parlor, which exuded a tangled combination of odors, among which I detected lilac and mothballs. Angelique's hospitality lived up to her heavenly name, and we felt snug in her cozy parlor. Still, I couldn't wait till the servants finished their preparations so I could bathe and climb into bed.

"My dear," Angelique said, "how different you look as a *jeune fille splendide* than that little boy with such spirit making sweet music at El Marinero Feliz."

"You remember me, then?" I was surprised. "Maybe Sylvia mentioned me in her letter."

"*Non, non, non, bien sûr* I recall like yesterday. How all our lives have changed since then. But *ma chère*, so little is your baggage. Sylvia wrote to tell of your mission, so ambitious, and I despair that you seem not to have all you need."

"We lost a great deal on the trail. If the need for finery arises, I'll have to acquire it here."

"Ah, I know *coutourières manifiques* here who would be happy to stitch together whatever you like. *Bien sûr* you need rest, and I am talking too much, but so I can help you on your way, what will be your first task once you are refreshed?"

"We must find out why my parents were here all those years ago and why they fled," I said.

"*Oui, je comprends.* But how will you do this?"

"We have a letter from the sheriff, so we hope to talk with him first," I said.

"One Andrew Carew, as we understand it," Luis said.

"Ah, and he is indeed the sheriff, and him I know quite well." She clapped her hands and smiled. "*Alors,* I will send him *la message personalmente*," Angelique said.

Another servant appeared at the bottom of the curved stairway. The woman spoke in the musical dialect of the islands.

"Mademoiselle, Monsieur, mo' betta dey dreams for you uppa de stairs."

"Very good, Monique," Angelique, said. "If you please." She nodded in the direction of the stairway, and we gladly followed, though I had no confidence that my dreams would be as pleasant as Monique suggested.

Chapter Three

Waiting for Carew

The next day dawned bright. It looked as if it there had not been a drop of rain for weeks, unless one lowered the eyes to the scattered puddles. The air was more humid than at home, but not uncomfortable, and the sweetness of the honeysuckle vine that surrounded Angelique's veranda replaced the thick, unpleasant odors of the day before. I managed to scavenge a presentable outfit from our remaining trunks—a wine-colored broadcloth dress with a muslin underskirt—that I thought would be suitable for our meeting with sheriff Carew.

Except, it turned out, our meeting with Sheriff Carew was not in the immediate offing. Despite our note of introduction from Angelique, he put us off over and again.

His letter to me, dated nearly a year earlier, stated that my parents, contrary to the wanted flyer issued by one Daniel Delacroix, were not being sought by the law in New Orleans for the theft of $5,000. We thought he'd be glad to see us and help correct the error. But still he kept us waiting. Three days hence, we secured an appointment. It was for three days later than that. At least we finally had a time.

And then the rains returned. We trudged to Carew's office at the appointed hour. That hour came and went. The new showers reinvigorated the stench of the mud. We waited and waited under a narrow parapet, its scant protection augmented by one of Angelique's umbrellas.

Finally, Luis said, "*Mira,* Monita. Look at that."

And indeed, it was something of a spectacle.

Sheriff Andrew Carew of Orleans Parish was a very fat man. Luis and I had first thought that he'd kept us in the rain because he was engaged in some important law enforcement business. When we saw him at last, we speculated that it might have taken that long for him to waddle his way out of the saloon and across Rampart Street to his office where the downpour washed over and around us.

His bulk forced him to swing his legs in semicircles as he mounted the two steps to the boardwalk, reaching under his Macintosh for a ring of keys as he approached the office door. A gesture toward his hat brim was his sole acknowledgement of our presence. The rude door swung open, revealing an office whose luxury contrasted with the roughness of the building's exterior. Another of the disagreeable odors I'd encountered in this new city drifted through the room.

A large desk faced us from the opposite wall. A brace of chairs upholstered in fine leather stood before the desk, a great chair behind it. A fine carving of blind justice, her scales raised high, adorned the front of the desk. I decided to take the carving for an augury of fair treatment, but my fists clenched and unclenched with anxiety. The strange odor I'd detected earlier intensified. After being put off for so long for no discernable reason, I suspected that justice was not what we would find here.

Carew hung his raincoat on a rack and his hat on a wall hook, gesturing to us to do the same with our dripping outer garments. He had yet to speak a word. He had apparently missed his lessons in southern hospitality.

I leaned over and whispered to Luis. "Will he help us, do you think?"

"*No sé,* Monita, but I am by your side as always."

We sat and waited for the sheriff to turn our way. But he was not yet ready for us. He grabbed a big ring of clanking iron keys from a nail, stomped to another door, a much heavier and more ornate one than that at the entrance, unlocked it, and swung it back to reveal a barred door close behind it.

My confidence began to falter once more. I whispered to Luis. "We should never have left San Francisco. They cannot refuse—"

Luis held his finger to his lips.

"But she is my own child."

He placed a finger on my lips. I clamped my teeth to quell my anger and sat back.

Carew kicked at the bars and yelled, "Bodine, you still in there?"

A guttural voice from somewhere in the shadows answered, "Now, where would I go, Carew?"

"I was hoping maybe you'd escaped somehow. I'm tired of you. Mabel feed you this morning?"

"Mabel ain't never fed nobody nuthin' worth eatin'."

"Don't like the food at this hotel, don't check in."

Carew selected another key from his clanking set, opened the barred door, rolled his way down a short hallway and around a corner.

Luis took the opportunity of the fat man's absence to say, "Monita, we have discussed this so many times. We have the letter." He patted the satchel that held the tantalizing note that had brought us to New Orleans. "We will find the proof you seek. Then Flora—"

"The make-believe mother," I said.

"Flora," he continued, "will then have no excuse to keep you from Margarita."

"*Bonita*, not Margarita, Luis, is her true name."

"*Bonita*," he said, smiling.

Carew emerged presently, following a short man in a coonskin cap with a nose red as a railroad lantern. Carew ushered him to the front door and pointed the way out into the rain.

"Now git you a jug and haul yourself up to Natchez or over to Alabama or anywhere else I don't have to drag your drunken self in here and look at your damnable mug."

"Now, you know you'd miss me, Andy."

"Watch your tongue. I'm Sheriff Carew to you just like to everyone else." He shoved the man out the door. "Now git." He slammed it behind him.

The prisoner gone, Carew finally plopped himself in his chair and turned his attention to us. Of a sudden, I knew where the strange odor I'd detected came from. The sheriff was not, apparently, a frequent bather. He smiled as if he'd been looking forward to our meeting for a long time. Perhaps this was the southern charm we'd been waiting for.

I took the lead. "As our note and the one from Angelique Chevalier explained, we have journeyed far and are quite anxious to talk with you."

"Yes, I received both of those missives. Intriguing, to say the least. Now, you're the famous Miss Kelly I've heard so much about. Or is it Richardson you go by nowadays?"

My anger had built so much that I was in no mood for niceties. "Since you know enough to ask the question, you obviously know the answer, so I'm wondering why you asked me to explain."

"It's not the kind of story you hear every day, and I wanted to make sure I had it right. You thought you were the Richardson niece till you found out your true parents, named Kelly, somehow made their way from here to San Francisco and got gunned down as horse thieves by the *vaqueros* of the man who raised you as his niece?"

"Yes," I said. "Correct. And I'm sorry for my sharp manner but we, my friend Luis Mendez and I, we've come a long way to find out the New Orleans part of my parents' story and we're anxious to get on with it. Can you help?"

"Your Mescan, is he?"

"Luis is neither Mexican nor my possession, Sheriff. He's as much a citizen of this country as you or I, and he's here to assist me in my search."

"You speak English, boy?"

Luis smiled, shrugged, and looked at me, as if he were asking for translation. I grew impatient with both of them.

"Sheriff, I've left my business and my niece behind in San Francisco, and I am anxious to get on with this." Why I'd referred to Bonita as my niece, I wasn't sure. Perhaps I wasn't comfortable revealing too much in front of this stranger. "Is there anything you can add to the information in this letter you sent? Can you put me in touch with this Delacroix person you wrote us about?"

I pushed toward him the letter he'd sent almost a year earlier.

September 4, 1853
Dear Miss Kelly,

Am in receipt of your inquiry regarding Michael and Fiona Kelly. I have more information than I could impart by telegraph. Hence, this letter.

The Kelly's are not wanted by the law in N.O. The poster you saw was manufactured by one Daniel Delacroix, a man of questionable reputation in these parts. There was some altercation between the Kelly's and Mr. D. regarding unpaid wages, and they apparently took it upon themselves to relieve him of what was owed, then disappear. Mr. D. claimed he was missing not only the amount in dispute—$500— but another $5,000 besides.

We were unable to verify any of his story, so dropped the inquiry. However, Mr. D. chose to pursue the matter himself. It is interesting that the poster has traveled as far as Calif. However, we have no interest in the situation and leave you to resolve it in any way you see fit.

Sincerely,
A. Carew, Sheriff, Orleans Parish

The paper was soft as cloth from my handling it so often, but the name in question was clear, right where my finger was pointing. He glanced at it, took the note, folded it and pushed it back toward me.

"We'll get to all that in due time. Just a caution for you, Miss Kelly. You'll find hereabouts it sometimes doesn't do to come in breaking down doors and breathing fire. You're likely to get less of what you bargained for in one way and more in another."

"Your tone is insulting to the lady, Señor," Luis said. I held up a hand to silence him, but it was too late.

"So, you have some English, do you?" Carew said. "But you wouldn't answer when I asked you."

"Your tone was insulting to me as well."

"Oh, was it now?" the sheriff said. "Look. Miss Kelly and Señor Mendez. I don't care an alligator's burp in the swamp whether you allow people to sully your honor or defend it to the last drop. That's beside the point. You're here to find some information, correct?"

I nodded.

"So, despite your rather abrasive manner, I'll give you a little primer on how to get it. Folks hereabouts are going to assume like I did you either own this Mescan or he's a servant. Best not to raise suspicion, which means he gets rid of that pistol. Slaves with weapons make folks nervous. The knife is okay. Just a tool. If you challenge the local assumptions, you'll get all argument and not a shred of knowledge."

Luis surprised me then.

"It is good advice, *alguacil. Cerrada la boca, los oídos abiertos. Es verdad,* Monita?

"Mouth closed, ears open. You have the idea, *hombre.*" Carew winked.

Luis and I sat in a moment of silent astonishment at Carew's understanding of the Spanish, then all three of us broke into laughter.

Since childhood, I've been possessed of a certain clairvoyance that allows me entry into the emotions and even the thoughts of some people. It took me some time to understand that not everyone is capable of this insight, which as a youngster I took to be as natural as eyesight itself. I couldn't understand when others found some of my remarks puzzling or even frightening. Over the years, I've learned to keep the knowledge to myself, but I still haven't learned to predict what, or who, will trigger it. The power had grown stronger since I'd reunited with Bonita, but, maddeningly, it was still something beyond my control. Thus it is both gift and curse because I sometimes find out that which I would rather not know, yet I'm often blocked from that I long to discover. I sensed a benevolence in this fat man, but there hovered a shadow behind his good will that I could not read.

I decided to follow his advice and remain silent, waiting for him to speak. Finally, he said, "Now, about that letter. You'll most likely find Delacroix in a mud hole of a bar a few blocks off Jackson Square, name of Adelita's. Anything you can do to get him out of New Orleans, we'd both be better off."

"Would you like us to get rid of anybody else for you? Your friend Bodine, perhaps?" I said.

Carew smiled broadly.

"I can take care of that cantankerous fool, thank you. However, another word of advice. Very few females enter that bar except for nefarious purposes, if you catch my meaning. It is a dangerous place, and what you see and hear could be rather shocking."

I presumed Carew didn't know about my stint as a piano player in Sylvia's brothel. At fourteen, I got away with disguising myself as a boy, and I'd seen more of life than I ever would have as an innocent in skirts. Nor did he know about some of the other depredations I'd witnessed and suffered over the years. I doubted anything I found at Adelita's would have the power to shock me. But I might need this man again, and the more important he felt, the better chance I had of acquiring his help.

"Thank you, Sheriff. I'll take care. And Luis will be at my side."

I stood, as did Luis. Carew remained seated, but he did lean forward and extend an arm across the desk.

"I wish you both the best of luck with that scallywag. He can be a dangerous man, but he's the place you have to start if you're going to solve your mystery."

We both shook Carew's hand, retrieved our raingear, and headed toward the door.

"Oh, by the way," Carew said, "since it's getting on toward dinnertime, you might want to try Pierre's down by the wharf. Gumbo like it's supposed to be."

Chapter Four

Adelita's

The worst thing about Adelita's was the smell. Or smells. Carew smelled of violets in comparison. It reminded me of low tide at home without the saltwater tang. I surmised that the flesh of multitudinous creatures and tons of vegetation lay rotting in the river mud that surrounded the hut of a building that looked more like a derelict shack than a proper business. Decaying planks bridged the puddles between the path and the front door. Luckily the rain had let up, and we were not further dampened on our walk from Carew's office. The improvised bridges sagged under our weight as we headed toward the entrance, often dipping into the pools they were meant to help one avoid.

In an almost comical attempt at elegance, a railing from a riverboat deck adorned the front of the roofline. I wouldn't have been surprised if the whole place was built of lumber salvaged from a wreck that had once shared the fragrant mud with the rest of the decayed matter.

Inside, the ceiling was low, the lighting dim. We could barely see through the tobacco and lantern smoke. There was just enough illumination to note six small tables, a rudimentary bar consisting of mismatched boards nailed to barrels and hastily varnished. Here and there I could make out shadowy figures in a variety of seated and standing positions. Another incongruous touch of sophistication was a large mirror, perhaps six by four feet, hanging behind the bar. Its reflection showed a couple in one corner who appeared on the verge of engaging in an activity not generally performed in public, even in El Marinero Feliz. None of the three men seated at separate tables took notice. Two of them stared at their empty glasses. The third sat with his face on the tabletop amid a scattered deck of cards. He seemed incapable of noticing anything. We crossed toward the bar.

The barkeep wore a shirt with French cuffs and ruffles. It had once been elegant, but now was ragged and soiled. Tall and thin to the point of emaciation, with his ragged mustache and a face that hadn't come within shouting distance of a razor in some days, he appeared as tattered and dilapidated as his shirt.

"Good afternoon," I said. "We are looking for a Mr. Delacroix."

The barkeep shrugged.

"Sheriff Carew said we might find him here," Luis said.

"Ah, Officer Carew." The bartender's speech was as elegant as his attire was tattered. "That corpulent gentleman is sometimes right, but often wrong. Mr. Delacroix may or may not be available. What is your pleasure?" He gestured toward the shelves back of the bar.

The thought of actually partaking of any beverage this place might sell turned my stomach. "Oh, I don't think—"

Luis poked me in the ribs and shot me a look. "The lady will have a glass of your finest beer. I'd like a boilermaker."

"Fine. From your manner of speech, Miss. . ."

"Oh. I'm forgetting my manners. I'm Miss Bonita Kelly." I held out a hand, which he grasped with his palm up. For a moment I thought he was going to kiss it. I was relieved that he didn't. "And this is my friend, Mister Luis Mendez." Luis nodded.

"You can call me Gator." He leaned over the bar, growled and chomped his teeth. I jumped a bit, startled. He bellowed with laughter, much beyond the appropriate degree of amusement for a rather anemic joke, I thought. "Always gets 'em, it does. Like I was saying, though, sounds as if you are not from these parts."

"San Francisco," I said. I raised my arms, bent my hands into claws, leaned toward him, and gave a bit of a roar. I was gratified to see Gator startled. "Grizzly bear," I said. "It would be interesting to see a combat between those two, wouldn't it?"

Gator changed the subject rather than acknowledge that my prank had gained me the advantage. "Milady, let me acquaint you with one of our local customs. You are welcome to partake of your beverage here at the bar or at any table. Your chattel here is welcome to drink outside."

"That's not—" I began. Luis nudged me again. I was not doing well in developing a subtle approach or in melding with the local way of things.

"Fresh air would be welcome," Luis said. "I thank you, Señor Gator."

The bartender talked as he drew my beer. "Most places, Miss Kelly, wouldn't serve a Mexican at all. Adelita's is a different kind of establishment."

"I'm beginning to sense that," I said.

The couple in the corner was in the process of rearranging their attire, their backs to the room. It was almost comical that they would show modesty after what had gone before. The woman disappeared behind a curtain at the back. He turned and headed for the bar.

I'd boasted that I could not be shocked. And if I'd been alone, I could have lived up to my words. However, with Luis there, I felt as if I'd been caught hiding a shameful secret. I glanced at him furtively. He was staring at the ceiling, apparently as embarrassed as I was. I turned my attention to the rest of the room. Two tables over, the man with his face on the table had pulled himself out of his stupor and was arranging his cards for a game of solitaire.

My beer was in front of me, and Luis had disappeared out the back door. I looked from the corner of my eye as the man from the back corner called to the bartender. "Whisky, Gator. Glass and bottle."

"Coming up, Mr. Delacroix."

A wave of disgust washed over me at the thought that I'd have to deal with this man, and that wave was followed by what I can only describe as a wave of light which emanated from somewhere within me. The first was no surprise, given what I'd just witnessed. But the second? I hadn't experienced anything akin to it since Luis had shown me my parents' graves on the California north coast more than a decade past. Their spirits, their auras, their presences, were in this dingy room. The experience of connecting with them, though intense, was too vague to assign shape or definition. What I knew was that my parents' presence had been and was still part of the ether that surrounded me. I would have crossed myself, but Adelita's wasn't the place and this wasn't the time. Then the feeling was gone, and the place was as bleak and revolting as before.

"By the way, sir," Gator said, "this is Miss Kelly. She was asking after you."

"Oh, was she now?" He reached for the bottle. I was afraid he would offer me his hand, but he was more interested in the whisky. He gestured toward a table. "This way."

I followed him to the small table. Sat in the bentwood chair. Delacroix poured himself his whisky and lit a cheroot which he pulled from the inside pocket of his swallowtail coat. Limp ruffles graced the breast and cuffs of his shirt. He wore no collar or tie at his throat. The ensemble gave the impression of a man who had been interrupted in the process of dressing.

"Call me Daniel," he said.

"I go by Bonita," I answered. I was anxious to get straight to the subject, but decided to try Carew's approach. "I'm from San Francisco," I said. "I have a number of business interests there. My friend, Luis, is the foreman of Rancho Sausalito, which is a sizeable *hacienda* on the north side of the bay. It seems we've made a poor choice of weather for our visit to your city."

"If you can't put up with a little rain, I'm afraid you would have a tough time living in New Orleans. Now, then. Whatever do you want with me?" Delacroix was apparently not a devotee of Sheriff Carew's indirect approach. "Forgive my lack of subtlety, Miss Kelly, but ladies of your stripe seldom pass through the doorway of Adelita's."

I wished Luis were at my shoulder, but I was on my own for what would perhaps be the most important conversation of our search. I sipped my beer and, much as I wanted to stay as far away as possible, leaned toward the man.

"For the early years of my life, I thought I was the niece of Captain William A. Richardson. The Captain owns Rancho Sausalito, where I grew up and where Luis is, as I mentioned, foreman. I discovered when I was twelve that my real parents had been killed when I was an infant, and that Captain Richardson had raised me, thinking it better that I never knew about my mother and father. Eventually, though, I learned that before they came to San Francisco, they lived here, Daniel, and that you knew them. I'm seeking to find out as much as I can of their lives."

I stopped, hoping that Delacroix would add questions and details. I sipped my beer while I waited. It was actually quite good. I had expected less. Delacroix tossed down a second glass of whisky.

"Kelly. Lots of Irish in this city. I suppose you reckon that somehow if you find out about them, you'll be finding something of yourself."

I nodded and sipped.

"I did the same thing. Thought maybe I was descended from French royalty or some such. The heir to land and wealth. What I inherited you see before you." He swung his arm around the room. "You could be chasing a nightmare instead of a dream."

"I've heard that warning before, Monsieur." I hoped I'd chosen the right way of addressing him and that my French pronunciation passed muster. He gave no indication that he noticed one way or the other. "I have no illusions. My parents are, as we sit here, branded as criminals. My hope is to clear their names. But my ultimate purpose is to find out the truth. Whatever it is."

"The truth, Bonita, is an elusive bird. Hard to track and harder to snare. Sometimes it brings cheer, like a spring robin. Other times, it's a bird of prey, like a falcon, that can rip your heart out. Sometimes it flies so high and far it's just a dot in the sky and you never do know what it looks like."

It was a poetic speech, but pretty words didn't begin to counter my distrust of this man who had put out a wanted poster on my innocent mother and father. My clairvoyance suddenly took over and I understood that his anger and frustration were born of pain. Interesting information, but I had no idea how to use it. Besides, my mission was not to assuage the hurt of an obvious degenerate.

"To help my exploration of the aviary you described, Daniel, I'm wondering if you might have known my parents, or could guide us to someone who might have?"

"Oh, I knew them all right, Miss Bonita Kelly, *neé* Richardson. In fact, I guessed who you were the minute I laid eyes on you, and I was certain of it when Gator told me your name. You look just like Fiona. Hardly at all like Michael, though there's a bit of him in the shape of your jaw."

I'd wondered for years how or if I resembled my parents. It was the first time I'd had any notion of the truth. My breath caught. I gulped. I sipped. I was surprised to see that my beer was half gone.

"What more can you tell me, Daniel?"

"Nothing, I'm afraid. I, too, have a number of business interests, Miss Kelly. And it is not in my business interest to reveal more than I already have." He threw down another shot. His fourth, I think, or perhaps his fifth. Who knows how many he'd imbibed before I arrived?

In earlier days, I would have taken Delacroix's words as a rejection and shuffled away in disappointment. However, my years as a woman of business enabled me to recognize in what he said the opening of a negotiation. Desperately as I wanted to ask him what it would take to open him up, I was in a weak position. My flash of clairvoyance had showed me something of his heart, but nothing of his mind. It would be foolish to reveal any of my cards without some idea of what he held in his hand.

I felt a breeze on the back of my neck. Delacroix's eyes lifted to the doorway. Luis couldn't have picked a better time to make his entrance. I stood and turned. I knew he wouldn't have entered unless something urgent had arisen.

"Is it time already, Luis?" I turned back to my adversary. "I have another appointment, Monsieur Delacroix, so I can't continue our conversation at the moment. Suffice it to say that I bring with me some information you will find profitable. Will it suit for me to return about the same time tomorrow?"

I hoped he wasn't too drunk to notice I'd switched from using his first name just as he'd stopped calling me "Bonita" when he delivered his rebuff.

He didn't get up. Simply poured another glass of whisky. "Suit yourself, *Miss Bonita.* Don't bring the Mescan, though. Can't stand 'em."

I shoved my ire down into my gut, where it felt hot as a dinnertime cook stove.

"We'll go, then, Luis."

"As you wish, Miss," he said in a servile manner I'd never before heard him use with anyone. Where had he learned it, and how could he bear it? The man surprised me constantly.

Chapter Five

Gumbo

Pierre's didn't want Luis polluting their dining room any more than Gator had wanted him drinking inside Adelita's. They were happy, though, to furnish us with a small bucket of gumbo and another of beer to take away. We found a place dockside and shared our first taste of Gulf seafood. It was all at once sweet and searing, rich in a way I'd never tasted or imagined. I'd thought we'd return home to California as soon as possible. Food like this could change my mind. But I was concerned about Luis.

"Are you sure you want to go on like this? How can you bear to be treated like a slave?"

He smiled in his way, as if the entire world amused him. As if he were in it but not of it. "I play a role, Monita. Such treatment does not touch me where I live, so if it is necessary, I will do it. Besides, I've found it is useful. I wanted to share what I learned as soon as possible."

"Learned what? Tell me." I spooned more gumbo onto my bowl of rice.

"Servants talk more freely among themselves than do their so-called betters. I crossed to the roadside while I was drinking my beer. I met quite a number of workers as they passed by on their errands. Our languages didn't always match. French is beyond me, but with some Spanish, some English, and the local patois I learned a great deal. Daniel Delacroix is quite well known in these parts."

"He told me he has a number of business interests."

"He provides insurance to barge owners, for one thing."

"You mean protection."

"If they pay, their barges don't burn."

"You said 'for one thing.'"

"He owns what he calls a troupe of Adelita's. The bar is named after his favorite. We saw her this morning."

Some small part of her, anyway, I thought. Such a pretty name, Adelita. I couldn't clearly make out her looks in the gloom of the bar, but the thought of the squalid life and sordid celebrity she endured made me put aside my gumbo.

"Up and down the river docks," Luis continued, "nearly every prostitute is under Delacroix's control."

"Sheriff Carew said my parents had worked for this man?"

"He also owns some legitimate businesses. A hotel. A store that sells outfits to hunters and trappers."

"He must be quite rich. Why does he use a place like Adelita's for his headquarters?"

"It is a question in everyone's mind."

"Wonderful work, *amigo*. However, we don't yet have enough to get Delacroix to reveal what he knows. Did you get the name of his hotel?"

"It is the Belle Fleur."

My first thought was that Luis and I should check into that hotel and try talking to the staff. However, Delcroix was sure to have spies aplenty and could easily feed us misinformation. Better we should stay at Angelique's, where we were sure to be among more trustworthy folk than at the Belle Fleur. Delacroix would know where we were in any case, but he might not know the connection between Angelique and Sylvia.

"What are you thinking, Monita?" Luis said after I'd been silent for some moments.

"Perhaps we should split up," I said. Luis listened to my idea, made a couple of suggestions, then agreed. I suddenly had my appetite back. Even cold, the gumbo tasted superb and gave me new energy for the tasks before me.

Chapter Six

Angelique

"I know not this Monsieur Delacroix." Angelique spoke as she and I enjoyed Dubonnet and *macarons* on the gallery of the boarding house. Luis was off somewhere with the servants, making friends and gathering information. The scene before us was a bit mysterious—dark lagoons and trees bearded with pale green moss. There were a few buildings and rude streets, but there was construction here and there. With the eye for development I had acquired during my years as a San Francisco entrepreneur, I suspected that the area would prosper before long. I even entertained the idea of investing some of Sylvia's and my capital here. But I dismissed the thought as a distraction from our goal of developing our San Francisco interests.

Angelique continued. "But everyone knows of him. He arrived *peut-être* ten years ago. At that time I was engaged in that other sort of business. You understand the one I mean."

I nodded.

"No one seemed to know the place where he come from. He float up and suddenly he is there, like a bubble going poof from the swamps."

She closed and opened her fingers in a sudden motion to imitate the bursting bubble.

"He went *rapidement* to Adelita's. It was called Le Diamant before. A *nombre comique, non?* For an establishment *sordide* as it was. So first the purchase from the one who serves the drinks now."

"Gator owned it?"

"*Mais oui*. Monsieur Delcroix have some money he bring with him from somewhere. Then came the Adelita sign and. . . " She made motions with her hands and fingers that it took me a while to decipher.

"The railing?" I said.

"*Oui, oui*. Yes. On the roof. He put it there from a riverboat. She is sunk down the current from here. Then *soudainement* like eye blinking, he own hotel too."

"The hotel came before the prostitutes?"

"Ah, *oui*. The rest of his business all come after Adelita's and the hotel."

"And yet, why do you imagine he spends so much time in a poor place like Adelita's since he must have a great deal of money?"

She shrugged. "Many have discovered that it is best not to become so very curious when the subject is Monsieur Delacroix. One thing I say. When this house changed from what it was to what it now is, some of *les femmes de moi* go to work for him. They all say he do good by them. Let them keep good per cent and protect them from harm. For myself, I don't know they tell me everything."

She offered another pour from the decanter that stood between us on a small tiled table. I accepted gladly. The tiles depicted a bucolic scene of shepherds and shepherdesses beside a brook. Not so different in its own way than the scene before us. However, both evinced a peace I did not feel in this atmosphere of confusion and contradictions.

I didn't need clairvoyance to sense that she was quite uncomfortable with the idea of Delacroix, even to the point of being reluctant to speak about him.

"Angelique, I have no wish to put you in danger. So answer this only if you can tell me without risk. If you were going to inquire about Daniel Delacroix without his finding out, where would you go?"

She was silent for a moment. "I also wish not to put you in danger, Mademoiselle Bonita. Such an errand. . . "

I turned and squared myself toward her and used one of the few French words I know. "*Ma coeur*," I said, "my heart yearns to know the truth at whatever cost."

She turned away, sent her gaze toward the distant swamp. She crossed herself. "*Mon Dieu, m'excuse.*" She turned back to me. "I will tell you one name."

I nodded.

"The person is not in the city. I will draw a map."

She rose and went inside for paper and pencil. I waited, staring into the swamps in the way Angelique had been doing, wishing I could see not only into the darkness beyond the trees, but into my future as well.

Chapter Seven

Magnolia

Luis and I left at sunrise. I figured it would do no harm to miss my makeshift appointment with Delacroix, who had made it clear he was unwilling to reveal anything. Luis had it from the servants that Magnolia Plantation, to which Angelique had directed us, was not an establishment in which they would be happy to find themselves "employed." We'd best be on our guard, lest the place present a threat to guests, as well as to slaves.

Perhaps this journey was a fool's errand. Perhaps I should have stayed in San Francisco and carried on my fight for custody of Bonita there. Surely the courts would hold with me if only on the evidence of our resemblance. Even if I brought back proof that my parents were the king and queen of England, Flora would find other objections.

Nevertheless, corroboration of my parents' innocence would remove that weapon from her arsenal, and she had no others. Anything I could gain here would be worth the journey if it weakened Flora. Not to mention satisfying my own hunger for knowledge of their past.

So far, Delacroix appeared to hold the key to the information I needed, but I had nothing to persuade him to use the key. Perhaps I would learn something at Magnolia that would prod him into opening the door.

After a two-hour journey, Luis steered our buggy into the magnolia-lined lane of the first grand southern plantation I'd seen. A splendid white mansion with Greek columns graced the end of the natural colonnade. An impressive sight in a setting doubtless meant to awe visitors. It cast that spell over both of us.

Suddenly the satin dress and simple jewelry I'd donned for the occasion seemed tawdry. I was almost of a mind to turn for home. Luis seemed to read my thoughts.

"It is for the show, Monita. If we must, we will know how to step behind the scenery."

"Surely we will," I said. "You must admit it is quite a show."

"Indeed so. I have never seen better."

A lithe Negro man in a black suit with a fork-tailed coat greeted the carriage. He spoke with what seemed to me a touch of arrogance.

"*Bonjour*, Mademoiselle. Is you expected?" He paid no attention to Luis.

"No. We have come to see Monsieur Gilles LeClerc on the recommendation of Madame Angelique Chevalier. Our errand is an urgent one, and we had no time to arrange a proper visit."

"Hmph," he said, his nose in the air over this breach of protocol. "Monsieur Gilles is tending to the indigo fields this morning. I don't expect him before midday, and then he has other activities scheduled for later."

"Well, we don't mind waiting, Monsieur. . . what did you say your name was?"

"I'm Xavier, Mademoiselle."

"If you would show me to a parlor, then direct Luis to the stables so he can care for our horses, we will be most happy to settle ourselves until Monsieur LeClerc appears."

My haughty manner succeeded in triggering his years of training to bow and scrape to white folks, especially ladies. I hated acting like this, but I would have hated more to be deterred from my purpose.

"And your trunks, Mademoiselle?"

"We have none. We are not planning to spend the night."

"Yes'm. Right this way, Mademoiselle."

He led me toward the marble steps leading to the front doors of the mansion. But wait. The steps were not marble. Wood cleverly painted to look like stone. Artistry or just deception? I'd soon find out.

***

The parlor was musty and airy at the same time. Windows were open for ventilation, but the sheer drapes intended to block the sun also blocked most of the breeze. Still, it was a pleasant room, dark walnut chairs and sofa adorned with maroon velvet upholstery and needlepoint pillows fringed in gold. A coal-black mynah bird hopped from perch to perch in a large cage at one corner. The creature emitted a shrill whistle from time to time. I had heard mynahs could speak, but apparently this one hadn't been taught.

The second I entered the room, Xavier disappeared, and a light-skinned maid in a black dress and white scallop-edged apron appeared in a far doorway.

"May I bring Mademoiselle something? A beverage perhaps, after your journey?"

I was soon lounging on the sofa holding a chilled glass of lemonade. The wing chair was not as luxurious as it looked, being much harder than I'd anticipated. Still, it didn't tip and bounce like the buggy, so my situation had improved. The maid, whose name was Rose, stood behind me, just inside the room, at my beck and call. I'd have preferred to beck or call her from somewhere that she didn't feel like a monitor, and I wanted to tell her so. But this was the milieu in which I found myself, and I had vowed to follow Carew's instructions and try to fit in.

This LeClerc, Angelique told me, had been in business with Delacroix, then had a serious falling out with him. It was her guess that he'd know a good bit about the man's past, though she wasn't certain. Whether I gleaned anything here or not, I would at least learn something useful about the southern way of life.

If one ignored the fact that all these "servants" were in fact slaves, it must be something to be waited on hand and foot. Not that you *could* forget about the slavery, but it was easy to see how a person could get used to all the service. With the menial tasks taken care of, think of how much freedom one would have to do the things that mattered.

I crossed myself and banished these selfish thoughts. I made a mental note to make a formal confession of them. Perhaps at the Saint Louis Cathedral in New Orleans.

My lemonade finished, I stood and walked toward the French doors leading to a veranda. Rose was right there to take the glass and inquire if I wanted another. I shook my head. The mynah whistled so loudly we both turned in his direction.

"Rose, I've never been here or on any plantation before. Perhaps you can help me." I stepped toward the French doors.

"If it please you, Mademoiselle."

Rose hurried over and unlatched them for me. At my gesture she followed me outside. The wooden veranda was raised, along with the rest of the house, about three feet above the ground. To avoid floods, and as a form of air conditioning by allowing circulation under the house, is the way Angelique explained it.

A riot of bougainvillea and morning glory swarmed around the posts in brilliant red and blue. Forty yards or so of greensward spread outward before the eye encountered some buildings in the distance. Where was Luis?

"Straight ahead, there, Rose. Are those the stables?"

"I don't rightly know, Mademoiselle. You have to ask Monsieur LeClerc."

"And where do you stay, Rose? You and your family?"

"I best get to the kitchen with your glass, Mademoiselle." And she scurried inside.

I thought at first this had been a very unproductive conversation. Then I realized I'd learned quite a lot. The slaves were so terrified of their master they couldn't dispense even the most basic information. I wondered what this augured for the success of this morning's journey. Though there was a small white wicker table and matching chairs, I felt too restless to sit. I paced the veranda until I tired of the sound of my own heels on the wood.

I headed back inside and crossed the entry hall toward some stairs. As I raised my foot to begin climbing them, I looked up to see an older woman, another slave in the black dress, scalloped-apron uniform, her arms crossed, shaking her head. The same sort of thing happened at two other doorways. I was politely but firmly trapped. Should I take this personally, or was it standard procedure for uninvited guests?

The grandfather clock at the foot of the stairs said two p.m. I had been waiting nearly three hours. My uncle had often invoked the need for patience. "You get a chicken by hatching an egg, not breaking it open, " he'd say. I'd understood his wisdom, but it failed to tame my nature. That native hastiness possessed me now.

I pleaded a need for the facilities with Rose, hoping to find an escape hatch. I was disappointed to find not a proper water closet, but a tiny chamber with a board, a hole and a chamber pot beneath a hole and a chamber pot beneath. Remarkably, the little room was odor free. A pitcher and basin rested on a small shelf behind the board. A small, high window above the board did admit some light. I set the pitcher and bowl aside and stepped up on the shelf to catch a glimpse of what lay beyond my tiny wall. I raised myself on tiptoes and saw a section of a formal garden. Paths, roses, statuary, but I hardly paid attention to all that. What caught my eye was the sight of a tall, thin man in riding attire—cutaway coat, straight pants, ruffles at his throat. All that, however, was incidental to the fact that he stood face-to-face with Xavier, threatening him with a quirt.

I could hear nothing of what he said, but he waved the whip beneath the slave's chin, leaned toward him with vigorous intensity. I longed to yell an objection, but how useless a gesture that would be. Eventually, the berating ceased, Xavier bowed, and the man—it had to be LeClerc—strode toward the house.

I jumped down to the floor, availed myself of the pitcher and basin, and opened the door. Rose had been waiting right outside. Naturally. I wonder what she'd made of what she'd heard, or not heard, outside.

We returned to the drawing room, where I expected to encounter LeClerc. Once again, I was disappointed. I accepted Rose's offer of another lemonade this time, and I sat and waited once more. Finally, he descended the stairs. How he had gotten to the floor above was a mystery. He wore a handsome burgundy coat with dark trousers, a pleated shirt and dark cravat. For whom did he dress so splendidly out here in the hinterlands? It surely wasn't for me.

"You are Miss Kelly, Xavier tells me." He lifted my hand to his lips, grazed it, and laid it back on my lap. "Gilles LeClerc at your service." He sat, taking care to spread his coat tails and adjust his trousers.

"I apologize for appearing without notice, sir. However, I have traveled from San Francisco in search of some important information. There are exigencies involved. Miss Angelique Chevalier suggested you might be able to help."

"Yes, yes. Angelique. Xavier said you'd mentioned her." Was that what had raised LeClerc's ire? "A lovely lady. Her retirement occasioned some sadness for me. She was a source of comfort when my Emily passed on a few years back."

I wanted to ask whether Emily was a wife or some other family member and exactly what comfort a madam could have provided, but what I couldn't guess, I could find out from Angelique. Best to press on.

"She seems a very kind woman."

The bird shrieked. I should have been used to it by now, but I turned toward it involuntarily.

"I apologize for Emily, Miss Kelly. She was my late wife's favorite. She used to be called 'Harriet' after a favorite aunt of Emily's. But after my wife passed on, I renamed her as a sort of memento. She doesn't seem to mind, and we let her carry on as she pleases."

I nodded and smiled.

"Let us retire to the veranda, Miss Kelly. Rose, would you bring me a whisky and something for the lady? Lemonade perhaps?"

Had they nothing else to serve guests?

"Would it be unfeminine of me to request a whisky as well?"

He smiled and shook his head. "You're the first woman I've met since Emily who enjoyed spirits. By all means. Rose, I presume you heard the lady."

"Yessir," she answered, then disappeared.

"San Francisco is it?" he said. "Never been there. If half the tales we hear are true, it's a lively place."

"It's settled down considerably now that the big rush is over. It's beginning to look and feel like a real city instead of a temporary frontier settlement."

"Still plenty of turmoil, though, I expect."

"Indeed."

Rose brought us our drinks. I sipped, waiting for LeClerc to change the subject. It was fine whisky.

LeClerc raised his glass. "To travel."

An odd toast, I thought, but I smiled and sipped.

"And just what led you to travel out here to Magnolia this morning, not even knowing whether I'd chosen to travel elsewhere? I might have been in Paris for all you knew."

"You've been to Paris? I would love to see it."

"I go there often. This coat was tailored for me there, as was much of my wardrobe. The French are known for their wine, but their whisky is equally fine. You are tasting a sample as we speak."

"Even had you not been here, Monsieur LeClerc, I thought it an opportunity to learn first hand something of life on a southern plantation. Magnolia is a marvelous place with a distinguished reputation." I'd had no time to inquire further than Angelique about Magnolia, but a man as vain as this one would believe me in an instant.

"It's been the work of decades. My grandfather walked into these swamps in 1797. He shipped over from debtor's prison in Paris, agreeing to sign on as an apprentice carpenter, bound to his master for seven years. He escaped at dockside and hid on these grounds, which were nothing but bayous and alligators, all the time building houses and appropriating land, which he farmed. By 1820, Magnolia was self-sustaining. My father took over, expanded, and I am continuing to improve what I inherited."

"A harrowing story, Monsieur. It is hard to imagine now that all this grew from such wilderness."

"Beautiful as is what you see before you, the perils continue. In wet years, the swamp tries to reclaim our fields. In all years, rapacious men challenge our land titles."

"And yet you prevail. I salute you, Monsieur LeClerc." I raised my glass, and he did likewise to share the toast. He smiled broadly. I didn't know if I could abide more delay, but he was beginning to relax, which might make him more amendable to sharing when we finally got to the core of things.

"My struggles," he continued, "are as nothing compared to Grandfather's, but they are no less important to the future of Magnolia. You yourself are on something of a quest, are you not? How might I help?"

Finally. I tried to remain calm and businesslike. I told about my parents as succinctly as I could manage, then ended with, "It came to my attention that they had some dealings with Daniel Delacroix. Angelique said you and he were partners at some point, and that you might know something that would help."

"There are men who don't know the meaning of honor, Miss Kelly. Daniel Delacroix is one of them."

"That seems to be a common opinion," I said. "Yet it is also said that he treats his… employees well. At least his prostitutes." The man started slightly at my use of the word in such a matter-of-fact way.

"Rose. I could use another, please. Miss Kelly?" Rose appeared as if she'd materialized from thin air. I began to think this service hand-and-foot business was more disconcerting than convenient.

"Later, perhaps."

"Daniel is capable of great generosity, but he is never, ever selfless, Miss Kelly. A thing it took me some time to understand."

"You know, Monsieur, you just told me the entire history of your family going back three generations. Yet, no one seems to know where Monsieur Delacroix came from. In San Francisco, which went from nothing to a metropolis nearly overnight, people can easily get away with hiding their past. But this city is much older."

Rose entered again, handed LeClerc his glass. I gave her mine, indicated I would like another. She nodded and exited. He remained silent, staring into his glass.

"I do know something of Daniel's antecedents, Miss Kelly. I hesitate to broadcast them because, despite the bitterness between us, he prefers to be treated as a man on his own terms, without reference to his heritage. In New Orleans, that is nearly impossible, but he's managed it so far. As for your parents, the story of the false wanted poster is interesting, but I know nothing of his dispute with them. And I don't see how revealing Daniel's past will help your case."

He drank. Rose brought my refresher. I was stalled, unsure how to proceed.

"If I am correct, Monsieur, Delacroix sullied my parents' reputation, then turned them into hunted outlaws. He forced them into hiding, then into a position where they were shot to death, apparently, but far from certainly, committing a crime. I believe they were innocent. Frankly, my own reputation is now at stake over all this. But I need evidence."

"Daniel's past will hardly provide such evidence."

"But it might provide information that will encourage him to reveal something helpful toward finding it."

"So, you are suggesting I tell you something you can use to extort him."

Ah, Carew's imprecations about subtlety seemed not so accurate. "Nothing so crude." I shook my head. "If, for example, I could compare my situation to his, show him how public knowledge or misinformation about some situation or another might harm him, he would be more understanding of my needs."

"Miss Kelly, I am expecting guests for supper. Madame and Monsieur Laurent from Belcoeur Estates not far from here. And their daughters, of course. I would like you to join us."

"I cannot impose on your hospitality. Doubtless the supper would end too late for us to begin our return journey. I could speak to Luis, but I fear I must decline."

"Luis? Ah, yes, your Mexican servant. Surely his wishes are of no concern."

"This is unfamiliar territory for us. He needs to be sure of the route."

"Of course. I will send a servant with you as a guide."

He had met all my objections except the one in which I wanted Luis to have a place at the table. But that was obviously impossible. As long as he was safe, he was perhaps learning more than I was.

"Then I cannot refuse, sir. I would be most honored." I finished my whisky and, feeling a bit lightheaded, I followed LeClerc into the house.

Chapter Eight

The Feast

As one might expect, the table was resplendent with crystal, silver, china, linen, and candles. The Laurents were a young couple, not much older than thirty, stiff and condescending in their manner. Even when they paid compliments, and they paid very few, they delivered them with a touch of superiority.

"So refined, considering her background," remarked Adelaide about some neighbor. "And he works harder than half his slaves," added Charles.

LeClerc found this banter quite amusing. For the first part of the meal, they paid no more attention to me than to the slaves or the furniture. And that was a gift for which I was grateful, for it left me to engage with the daughters.

Venus was just my Bonita's age. I was sure those two eight-year-olds would get along famously. Diane was two years younger. Both of them wore their hair in long auburn ringlets, and Adelaide had dressed them in silk brocade as fine as ball gowns. Even with the hair style and attire, they had so far avoided copying their parents' haughtiness.

"I have three pet bunnies," Venus told me excitedly. "Nelly, Alice, and Sammie. They are so soft. I wish they were here so I could show you, but Daddy wouldn't let me bring them."

"I don't give a hoot in a handbasket for your silly rabbits," Diane said. "My kitty Beauregard is worth six of them. Besides Sammie is a girl and you gave her a boy's name."

"Excuse me, miss know-everything, but Sammie is short for Samantha."

"I would love to visit Belcoeur and meet all of them," I said. "And to bring my daughter from San Francisco as well. Would you like that?"

Their dark eyes sparkled as they turned toward me.

"How old is she?" Venus asked.

"What's her name?" Diane added.

Such simple questions. In a split second, I spoke her real name in public, and it dizzied me almost as much as the whisky. "She is called Bonita," I said. "The same as I am. And she is eight, Venus, the same as you."

"Oh, you must bring her soon," Venus said.

"We don't have any real playmates except the slave children," Diane said.

My mind went back to that day, not long after I met Bonita when she and Flora's daughter, Rosita, two years younger than my Bonita, all went to the beach. Flora was there, of course, along with their old useless *niñera* who tagged along everywhere.

"Don't let them near the water, Lila," Flora told her. Imagine going to the seaside and avoiding the sea. It's as ridiculous as to hold a rose and avoid smelling it.

Still, we had a wonderful time. Bonita and Rosita and I, building sand castles—more than castles, a whole kingdom—and chattering away like the seals on the great rock offshore. I carried bucket after bucket of water and wet sand to the site we'd made our own.

"Tía, Tía, Tía," Bonita called. "*Más agua.*"

"*Sí, sí. más, más,*" Rosita squealed jumping up and down.

"Miss Bonita, what are those scars on your cheek?" Diane asked.

"Why, one evening when I was not much older than you, I had a wrestling match with a grizzly bear."

"No you didn't, Miss Bonita," Venus said.

"Did you win?" Diane was sincere and excited.

"Of course," I said. "But he did leave his mark, as you can see."

"What was his name?" Diane asked.

"Don't be silly," Venus said. "Miss Bonita, what happened, really?"

"Girls, quit bothering Miss Kelly," Adelaide called.

"*Au contraire*, I said. They are delightful."

But Adelaide was not to be deterred. "Is it true, Miss Kelly, that gold was so plentiful in San Francisco that you could pick up nuggets from the creek bed?"

I whispered to the girls, "We'll save the bear story till later." Then I turned to their mother. "Alas, no, Madame Laurent," I said. "The nearest gold from San Francisco was a hundred miles away, and that has grown quite scarce since '48. A few discovered bonanzas, but the true riches came to the merchants who supplied all those starry-eyed prospectors with their equipment."

"It is ever so," remarked her husband. "How many explorers died at sea or ashore in poverty while the shipbuilders prospered safe ashore?"

"Safe ashore," she said. "Rather a dull notion, isn't it?"

"Are you preparing to embark on some grand adventure, Adelaide?" LeClerc said.

"To borrow a phrase from Miss Kelly, alas, no. I have my little ones, and they have their rabbits and cats, and I am thus bound safe ashore. Still, one can dream. Have you read *Robinson Crusoe*, Miss Kelly? Or *The Swiss Family Robinson?*"

I confessed I had not, though I mentally put those books on my list for future reference. Since my early tutelage had been in the classics with my beloved Horace as a centerpiece, I had not ventured into novels. Perhaps it was time to branch out. Even Horace advised *stultitia ad sapientiam misceat*. Mingle a little folly with your wisdom.

"These tales will take your mind and your breath away, Miss Kelly. The nearest thing to true adventure."

"So you wish to be marooned, my dear?" Charles asked.

"Sometimes I feel that I am," she said. "Life is so comfortable. When I read these tales I almost feel that we're cheating by insulating ourselves from adversity." She held up her glass. "Rose," she called. "I asked that you keep my glass full."

Rose glanced at Charles. He nodded, though with tight lips, and Rose did as requested.

I glanced down at my plate and grew suddenly famished. I realized that I'd been so engrossed in conversation I'd failed to put a fork to what had been described as crayfish *etouffée*, served over rice grown on this very plantation. I had never heard of the dish and now I had allowed it to grow tepid. Nevertheless, I took a bite and was rewarded enormously despite how long it had sat unattended. Gumbo one day, etouffée the next. I wondered what other culinary miracles awaited.

"And are both novels about people who are marooned, then?" I asked Adelaide.

"Oh, yes. Robinson Crusoe is alone except for his servant, Friday. Isn't that just the most delicious name? Friday, come here. Friday, build me a fire. Friday, make my dinner."

"It could lead to confusion, though," LeClerc said. "If you gave the order on Monday, you might not get your meal until the end of the week."

Everyone laughed except Adelaide.

"Very amusing, Gilles. 'I prithee, do not mock me,' to borrow a phrase from the Bard. And Miss Kelly, as the title suggests, *The Swiss Family Robinson* concerns a whole family who are thrown upon their own resources on an isolated island. They create a whole little civilization out of practically nothing. Their ingeniousness is fascinating."

"Not quite so ingenious," Charles said. "The author provides them with a number of handy tools from their ship."

"Ha! How would you do, Charles, trying to build a house from a few boards and some rope?"

"I'd venture to say Mr. Wyss never had to do so either. Easier to put the words on the page than to do the deed."

"Well, I for one would like to try my hand. Perhaps I'll venture into the Belcoeur woods and give it a try. What do you think, girls? Are you game?" She held up her glass. "Rose." Again, the glance at Mr. Laurent. This time, he shook his head.

"Gilles, perhaps, we can retire to the drawing room?" Charles said.

"We haven't had dessert yet," Venus objected.

"You are speaking out of place, Venus," Charles said.

"Venus is right," Adelaide's tone carried a challenge. "Rose, where is our dessert? And the sherry?"

"Adelaide, my dear, Rose is not our servant. She belongs to Gilles."

"Quite all right," LeClerc said. "Rose, would you serve the Charlotte Russe in the dining room, please?" He turned back to the guests. "The cherries, you will find, are quite fresh, and Madeline is the best baker I have ever had on the estate."

"Girls, you may be served here," Charles directed. "Adelaide, come along."

"Monsieur LeClerc," I said, "I have enjoyed myself immensely, but I beg please to be excused." I turned to Charles. "You and your family have been a delight. However, we must return to the city this evening, and the hour grows so late."

"Just a few more minutes, Miss Kelly. Take my word, you do not want to miss the Magnolia Charlotte Russe. It is the best outside of Paris."

I'd found the Louisiana food delightful, but, so anxious was I to find Luis and be on our way that I cared nothing for dessert. Still, I was loath to pass up the chance for at least a particle of information. So far I had learned next to nothing. And, if I were to stay, my heart pulled me toward the room where Venus and Diane were being served. They reminded me so of Bonita and Rosita. What would the two sisters do without one another if I were to pry Bonita away from Flora? A question for another time. My duty called me to follow the adults.

The drawing room turned out to be nothing more than the parlor in which I'd spent most of the afteroon, with a few extra small tables added for serving. The sherry glasses were smaller than the wine glasses, so Rose would have to scurry to keep up with Adelaide's thirst. After her second glass, however, Adelaide's chin dropped to her chest, and she appeared to slumber, with occasional returns to consciousness. The mynah bird's cage had been covered for the night, or it would no doubt have squealed its approval.

Charles turned his attention to me.

"It must be distressing to have so little knowledge of one's parentage, Miss Kelly. My ancestry goes back to Louis Seize and beyond."

"Mine may go back that far as well," I said. "I don't know. For the most part, that sort of thing doesn't count for a great deal out West. But my case is somewhat different."

"In what way?"

LeClerc had told them only that I was seeking information. How much more did I want to explain?

"My parents stand accused of a crime. It darkens their name and mine. I wish to prove their innocence."

"Intriguing," he said. "Would it be intrusive to inquire as to the nature of the crime?"

"Theft," I said. I decided to leave out the horse rustling for the moment. "From a Monsieur Daniel Delacroix."

"Delacroix?" Charles said. He laughed. "Anything stolen from him would be stolen twice because he's sure to have robbed it from someone else."

I was about to ask my next question, but LeClerc spoke before I had the chance. There was a warning in his eyes and voice. "Miss Kelly seems to think that it would be advantageous to her search if she could learn something of Delcroix's background."

Adelaide suddenly sat up straight. "Delacroix. I know about him. He was in the French Revolution. Guillotines everywhere. Chop. Chop. Chop. Chop." She sliced the air with her hands. She sat back, smiled, then her eyes glazed and her chin dropped once again.

Charles and LeClerc shared a glance. I had the feeling I had learned more in Adelaide's brief expostulation than I had in all the preceding hours of conversation. Charles rose quickly.

"I believe we had better retire," Charles said. He stood and crossed to his wife. "Adelaide, dear." The word "dear" had a distinct edge to it. "Come along now."

"Rose," LeClerc said, "the Laurents will withdraw now. Would you call the bedservants, please, and gather the girls."

"As you wish, sir," Rose said, and disappeared.

"A delightful evening, Gilles, as usual." Adelaide was on her feet and conscious, holding her chin up and shoulders back, though wavering a bit.

"Till the morning, then," LeClerc said. We watched them go, then he turned to me. "Perhaps you would like to retire as well," he said.

"I'm afraid I must insist upon the servant you promised to help us navigate back to our boarding house," I said.

"Nonsense. A comfortable bed awaits upstairs. You can get an early start tomorrow."

"We hadn't planned to stay, Monsieur. I have no change of garments, no toiletries."

"Rose will provide whatever you need. And you needn't worry about your servant. There are ample quarters and services. I thank you for your delightful company at the table."

And with that, I was dismissed. I had to trust that Luis was all right and that his sleuthing had been more productive than mine. I'd learned something of Delacroix, but it was clear that even that bit of information was imparted unintentionally. Further slips were unlikely.

"This way if you please, Mademoiselle." Rose gestured toward the stairs.

It was as much an order as an invitation. Well, LeClerc was in for a surprise if he meant to keep me caged like his mynah.

Chapter Nine

Secret Passageway

As much as my own semi-captivity concerned me, I was even more anxious about Luis. I'd received no communication since we arrived, and my inquiries had been deflected, as if the welfare of a mere servant was of no moment.

Though I was able to sneak easily past Lily, who was slumbering on her pallet at my bedside, I knew she wouldn't be my only obstacle to finding Luis, for I was certain there were many spies lurking at Magnolia. Sure enough, as I sneaked down the hall to the top of the staircase, I saw a slave sitting in a chair at the bottom, knitting by the light of a kerosene lamp. I recalled that LeClerc had somehow reached this same staircase without coming through the house below. How had he done it?

Five doors opened onto this hallway. I had to assume they were bedrooms. I reasoned that in addition to mine, one was LeClerc's, one for Adelaide and Charles, and one for the girls. That left one that might lead to stairs. Which one? I crept to each door, listened carefully for breathing and snoring. Only one was silent. Whether because it was unoccupied or because whoever was sleeping there was particularly quiet, I had no way of knowing. My clairvoyance had its limits, and it didn't seem active in this case. I turned the knob and pushed slowly.

There was enough light to discern a child-size bed, its mattress surrounded by mosquito netting and covered with a quilt. I couldn't tell if the quilt covered a human form or not. I listened some more. Silence. I closed the door silently behind me and headed toward another door on the far side of the room. Its knob turned without a sound, and the door made no creak as it swung open to reveal a closet, hung with children's garments. I was about to back up and look for another way out when a scream cut the air.

"Monster. Monster. Monster," the child in the bed yelled. I swept aside the netting, climbed on to the bed and took the girl in my arms. Venus. So the girls had separate rooms. So much for my counting the doors.

"Shhh," I whispered, rocking her back and forth. "There's no monster here. Only me."

"Miss Bonita?"

"Yes. No harm will come while I'm here. I promise."

She embraced me, buried her face in my bosom while she snuffled. I heard footsteps, froze. A knock. The door opened a few inches.

"You all right, Miss Venus? I thought I heard you call out."

"I'm fine, now, Sherry," she said.

The door opened. I put a finger to my lips and slid off the bed to the floor on the side opposite the door. If I were discovered, I could claim that I had heard Venus yell and come to investigate. But I was fully dressed, and I didn't care to answer any questions about my intent. Either Venus was quick or she was practiced in deception. A brief smile crossed her face, then she joined my game.

I could hear the maid's footsteps as she approached the bed. She was not shod in slippers, but in hard-soled shoes that clicked a bit when the heel came down. She'd been on duty, not asleep in bed.

"Please tuck me in, Sherry. That would be nice."

"What frightened you so, child?"

"A silly thing. I just dreamed there was a monster in the closet."

"I swear, your mama said she put you girls in separate rooms, so you wouldn't make so much noise, but it couldn't get much noisier with both of you than you by yourself."

"I'm sorry, Sherry."

"Well, let's just see, then, Venus, darling." The closet was only a few feet from where I crouched. I slid under the bed. I could barely make out the maid's feet.

The door opened. Candlelight swept the enclosure.

"Nothing here now, child." The door closed. The footsteps retreated. "I'll just stay here with you, child, until you're asleep again."

"Thank you, Sherry."

That was nice for the little girl, but I was in no mood to thank Sherry, for I was trapped now. I might be able to sneak out of the room of a sleeping child, but not while Sherry remained on duty.

After what seemed like forever, I heard regular deep-sleep breathing. I figured I could get out at last, but it was not to be. When I pushed the bed skirt aside, I found myself face-to-face with Venus. So, it was Sherry whose breathing I'd heard. Venus put a finger to her lips. She motioned for me to follow, then crawled toward the closet. Once inside, she pawed her way through the hanging clothes to the back wall. There were several hooks in the wall with belts and bonnets hanging from them. Except one of the belts wasn't a belt. It was tucked into a hole behind one of the hooks, and when Venus pulled on it, a hidden door opened on to a descending staircase.

Venus turned to me and smiled. "I want to hear the story of your bear," she said as she started down the stairs. I had no choice but to follow.

The treads were solid and silent, as befitted a secret passageway. The door at the bottom opened into a hallway, at the end of which was not another conventional doorway, but a ladder leading to a trap door. It was equipped with a hasp, but no padlock. Venus pushed up the door, and led me up a small ladder into a pantry filled with dry foodstuffs—flour, beans, sugar, and the like. Quite naturally, this storeroom opened onto the kitchen. I had heard that the kitchens on these mansions were sometimes located away from the main house because they were often a source of fire, and the distance might save the primary building in case of flames. We had apparently crossed from the main house through an underground tunnel.

The fire in the huge fireplace was banked for the night, and only a single servant slept beside it. I hoped she was the only guard as we slipped past and let ourselves into the yard. A few steps across a graveled walkway took us to a small shed, secured only by a peg and a hasp, and Venus quickly let us inside.

"Where are we?" I said.

"It's our playhouse. Monsieur LeClerc had it built for when we stay here. They don't watch us here like at home, so Diane and I get to explore all over."

"Well, good on you," I said. Which was true as far as it went. She'd showed me the way out, but I couldn't keep her with me as I searched for Luis and arranged to escape from the plantation altogether. I had to devise a way to rid myself of her. "Now, about that bear," I said by way of distraction.

"Yes, yes, yes," she said. I could almost see her eyes sparkle even in the near complete darkness.

"On our ranch, the *vaqueros* used to capture grizzly bears and set them to fighting bulls."

"Why?"

"It was entertainment to see which animal would win." I could feel she was ready to ask another question, but I plunged on. "Anyway, one night when I twelve I followed the *Vaqueros* on one of their bear-capturing excursions. I fell into the gully where the bears were feeding, and one of the cubs gave me a swat. So that's where the scars came from."

I expected her to giggle with fascination at the adventure, but she stayed quite silent for a moment, then reached out and touched my hand. "You must have been very frightened."

"I was too surprised to be scared at first, but afterwards I cried more with fear than with the hurt of my wounds. I was lucky that my friend, Luis, was there to scare the bears away and bring me home safely. Anyhow, that's my story. Now, it's back upstairs with you before Sherry wakes up and finds you gone."

"Why were you sneaking into my room?"

"I was. . . exploring. Just like you and Diane. I suspected there was a secret way into the house and I was curious to find it. Now, you must return before Sherry misses you and we both get in trouble."

"You must come with me."

"No I'm going to take a little walk."

"I could walk with you."

"Think how hard it will go for poor Sherry if they discover she fell asleep and lost you."

"You are right, Miss Bonita. Monsieur LeClerc is much more cruel to his slaves than Daddy."

"Do you think he might even whip her?" I had no idea if that was a possibility, but I had to free myself from this delightful child and get on with finding Luis. Playing on her sympathetic nature seemed the best tool I had at the moment.

"It could be," Venus said.

"Then quickly, now, before Sherry gets in trouble."

I rose and grabbed her hand. We dashed out of the playhouse, back through the pantry and through the trap door. At the foot of the stairway, I knelt and embraced her. I imagined for a moment I was hugging my own Bonita, and she hugged me back just as Bonita might have. "Now, off with you, my love. And thank you."

"Good night, Miss Bonita."

I yearned to call her back as she started up the stairs, but I closed the door to the stairway and sneaked back up through the trap door into the yard.

Chapter Ten

Seeking Luis

It was dark as the inside of a cave as I hurried across the wide lawn toward the flickering light in one of the distant buildings. I wished for even a sliver of moon. All it would take was an unseen gopher hole to sprain an ankle and spoil my mission. As much as I wanted to find Luis, I wanted answers to the mysteries the night's conversation had raised.

Delacroix and LeClerc may not have been friends, but there was much more to the story than a simple business falling out. And this story about the French Revolution, over and done with these fifty years and more?

By the time I was more than halfway to the outbuildings, my eyes had grown accustomed to the darkness and I saw the knee-high hedge of thorny brambles blocking my way at the lawn's edge.

Then I heard the crack of a whip and a cry of pain. Luis? I couldn't tell, but I had to find out. I moved to my left, toward what I thought was the road from the entrance to Magnolia to the outbuildings, looking for a way around or through this thicket. It was only a guess, but from what I'd been able to see from the veranda earlier, the other direction seemed to lead only to forests and fields.

I'd guessed right. Twenty yards or so later, I came on a path that led in the right direction. Another crack. Another cry. The brambles tore at my skirt. I didn't dare start running, but the delay was agonizing. I came to a padlocked gate nearly ten feet high. Daunting, but far from impossible to scale even in my dress.

When I dropped down on the other side, I had cleared the brambles, and the hard-packed earth offered quick access to my destination. I passed a barn that was completely dark, then crept around to the door of the building with the light. A couple of the stall windows were open, but I passed them by, afraid of startling an animal and telegraphing my presence.

The men had their backs to the door, and I was able to scurry inside and hide behind a cluster of pitchforks and shovels. Luis was hanging by his wrists, which were bound together. He was bare to the waist, and his feet barely touched the floor. He was facing the door and saw me enter, I was almost sure. But in the next moment I was mortified to see him twist around slowly, like a hanged man I'd once seen dangling at the end of a rope. His back was a sorry mess of welts and cuts from the whip that Xavier, the supercilious house slave, had been wielding. A huge white man stood to the side, watching the spectacle. Perhaps he was an overseer of some sort. My love, Carter Maxwell, had taught me how to use a bullwhip, a weapon that would make what that man held in his hand look like a shoestring. I had neither Carter nor the bullwhip, but I still had my pepperbox derringer, which I thought might purchase me the chance to deliver these torturers a taste of their own brutality. I pulled the pistol from my stocking holster, intent on creeping within its limited effective range.

The white man stepped toward a cleat on the wall where the rope that held Luis was anchored after running through a pulley. Xavier spoke. "Jonathan could lower you to your feet in a few seconds, Monsieur. Are you prepared to go to the grave over this?" He said it softly, as if he sympathized with his victim. "Surely the information can't be that precious."

"The swamp is deep, *mon ami*, and the crocodiles hungry," Jonathan added. "Your mistress nor no one else will ever know."

"Jonathan is right, Luis," Xavier said. "We don't want to do such a savage thing, but if we must, we must."

I estimated I would need ten steps before I could throw down on my quarry with any chance of success. The one called Jonathan had a pistol shoved into the back of his belt, but he wouldn't have time to draw it. I ventured forth from behind my shield.

Just then Luis drifted back so that I was once again in his sight line. He looked straight at me and shook his head, yelling, "No, no," as if responding to his tormentors, but clearly talking to me. I stepped back out of sight. Xavier cracked the whip again.

"Would you not feed me to the reptiles regardless?" Luis said, once he had caught his breath from the latest lash.

"Monsieur LeClerc would rather deliver you to your mistress in the morning than have you perish," Xavier said.

"Why?"

"This," Jonathan said, "he has not shared with us."

"All right. All right." Luis groaned. "Just let me down."

Xavier said, "Not until. . ."

"Until what?"

"You know," Jonathan said.

"I would be a traitor to tell you."

"Better than dead," Xavier said.

"Of that, I am not so sure, Señor Xavier. But here is what I know. Bonita came here looking to prove her parents innocent."

"So she says."

"And she is not lying. But there is more that Bonita does not know."

Jonathan and Xavier looked at one another.

Jonathan said, "It is as Monsieur LeClerc supposed. They were not innocent at all. They escaped with a large sum of money, did they not?"

"*Sí*. But it was money ripped from the hands of the poor and downtrodden. Bonita's parents wanted to give it back. And that is not all. Please cut me down." He groaned. "There is no blood in my arms. I will be useless."

Xavier said, "Speak quickly then. Why did they go all the way to San Francisco?"

"Bonita's mother was with child. They had to find someone they could trust. That person was my grandmother."

Jonathan said, "And they left the baby, Bonita, with her?"

"*Sí, sí*. They told *mi abuelita* there was a paper. Delacroix has a huge cache of money."

"As Monsieur LeClerc suspected," Jonathan said. "And where is that money?"

"They did not say."

Xavier sounded suspicious. "And you didn't tell your mistress about it?"

"He meant to keep the money for himself, obviously," Jonathan said. "Isn't that right?"

"She has plenty. I am a poor man."

I was jumping from my skin. I knew he was lying for some reason I didn't yet know. But it still shocked me to think Luis might have the power to keep something from me. Such is the force of evil that it can make one doubt even the most devoted of those close to us.

Xavier wielded the whip once more. I jumped along with Luis. Jonathan took up the interrogation.

"Where?"

"Yes. Yes. I was lying, but I can't take any more of this. I do know. Now cut me down."

It was Xavier's turn then. "Certainly, Monsieur. When you tell us what we want to know."

"It can't be told. I must show you."

"You're about to become 'gator bait, Mexican," Jonathan said.

"Dump me in the swamps," Luis countered, "and you will never know. Only when I am free will I tell you."

Xavier and Jonathan traded a look. It was the big man who finally spoke. "We will speak to Monsieur LeClerc." Jonathan said.

Chapter Eleven

Exodus

Hurrying back toward the house, I made no effort to conceal myself. It was probably too late for that anyway. Lily had surely awakened and spread the alarm of my absence. I was astonished to see no sign of a commotion. I climbed the steps and flung open the door into the parlor. The knitter at the bottom of the stairs jerked awake. I took a chance.

"Sherry?" I said.

"How you know me?"

When she awoke, she'd appeared confused, now she seemed terrified. "Shh." I put a finger to my lips, then whispered, "I'm going up to my room. In a moment, I'm going to ask Lily to awaken Monsieur LeClerc. I won't mention you were asleep if you won't mention I was here just now. Can we make that bargain?"

She looked around, still afraid, then nodded.

"Good," I whispered, then hurried past her.

I'd been mistaken to think that Lily would arouse the household. I found her cowering on her palette, sobbing. She started to a sitting position when I entered.

"You back, miss? I was scared you was gone for good."

"No, Lily. Why in the world are you so terrified?"

"I'da been whupped for sure and maybe sold away from Mama on top of it."

"Well, nothing's going to happen if neither one of us tells, and you can count on me not to say a word."

She just nodded, wiped her tears away, and let her sobbing subside.

"Now, I want you to go awaken Monsieur LeClerc." She froze again, and her eyes opened in new terror. "Don't worry. Tell him I ordered you to do it. I want my carriage, and I need to leave immediately." She shook her head, but I wasn't to be deterred. "Now," I said sternly, "or I'll wake him myself and tell him you refused."

That launched her into action. I headed down the stairs. As I passed Sherry, I said, "Tell Monsieur LeClerc that I will expect my carriage and servant on the front veranda in short order." The redundant message might do no good, but it couldn't hurt.

I paced the veranda, a shawl wrapped around my shoulders. From inside, the babble increased by the second. I took in huge gulps of air, both to calm my stomach at the spectacle of my beloved Luis being flayed alive and to clear the choking anxiety over whether we would both escape from Magnolia without further injury. Or at all for that matter.

After what seemed an age, LeClerc appeared, followed by Xavier, who was holding a lantern. LeClerc was in a maroon robe and a nightshirt. I noticed, however, that he wore boots rather than slippers.

"Well, Miss Kelly, whatever occasioned this startling turn of events?"

"I apologize for this untoward demand on your generous hospitality, Monsieur LeClerc, but I have urgent matters to attend to. They cannot wait. Now, if I can please have my carriage and my man, Luis, we will be on our way."

"I am afraid I cannot permit that, Miss Kelly, it being so dark and you unfamiliar with the area. I would never forgive myself if you all came to harm."

"I am grateful for your concern, sir, but I insist. The responsibility for my welfare is mine alone. None of it rests with you. I expect my carriage and Luis Mendez to appear presently, if you please."

Xavier spoke. "Mr. Mendez, he indisposed, Miss Kelly. Got no one to drive that carriage."

"Then I will drive it myself," I said. "I am quite capable." I stepped off the veranda and down the stairs. I headed toward the stables where

I had just seen Luis flogged. I heard rapid footsteps, saw Xavier speed past me then cut in front of me to block my way.

"Monsieur LeClerc refuse to permit this, Mademoiselle, to have you drive your own coach. Please to wait here. I will return presently."

"Things are beyond that point, sir. Please allow me to pass." I stepped to the side. Xavier continued the blockade. Footsteps approached, and LeClerc appeared.

"Why are you prolonging this, Monsieur?" I said.

"As I said, my honor, my reputation, is at stake. Madame Angelique would be offended to have you sent into the night. And she has many friends. The word would spread quickly. At least allow me to provide an escort so you don't lose your way."

Suddenly, I dropped all pretense of civility. "I'd as soon have Blackbeard himself for an escort as one of your men, LeClerc. And you can quit worrying about your reputation. That's as cooked as a Christmas goose already. If it's southern hospitality to hold your guests prisoner while you whip their friends, then give me the North every time."

It was dark, but I could see LeClerc's face grow even darker with rage.

"Whipped? Is this true, Xavier? Was Miss Kelly's man mistreated?"

Xavier hung his head. "I believe so, sir. I come upon it of a sudden and hoped to restore him before first light to avoid unpleasantness."

"And the culprit? Jonathan was it?"

"Yassuh."

"Take care of it, Xavier, forthwith. Miss Kelly, my deepest apologies. I had no idea. Would you care to be seated on the veranda? Xavier will fulfill your request with all deliberate haste. And perhaps you'd care for another sip of our bourbon while you wait."

I would have liked nothing better, except that it came from this man. I wanted nothing that might be construed as our being indebted to Magnolia.

"I will wait right here, Monsieur."

"As you wish. I'll have Rose bring you a chair."

"I've troubled your servants enough, Monsieur. But if my Luis and my carriage don't appear instantly, everyone in Orleans Parish, including Angelique and her friend and mine, Sheriff Carew, will know how we were treated at Magnolia."

"Of course." He spoke through gritted teeth. He strode off in the direction of the barns, leaving me standing alone in the driveway.

I thought invoking Carew might have been a mistake. Was Magnolia even in his jurisdiction? Never mind. Even isolated as it was, Magnolia couldn't possibly operate under its own law, whether Carew was in charge or not.

I stood at the spot until I couldn't bear it longer, then started pacing until I could no longer bear that, so I started off toward the barns. Luis's groans led me to the spot. The horse was hitched to the carriage, and Jonathan and Xavier were helping Luis to the seat. He was wrapped in a blanket to hide his wounds, but I knew they could not have been dressed yet, and that he must be in great pain. He was conscious, if unsteady. He caught sight of me and essayed a brief, very brief, grin. I pulled myself into the driver's seat, grabbed the reins, and slapped us into motion.

Xavier tried to climb up with us, but I whacked him with the buggy whip. He managed to grab it and wrest it from my hand, but he fell back when I let loose of it, and I managed to pick up speed during the tussle.

Still the struggle did not end. LeClerc stood in the driveway by the house, and tried to flag us down, but I gave our horse an extra slap of the reins and steered around the slave master as if he didn't exist. He reached out as we sped past him, but we were beyond his grasp, and we galloped away unmolested.

I breathed deep, trying to quiet my fear, and turned my attention to Luis as much as I could while still controlling the vehicle.

Chapter Twelve

Country Roads

The colonnade of magnolias which had looked so majestic on our arrival now appeared ghostly and ghoulish. Once out of the drive, I slowed the horse to a walk and continued a few hundred yards before I stopped and turned toward Luis, thinking to ask how I might comfort him. I was close to tears myself, but it is ever true that helping others is the best way out of grief and fright. It proved so this time.

"Drive on, Monita. We are not out of danger yet."

"Surely we have time to pause and tend to your wounds."

"No, just go. I will explain."

So I clucked the horse back into motion and slid closer so I could hear Luis's words. The debilitation of his usually strong voice was even more disturbing than the wounds hidden under the blanket.

"We will come upon a crossroads before long. I cannot say how long. They will be waiting for us there. They want the information I supposedly have. And, Monita, something they do not know. There was a map on the wall. They do not know I saw it. They may not understand its significance themselves."

"What kind of map?"

"A map of Rancho Sausalito."

I was stunned into a momentary silence.

"Do you think they believe the money is there?"

"I don't know what it means."

"Well, your wounds must be our first concern. They wouldn't dare attack us now. Angelique knows we came this way. Questions will be asked."

"They will claim ignorance. They offered an escort. We refused. There are bandits abroad."

"So we are not yet safe. What are we to do, Luis?" I managed a check of the watch at my waistband. "It is nearly two a.m." Silence. I feared he had passed out. "Luis?"

"We could stop, wait for daylight," he said.

I considered the suggestion. His wounds needed treatment. The sooner the better. I climbed down from the carriage and undid the traces. We would abandon the vehicle. Luis would ride. I would walk. Judging by the leisurely pace we had taken from Angelique's stables to Magnolia it would take us not much more than two hours on foot to return. Whoever was waiting in ambush would be looking for a carriage. I didn't know what we would do when our attackers appeared, but out of the carriage we made less of a target. Luis approved of my plan.

My shoes were not as utilitarian as I would have liked, but I was confident they would hold together for a short journey where the stones were so few. Another advantage of our current mode was lack of all the creaking a carriage makes in transit. A minor problem was water. We had none. But we also had not far to go.

All we had to do was to put one foot before the other until we arrived at Angelique's. Eventually I made out intersecting tree rows in the distance. A crossroads. I drew close to Luis. He was half-asleep, but managed to raise his head. I had thought we were close to escape, but was now terrified that neither Luis nor I would get out of this fix after all. I breathed, calmed myself, and tried to think. Luis roused himself. Even though he was a bit groggy, his rationality reassured me. We discussed leaving the road and trying to go through the fields to circle around those we supposed lay in wait. But the unknown terrain made for too great a risk. In the end, Luis went on alone, hoping they wouldn't be on the lookout for a single man on horseback.

I crossed myself, uttered a short prayer, and continued on foot. I hugged the side of the road, hoping to slip past our adversaries that way. Presently Luis stumbled into the scene, swaying in the saddle and singing like a drunk.

Juanita
Nita Juanita

Even terrified as I was, I had to smile at his masquerade. He could have been an actor, and, with his fine tenor voice, a singer as well as a *vaquero.* It was a side of him I'd never known.

He was challenged, of course, when he got to the intersection. Three men surrounded him, pistols drawn.

"Senores. *Estoy muy feliz de conocer a todos ustedes. ¿Es este el camino de Texas?*"

Unfortunately, our friend, Jonathan, was one of the group. He wasn't fooled by Luis's ruse of asking about the road to Texas.

"It's the Mexican. I recognize the horse, too. Grab him."

It was time for me to join the action instead of just sneaking around it as I'd planned. I uttered yet another prayer, sneaked up to the rear of Jonathan's horse, and slapped its haunch. The animal lurched and spun, and the other two men froze in confusion. While Jonathan was fighting for control of his animal I dashed over and slapped another of the horses.

The turmoil created the confusion I'd hoped for, and all at once, Luis and I became a team in combat. The fear in my heart gave way to elation. Luis put his heels to the carriage horse and slammed it into the third man.

At this point, I thought I had done all I could with my bare hands, and I longed for a weapon. I saw Luis rip a revolver from the holster of the man with whom he had collided, point, and fire. The man screamed, grabbed his belly, and slumped in the saddle.

I was desperate to do something other than stand and watch. I longed for a weapon, even the buggy whip Xavier had yanked from my hand would be welcome.

Then Providence showed me there was plenty I could do even without a weapon. I reached up and hauled Luis' shooting victim to the ground. Now I'd have a mount even if I didn't have a gun. I was pulling myself aboard the man's animal when more shots rang out. They came from Jonathan, but his horse was still pitching, and he missed. Luis fired again, and Jonathan dropped his gun and clutched his arm.

Our teamwork was a success. We were going to escape after all. I laughed with joy as we kicked our mounts into a gallop and fled the scene.

More gunfire. Something tugged at my skirt, but I felt no pain. It seemed, except for Luis's lash marks and perhaps a bullet tear in my skirt we'd come away unscathed. Luis's wounds were serious, but I felt sure they would heal in time. We still didn't know who had come after us or for what reason, but I knew we were getting closer to the truth. The truth we'd come nearly more than two thousand miles to find.

Chapter Thirteen

Delacroix Once More

The eastern sky was pink behind us, and I was near to slumbering when we finally approached Angelique's gate. I wrapped the horse's reins around a fence post and helped Luis from the saddle. Miraculously, he seemed a bit better, which was fortunate, for I could never have borne his weight alone.

"I am accustomed to sleeping in the saddle, Monita," he said.

How he could have slept even in a feather bed given the pain he was surely in, I still could not fathom. We struggled down the walk and up the steps, he leaning on my shoulder. I reached for the door handle. It swung open, and we found Angelique with arms ready to embrace us.

"Luis," I said. "He—"

"Yes, yes. I know. *Dépêchez, mon ami.*" She stepped to Luis's other side to help support him as she closed the door.

"How could you know about Luis, Angelique? We have only just—" Then I caught a glimpse into the parlor, where I espied Daniel Delacroix lounging in a brocade upholstered armchair, a china cup of coffee in his lap. He smiled and sent us a perfunctory wave.

"*Bonjour*, Miss Kelly."

I tried to ignore him, but I am sure my countenance must have betrayed my surprise and fright. "I believe," I said, "that Luis can reach his room with our assistance, but he needs a doctor without delay."

"Le Docteur Beauchamp is on the way, *chérie*," she said.

We struggled up the stairs, Luis easing in and out of consciousness. Delacroix had obviously heard from Magnolia, knew all that had happened there, and told all to Angelique. Otherwise, they would be asking what happened to him. So Delacroix must be in league with LeClerc. But if that was so, why was he arranging help for us? Or had Angelique been the one who received the information about us and notified Delacroix herself? In perilous circumstances such as these, trust is essential to survival. But we were so far from our familiar circles that faith in others had become a will o' wisp, hovering always just beyond our grasp.

***

An hour or so later, when Doctor Beauchamp had treated Luis's wounds and departed, I sat with Delacroix and Angelique in the parlor. A sense of danger and mystery had banished my exhaustion, and I was alert and on edge as I sipped the coffee, thick and sweet with molasses, that Angelique had served with one of her flaky croissants. I nibbled at the butter-rich pastry, more out of politeness than appetite. I should have been ravenous, but I was fearful of the conversation to follow. I wanted desperately to ask questions, lay my cards down face up. But I heard Sheriff Carew's voice and simply thanked Angelique and Delacroix for their help, then sat back to listen. There was a period of silence, but I was determined not to be the one to break it.

Finally, Delacroix spoke. "I was disappointed at your absence from Adelita's yesterday, Miss Kelly."

"My note of regret did not reach you, Monsieur?"

He smiled and shook his head.

"It must have gone astray somehow. I do apologize."

"Of course."

A moment of silence ensued. Delacroix said, "I understand that you exited Magnolia rather abruptly."

"You have excellent information, Monsieur. I congratulate you. Perhaps you could avail me access to your admirable sources of communication. They might aid me in my quest." I smiled, sipped, nibbled. Delacroix and Angelique shared a glance. Delacroix continued.

"It was most unfortunate, whatever happened to your man. I hope he will recover."

I began to understand a little of what was happening here, and I began to appreciate Luis's craftiness. He had phrased his lies to Xavier and Jonathan in a way that left his loyalties ambiguous. They couldn't be sure how much he had told me. As long as Delacroix did not know how much I knew, I had a bit of leverage. I hoped I could exploit it.

"Luis is a very resilient fellow," I said. "He will be back at my side before long." Another moment of awkward silence followed. Angelique filled the gap.

"Monsieur Delacroix came here much distressed. He wondered what inspired you to go to Magnolia at all."

Since Angelique herself had sent us to the plantation, I took this as a signal that she and Delacroix had not been in cahoots. It didn't explain his presence here this morning, but at least I knew I could continue to trust Angelique. Wheels within wheels. I confess, I'd begun to rather enjoy the little game we were playing.

"My inquiries after we met at Adelita's, Monsieur, gleaned a suggestion that LeClerc might have useful information. I heard nothing else of value, so I decided to pursue it, hoping I would learn something that would inform our subsequent inquiries."

It was Delacroix's turn. I waited. He waited. He finally spoke. "And did you find any such information?"

"Monsieur LeClerc was the very picture of southern gentility."

"And yet—"

"And yet, we departed in haste. Luis needed medical attention that was unavailable at Magnolia. I'm sure everyone understood the urgency of our situation." I smiled. Finished my coffee. "We are grateful for your summoning Doctor Beauchamp." I waited. Delacroix looked toward Angelique. She did not meet his eyes this time. She spoke to me instead.

"It is the least we could have done, Bonita. I am sure you could use some rest yourself." She rose. I followed her lead, and she ushered me toward the staircase. Delacroix stood as well, but stayed near his chair. I placed my foot on the bottom tread and turned in his direction.

"Thanks to our excursion to Magnolia, I do believe we are a step or two nearer to discovering the truth about my parents, but there is much left to learn. If you happen to think of any other helpful information, you or Monsieur LeClerc, I would be most gratified if you would see fit to share it when we meet again."

I ascended to my room, my mind blurred with a fatigue even fear could not overcome. Delacroix had learned nothing from me. His presence and his questions, however, told me plenty. At least it seemed so, but the time for sorting it out was after, not before, I'd gotten some sleep.

Chapter Fourteen

Convalescence

My confidence in Luis's recovery proved rather optimistic. He was able to walk in a rather shuffling manner the next day, but he wasn't able to approach his full and confident stride until a few days later. I became his nurse, cleaning and dressing his wounds, supporting him as he walked the hallway to regain his strength.

It was frightening to see him so weak, this man who had been my strength from childhood. He'd been twenty-two to my twelve when we first met. A wide gulf in age for a young mind. But now, fifteen years later, I realized we were both adults, nearly contemporaries, though I'd never before thought of us that way.

We are all of us mortal, and I, of all people, surely knew that. But in my heart, Luis had seemed no moreso than the oldest and staunchest of the redwoods that graced our western slopes at home. And here, his hand resting on my shoulder as he tentatively placed one foot in front of the other, he was as dependent on me as I had been on him these fifteen years. He was suddenly as vulnerable as anyone.

One morning, exhausted after our short stroll, we made our way to his room where he would rest until our next excursion, two hours hence. Our schedule was strict because our situation was urgent. I held his arm while he lowered himself to the bed. Once his boots came off, the next step was to swing his legs up. With some effort, he succeeded with one leg, strained to lift the other. He failed, then tried to reach down and interlace his fingers under his thigh. The wounds on his back wouldn't allow him to reach that far. Finally, I grasped his ankle and lifted. As I laid the leg on the mattress, I shifted my gaze to his face. He turned his eyes away. They were filled with tears. And with something else. Shame, I think.

"No, Monita," he said. He turned away. "No," he repeated.

I covered him with a quilt and left the room. Outside the door, I paused to collect myself. I heard a soft thump. Alarmed, I opened the door. His back was to me so he couldn't see me. I felt a little like a voyeur as I watched him, sitting on the bed with his feet resting on the floor, lifting first one leg, then the other, with agonizing slowness and pained grunts, to the bed. He then lowered his feet to the floor and repeated the torment.

I closed the door softly. The Luis I knew, the one who appeared lost a few moments before, was returning.

Chapter Fifteen

What Next?

Sheriff Carew was again not in his office when Luis and I dropped by four days later. This time, however, I was prepared for his absence and had written a note to slip under his door explaining that we were headed for Adelita's and promising not to leave town without notifying him.

We had decided on this precaution the day before as we sat on Angelique's porch. Luis was well on his way back to his old self, but nevertheless he perched on a stool because his back still hurt too much to lean back in a chair. His stride was not yet as swift and sure as customary, either. Over his objections, and as I supported him while he eased himself to his seat, a most unexpected moment occurred.

Our eyes met, as they had in his room a few days earlier, but this time a feeling passed between us that was different than anything we had ever before shared, close though we had been for so long. Never had there been a hint of romance between us, but suddenly, there it undeniably was. My breath caught. He was the first to look away. I finished arranging the blanket and sat down, shaking, in my own chair. Probably, I thought, it was the age-old emotional attachment that I'd understood often grew between nurse and patient. We immediately went on to more concrete issues.

We discussed the note to Carew, then he had a request. "And Bonita, I need a knife to replace the one Xavier and Jonathan stole." My spirits lifted to see that he felt ready to return to action. I wished we could add the .44 revolver we had stored in the luggage to his arsenal, but circumstances wouldn't allow.

During his recovery time, I had strolled down to the waterfront seeking information from some of the ladies in Delacroix's employ. I met with no success at all on my errand for quite some time. But here, like everywhere else, perseverance paid.

It was the liquor in her step that first drew my attention, but when she turned in my direction, I was surprised, then not at all surprised, to recognize an old friend and enemy from San Francisco. Rebekkah— two "k's" she'd always remind people. Maybe even her clients for all I knew. She had years earlier pulled me out of the rain and cold of a San Francisco winter into El Marinero Feliz, where I spent those many months playing piano while disguised as a boy. She later negated her good deed by betraying me to kidnappers. However, forgiveness is at the heart of my faith, and in my mind, I had absolved her, knowing she was the victim of men and drink. When I saw her that day in New Orleans, all my kind thoughts fled. I had an urge to shove her into the waiting current and entertained thoughts of hungry fish pursuing her through cold waters. Thus can Satan strip us of even our most holy impulses.

I tightened my fists, whispered the Our Father, and approached her with a smile. She was fearful at first, and untrusting. But a coin or two, some friendly talk, and a free libation convinced her of my good intentions. She seemed to have kept herself informed of San Francisco events. She knew that Sylvia had closed the brothel and that she and I had become successful in legitimate business.

"What d'ye think I'm doing down here in this sweatbox?" was the way she put it.

"I'm sorry your life has taken an unfortunate turn, Rebekkah. But perhaps I could help make it a bit easier." I held out another coin. She reached. I drew back. Eventually, my hesitation led to some very useful information. Not all I wanted, but enough to advance our cause a step. She even proved able to help fill Luis's need for a weapon, Mexican though she knew he was. Was I merely exploiting the weak and vulnerable, or had the Lord sent her to our aid? I chose to believe the latter.

***

"They will be coming after me soon," Luis said, "to collect the money Delacroix talked of in that wanted poster for your parents. When I meet them again, I must have more than words to show them."

"And who knows if that money even exists?" I said. "You certainly didn't find it anywhere near your grandmother's cabin on Rancho Sausalito, and my parents didn't tell your *abuelita* about it."

"So if the money exists at all, the secret lies with them in the grave," Luis said.

"Well," I continued, "LeClerc seems certain it does exist. Or did. And, as the saying goes, they tried to take it out of your hide."

Luis tried on a grin, but it didn't fit well. I hurried on with the discussion. "All we know for certain is that one way or the other, that money, LeClerc, Delacroix, and my parents are all linked. I believe the time has come to at last keep my appointment with Monsieur Delacroix. It will be risky. We could both be dumped in a bayou for the alligators as they threatened, and who would know?"

The customary look of concern he gave me now carried those new overtones for which I was still unprepared. Not that I found them unwelcome, which was even more disarming. We quickly got back to business, and I penned the precautionary note to leave with Sheriff Carew before we visited Delacroix. If we disappeared, at least some official would have an inkling of our intentions. And like the grain of wheat of which our Lord spoke, our actions would later bear fruit even though we might never know of it.

***

It was with a prayer on my lips and fear in my heart that I once again approached Adelita's. The noon sun was out, though the ground was still muddy from night showers. I feared first for Luis, knowing he'd have to wait outside during my sit-down with Delacroix. He had his weapon, thanks to Rebekkah, but it wouldn't be much help in an ambush that included firearms. I feared for myself as well, facing this rattlesnake of a man without my knight at my side.

The place seemed exactly the same, as if I had just stepped out for a moment instead of for days. The same vaguely rotten smell emanated from everywhere. Gator was at the bar. The same men sat in their places, same beers, same cards. Delacroix was at the bar instead of up against the wall with his lady friend, but she was at his elbow, clinging, seemingly ready for another go any time he felt the urge. Or anytime she herself felt one, perhaps.

All eyes turned my way when I entered, as much, I think, for the light that followed me when I opened the door as for my person. Instead of stepping up to the bar, I looked at Gator, raised my arms, and repeated my grizzly bear roar. He laughed and answered with his alligator imitation. Laughing myself, I waved to indicate I was headed for the table where Delacroix and I had met the first time. Gator nodded with a grin, understood I was asking to be served at the table instead of the bar. He picked up a mug and began drawing a beer. Delacroix whispered something to his companion and wandered in my direction. The woman, the "Adelita" after whom the bar was named according to Angelique, turned her back to the bar, propped herself on her elbows, and threw a smile, or a smirk, in my direction, though not to me or at me.

"Well, well, Miss Kelly," Delacroix said as he sat, "I was beginning to think you were avoiding me."

Two things happened before I could answer. Gator arrived with my beer, then Luis entered. We had decided to come in separately to give him a chance to scout the area outside before he joined me. Gator started to object to his presence, but I reminded him of our relationship, and he made the same arrangement he had before, to serve Luis as long as he drank outside. I held up a finger to pause Delacroix and joined Luis as he exited, a signal to any kidnappers, that whatever they had in mind, separating us was not an option.

The coast seemed clear, and there was plenty of open ground. "Please stay near the door, Luis," I said. He nodded, which I knew meant he would do whatever he thought best.

I rejoined Delacroix and sipped my beer while he shooed his woman off his lap and sent her back to the bar. I decided to dispense with all the indirect niceties. "I don't have your five thousand, Delacroix. I don't know where it is, or if it even existed."

He smiled, eyes flat as a snake's. "Oh, you can be certain it existed, Miss Kelly, and still does. And you can be certain that I intend to get it back."

"Good." I tossed him what I hoped was a fetching smile. "I believe I can help you."

That surprised him. It was the first time I'd seen his face register anything but cynical indifference or an equally cynical grin. He recovered quickly, though, and painted on the grin.

"Now why would you do that? And how?"

"Monsieur Delacroix, I'm going to violate a southern tradition here and come right to the point. I have no interest in that money. What I'm after is my parents' story, and I am just as determined to find that as you are to find your cash."

He paused, signaled to Gator, who delivered a full shot glass to the table. Delacroix looked at it, shoved it aside. "Water," he said.

Gator froze, mouth agape.

"I said *water*," Delacroix repeated.

"I heard you," Gator said. "Just caught me off guard is all." But he still didn't move.

"Well?" Delacroix shot menacing look at his bartender.

"Right away."

Gator vanished. I rose and told Delacroix I would return shortly. I found Luis just as I'd left him. "Everything calm?" I asked.

"As a summer pond," he assured me. "And you?"

"I'm making some progress. I'll check back before long."

He nodded. I returned to the table. Delacroix's lap was still unoccupied. He leaned toward me and spoke in a near whisper.

"All right. You've answered the 'why' part of my question. What of the 'how'?"

His movement implied that he was ready to share confidences, but I judged it to be too early for that. "First, I need to verify a couple of things. I believe you have no more interest in the money than I have. What matters to you is the honor, the principle of being somehow duped or tricked. It's a thorn that will fester until it's pulled. Am I right?"

"Let's just say you have a vivid imagination, my dear."

"And, sir, if we are to be partners, it is a business arrangement, not to be infected with words like 'my dear.'"

"My goodness, you are a ferocious one."

"Nor will there be any such condescension."

My words may have seemed petty to a casual listener, but I had learned that in dealing with men, it is utterly essential to make one's position on such matters clear. Women enter these relationships at a disadvantage when it comes to respect, and without respect, we will be exploited as sure as storms come in winter.

Delacroix took a breath. I'm sure there was another bit of sarcasm coming, but I cut it off.

"You and Monsieur LeClerc had a falling out that involves this money, and the bad blood will continue until your mutual honors are satisfied. Frankly, I am surprised you have not fought a duel over it."

Delacroix actually laughed aloud. He'd finished his water and turned now to the liquor.

"Well, it is now my turn to break a southern tradition, Miss Kelly. As you have surmised, this is a sore affair between LeClerc and myself. But we are both of us too intelligent, or perhaps too cowardly, to fall prey to the dueling custom. At least in the normal manner."

It was my turn to laugh. "One more item, then, and we can perhaps make a plan together. I'm sure you know that a pair of Magnolia thugs tried to whip the story of the money out of Luis."

He nodded, confirming my previous suspicion that he had spies virtually everywhere.

"And they think they succeeded. They believe Luis knows the hiding place and that he's willing to betray me to reveal it."

Delacroix was again surprised. The look on his face passed more slowly this time.

"You are a devious man, Delacroix. Even, by my lights, a degenerate one. But you are neither a brute nor a killer."

"And how have you divined these secrets of my character, my dear, er. . . excuse me, *Miss Kelly?*"

"It was not divination. You have a reputation, sir, among your associates. You are willing to resort to trickery and subterfuge to get your ways, but you would not have sanctioned the beating that Luis suffered."

"Without admitting the truth of your words one way or another, what might this mean about how we proceed?"

Thus, was Delacroix in my confidence and primed to take direction from me. Flattery, especially if it is also the truth, is a precious tool the Lord has provided for our sex.

Finally, I leaned toward him across the table. "Let me explain what I have in mind."

Chapter Sixteen

A Bit of Voodoo

I had barely begun my proposition to Delacroix when yells and curses sounded outside the entrance. *Luis.* My fears were well-founded. Near the doorway, Luis stood over Jonathan, one of his torturers from Magnolia. Blood dripped from the blade of Luis's new knife. His beer mug lay in a pool on the ground. The men from inside the bar gathered around quickly, their torpor suddenly vanished.

"Mexican stabbed that white man."

"Hang him, then."

"Sounds like fun to me."

I stepped between Luis and the crowd, wielding my little pepperbox. Not exactly a hogleg revolver, but threatening enough at close range. I was near enough to the lead attacker to smell his foul breath.

"Call a doctor, and call the law, but none of you is touching this man," I said.

"There's no need for either one, Miss Kelly." It was Delacroix suddenly at my elbow. "Take him inside, Gator." He raised his voice and addressed the crowd. "The man's under our care now, gentlemen. Rest assured that justice will be rendered. Gator, each of these fellows deserves a free drink for the shock they've been through."

The barflies were at first confused and uncertain. Delacroix took Luis's arm and hurried him inside. The crowd slowly followed. Thus were their passions easily purchased.

Gator and Luis lifted Jonathan and laid him face up on the bar at one end. Gator set about pouring the refreshments for the men at the other. Jonathan was bleeding badly, rolling and bucking with pain. Someone had stuffed a bandanna in his wound, but it was soaked and dripping now.

"Addie," Delacroix called. "You get some of those herbs of yours and come on."

"On my way," came a voice from somewhere in the back.

It rather surprised me to see Delacroix's paramour emerge with a cloth sack and a crock jar. Luis stepped aside.

Adelita—Addie, as Delacroix had called her— yanked the bandana from the wound and tossed it aside. Jonathan yelled and grabbed for the injury.

"Hold the varmint, for Christ's sake," she growled. Luis leaped up on the bar, grabbed Jonathan's hands, and put knees to his shoulders. Gator left off his bartending for the moment. He whipped off his belt, wrapped it around the big man's ankles, then climbed on top of him and sat on his thighs.

I was at a loss for how to help, but Gator said, "Keep pouring drinks, girl."

It didn't even occur to me to object to the man's language. I just took drink orders and grabbed bottles. I paid little attention to whether what I poured matched what they requested. I'm sure many of them got well more than the single drink Delacroix had promised. The smells of liquor, blood, tobacco and stale sweat battled for dominance as the men pressed to the bar cussing at me and yelling for more drinks while Jonathan screamed in pain, and Adelita called directions for Jonathan's treatment.

"Daniel, tell Helmina to close the shop and bring candles," Addie ordered. Delacroix disappeared without objection. Addie drew a handful of herbs from her sack and began chanting. It was a chore to keep track of all this and tend bar at the same time. The torrent of bellowing and hollering redoubled as I slowed my liquor-pouring pace, but I wasn't about to let all the name-calling in the world keep me from missing a single detail of what Adelita was doing.

Presently, a black woman, undoubtedly the Helmina of which Adelita had spoken, appeared. As beautiful and exotic looking as she was dark, she wore a long necklace of garish glass beads. On her head she balanced a tray bearing three lighted white candles. She set the tray on the bar, and Addie used the candles to light the herbs. The whole place filled with the smell of hot wax and an aromatic smoke that blotted out even the resident stench of the bar. The odor was dominated by sage, but there were other smells I couldn't identify. Helmina swayed behind Addie, adding her own chant and hand motions while Addie waved her incense around Jonathan.

Addie handed the smoking bundle to Helmina and drew some foul-smelling wet herbs from the crock jar.

"Hold him down tight now," she warned. She stuffed some of them into Jonathan's wound. He began bucking and writhing again, but the women paid no attention to his distress. Addie poured some liquid from the crock jar into a glass. Helmina held Jonathan's nose and forced some of it down his throat. Addie then applied some dry herbs from the cloth sack directly to the wound. After that, she drew from her bodice a bone needle and some catgut thread.

Jonathan had ceased his paroxysms, but resumed them when Addie started her sewing. Again, Helmina and Addie remained indifferent to his reaction. Soon, the whole operation was complete. Luis's handiwork lay mended like a ripped and repaired shirt. Addie stepped back while Helmina made one more pass over Jonathan with her candles, and they exited toward the back.

Curious about where they were headed, I announced, "Gator will take over, gentlemen," and followed the women toward the back until I felt a hand on my shoulder. It was Delacroix.

"You won't be welcome, Miss Kelly."

"Why not? What's going on back there?"

"It would be best, Miss Kelly, if we resumed our discussion at another time and place. I will send word to Miss Angelique's as soon as I have arranged something."

"What of Jonathan?"

"He is about to embark on a voyage."

"Voyage?"

"To a place where he can heal properly and in seclusion."

It was clear that Luis and I had outstayed our welcome at Adelita's for the time being. Delacroix would tell us nothing more.

"And when might we expect your communication?"

"Patience, my dear Miss Kelly, is a virtue too little observed among those of both sexes. Now, if you will please follow me."

With that, he led Luis and me toward the rear of the bar. I thought I might see what Addie and Helmina had been up to after all, but there was no sign of them or of any herbs or potions in the hallway we traversed. There was, however, a closed door from which emanated some interesting and unidentifiable smells. The exit door at the end of the hallway opened on to a boardwalk that led directly to a quay. No one entering or leaving Adelita's by the front entrance could have seen us walking toward the ship called *Marat* that was docked at the foot of the path.

"What do you think, Luis?"

"*Esperamos,*" he said. "We wait, Monita."

It was a wise answer, but it did not suit my mood or my temperament. "We will wait, my friend," I said, "but we will not rest."

Chapter Seventeen

At the Altar

The splendid cathedral that stands in the center of New Orleans is, in its own way, even more grand than our cathedral at Mission Dolores in San Francisco. Its three conical spires lift one's eyes and heart toward heaven. Such is a proper attitude for those approaching a holy service through the grand nave, above which soars the central and tallest spire.

Luis and I knelt together, then joined the queue to the altar to partake of the holy bread and wine. The congregation was a diverse assembly of races and attire. All the antipathy we had experienced at Adelita's, and which Sheriff Carew had described, seemed to dissolve here into a common yearning for the favor of the Almighty. I wondered that so little of this common spirituality transferred to life outside the cathedral doors.

I made a brief stop at the confessional before we left, but my purity of spirit was compromised, and I made a botched job of it. Still, I figured it was better than nothing.

Back at Angelique's I expressed my puzzlement over glasses of her excellent sherry.

"You are a lady *très intelligente* Mademoiselle Bonita, but your learning is *plutôt,* slow in some things. You are no longer in the Ville de Saint Francis. Here, things that appear obvious are often not so. You assumed that all the dark faces you saw at mass were in bondage.

In truth, there are a great many free people of color here, people who own property and appear to prosper side by side with white people."

"And yet, there is such hatred," Luis said.

"And yet these free people cannot vote. They cannot testify in the legal courts. But they can all gather at the cathedral," Angelique said.

"I feel fortunate to live where there are no slaves," I said.

"Ah, again you have the *naïvité*. You forget that I have resided in your city. Black slaves to buy and sell you do not have, but some who brought slaves with them before the Americans seized California still hold them, no? And for the Indians, there is not protection even yet."

"Angelique is right, Monita," Luis said. "And you know it well."

I realized that in my desire to inhabit a world of right, I had created a truth for myself that was decidedly untrue. We may complain when others deceive us, but in matters of self-deception we are willing and unwitting victims. I had ignored all that Angelique and Luis described, even the mistreatment the Miwok people had suffered on Rancho Sausalito. Luis's own grandmother had been among those. My uncle had helped ameliorate their plight. But the well-being of that small village was an exception. Their brethren far and wide endured state-sanctioned proscription and forced labor.

And as for that hatred that Luis described, I recalled how often my own Sylvia had turned away black and brown men from her brothel and redirected them to "your own establishments." Even though our ladies represented all colors to cater to the varied tastes of our white clients, the colored clients were not eligible to partake at The Happy Sailor. Even in the lowest places, then, were the races kept subservient. And even if San Francisco had been narrowly blameless in the matter of Negro slavery, I held little of the moral authority I had assumed in objecting to what went on in New Orleans. Even accepting all that, however, I thought I could turn the situation to our advantage.

"What do you say, Luis," I asked, "to another trip to Pierre's? Suppertime is near, and I'd like some more of that gumbo."

"But—" he started to object.

I held up my hand in a "halt" signal.

"I know," I told him. "I'll explain on the way."

***

It was dusk, and I was seated in the dining room at Pierre's. Luis, of course, would not have been allowed inside, so we didn't even try. He had gone on another mission to Adelita's.

I had remembered Carew's recommending Pierre's. It had occurred to me that, knowing of our purpose, he had suggested the place for more than its cuisine. Why it had taken so long for the idea to dawn on me, I have no idea. *Plutôt,* slow, as Angelique had said, was the only explanation.

Even in cities as broad-minded as San Francisco and New Orleans, the appearance of a lady dining alone attracted some attention. Not only did I not mind, I was depending on it. The ploy had worked admirably for launching my career in San Francisco, helping arrange acquaintances with prominent business people I could never have met otherwise. It was sometimes difficult to embrace the monetary side of the relationships while avoiding unwanted romance. But with Sylvia's help, I had managed. I saw no reason why the tactic wouldn't work to further my goals in New Orleans.

It began with furtive glances, of course, then not-so-furtive staring. Finally, true to a script that was apparently followed on both coasts, a waiter delivered a glass of unrequested wine.

"With the compliments of the gentleman, who assures you it is the very best pairing with the gumbo of the house. I cannot disagree." He nodded in the direction of a not-so-distant table where a man in rather soiled buckskins sat with a full decanter before him.

I pushed the glass away with a smile. "Thank you, François. Please tell the gentleman I appreciate the offer, but that I cannot accept such a gift from a person not of my acquaintance."

"As you wish, Mademoiselle." The waiter adjusted the towel on his arm, straightened, and strode to the man. I turned my attention to the gumbo and to the wine I had already ordered. The exotic combination of spices tickled both my nostrils and palate. It was like nothing I had ever tasted. The lunch Luis and I had sampled at wharf side was a mere shadow of this.

Presently, the waiter interrupted again. "Mademoiselle, the gentleman sends his apologies for his presumption and asks if an introduction *par moi même* would suffice as proper in this circumstance."

This was a new one. A San Franciscan would have stepped up to my table and made his own introductions. I wasn't sure whether an acceptance would mark me as an easy woman or merely a polite one. I despaired of ever learning the codes around here. I decided the waiter might be my best guide in this case. I stole another glance toward the gentleman in question. He was a handsome specimen indeed. One I might find difficult to refuse in other circumstances.

"François, you realize from my accent that I am a stranger in your city."

"*Mais oui.*"

"As such, I am placing my trust in you. I hope you are worthy of guarding my reputation."

His eyes opened wide with puzzlement. "I. . . I hope so, Mademoiselle."

"First, would that man be someone you would consider worthy of introducing to your mother or sister?"

"Oh, *certainement*. His appearance is not of the best quality at this moment, but he is indeed a proper person."

"And would it be considered forward of me to accept such an invitation from him?"

"*Mais non.* You can be confident that you would remain *dans la meilleure réputation.*"

"Then you may deliver my assent to his invitation and ask him to join me following your introduction." I had no idea what might come of this encounter. It might lead to nothing, or it might open doors to the mystery I was pursuing.

"As you wish, Mademoiselle."

Thus, after this rather tiresome dance did I find myself sharing my table with a tall and muscular fellow named Cat McGhee. "Cat," short for "Catamount," that feline predator we in the West might call a cougar or mountain lion. I judged him somewhat older than I, perhaps in his late twenties or early thirties. His features were elegant in a rough-hewn sort of way, so his physical attractions were both sophisticated and primitive. How one achieved such a combination I couldn't quite fathom, but there it was. His buckskins, though far from pristine, gave off a rich, not unpleasant, odor of forests and flowers.

He hailed, he explained, from "back East." Boston, specifically. But his parents had in their youth decided to forsake the city for the wilds of Tennessee. It was there he was christened with a name meant to invest him with the feline qualities of stealth and power they admired in his totem animal.

"My folks eventually tired of frontier life and returned to Boston, where I spent most of my youth. But the name stuck, and so did a taste for life outside the urban crush."

A colorful tale, though not one I accepted at face value. We would see what the future brought.

"I was under the impression there were no mountains in Louisiana," I said with a smile. He gave me a puzzled look. "Your attire. You look like a man roaming high elevations on a quest for beaver."

His laugh was hearty. "And doubtless I smell a bit like that man as well. I am fresh off the trail and considerably underdressed for a place like Pierre's, but I was starving for something more than pemmican and squirrel."

"I've been reduced to those dishes a few times myself," I said. "Distasteful, of course. But survival always trumps flavor, and I agree that Pierre's is more than a step or two removed."

"You surprise me," he said. "There are some mysteries behind your elegant appearance, then."

I gave him a carefully edited version of my own history. Both of us left hanging the question of what we were doing in New Orleans at the moment. I broached the question first as François was clearing my place settings. Cat and I ordered brandies.

"Do you live in New Orleans, or are you on a visit?"

"I come rather often. But no, I do not live here."

"Where do you call home?"

"I confess 'home' is a rather catch-as-catch-can proposition for me, which depends on the circumstances of the moment."

"And what employment takes you hither and yon?" I asked.

"I do indeed spend some time on mountain traplines. Despite the tiresome diet, I from time to time get the urge for mountain air and the solitude and occasional encounters both with nature and other rough and ready fellows. The pelts help finance my expeditions. After a time at the higher altitudes, I find myself yearning for civilization, so here I am. I do some building and some lawyering. So I am a bit of a wanderer, Miss Kelly. Much different than you, I am guessing."

"How so?" I answered. He was spilling so much about himself at first meeting that I found myself shifting uncomfortably in my seat.

"You do have a fixed home," he said, "yet you are far away. And apparently alone. I am intrigued."

"You already noted that I am a woman of mystery," I smiled in what I hoped was an enigmatic manner. Cat awakened my clairvoyance. I sensed an almost pure benevolence about him, a quality I had seldom encountered in man or woman. And no shadow behind, such as was the case with Sheriff Carew and other such persons of apparent benevolence masking malevolent intent.

François appeared with our brandies and a note.

"For you, Mademoiselle." He handed me the folded piece of paper. It was from Luis.

Meet me on the wharf.

I instinctively folded the note and checked my surroundings for imminent threats. My countenance somehow betrayed my anxiety.

"And now you are engaged in secretive correspondence," Cat said. "My fascination grows apace."

I tried to hide my apprehension behind another enigmatic smile. I spoke in a throaty whisper. "As well it might. Now, if you'll excuse me." I started to rise, only to find him behind me, pulling my chair back. He moved with a silence and dexterity that did honor to his name.

I nodded and stepped toward the exit. I am far from a whimsical person, but defying reason and my own nature, I chose, guided by my clairvoyant sense, to follow an impulse. I turned back to this man who claimed to be a trapper, a builder, and a lawyer all in one package.

"If you'd care to indulge your appetite for intrigue, Mr. McGhee, perhaps you'd like to accompany me."

"By all means," he said.

***

When we arrived at the wharf, Luis was nowhere in sight. I wrung my hands, turned and looked in every direction. What had happened at Adelita's? Cat and I stood in place as the shadows deepened. The mighty current slipped by with barely a whisper, leaving muddy wavelets behind.

"Am I allowed to know more about this Luis or about your errand here?"

"I'm afraid not, Mr. McGhee. In fact, perhaps it would be better if you departed."

"And leave you alone here? That would not be chivalrous."

"I'm quite prepared to defend myself." I patted my thigh where the derringer was concealed beneath my skirts.

He hesitated. I was suddenly more anxious to get rid of him than I had been to invite him along.

"It would be even less chivalrous to refuse a lady's request, would it not?"

"As you wish, Miss Kelly." He touched the brim of the low-crown, trail-stained, leather slouch hat he had donned when we left the restaurant, a ceremonial gesture meant to suggest tipping said hat without actually performing the action. "May we meet again?"

"I will look forward to it," I said. I tipped my eyes toward the ground in the shadow of a curtsy, a gesture I meant to reflect his own token action.

He smiled, took one more look around the area, and strode into the shadows.

"Monita."

Luis's loud whisper came from behind a cargo shed a few yards from where I stood. I hurried to him. He crouched on a narrow ledge behind the shed, water lapping at his boots. A coolness rose from the river. I knelt beside him, unmindful of the splashes wetting my skirts.

"Luis, you look dreadful. What's wrong?" I said.

"Who is that man?"

"Just someone I met in the restaurant. He's of no consequence. Tell me what's happened."

"Gator is dead."

I gasped. It was an effort to keep my voice down. "The bartender at Adelita's? How?"

"All I know is that someone shot him and that the law wants to hang me for the crime."

Chapter Eighteen

Fugitive

"I walked into Adelita's," Luis began.

I had never seen him so frightened, even at the hands of Xavier and Jonathan. He time after time looked over his shoulder as he spoke, leaned against the wall as if he were trying to merge with it. I took his hands in mine. Once more that surge filled me. Did he feel it as well? I couldn't tell. I wished, perhaps for the hundred-thousandth time, that I could learn to invoke my clairvoyance at will.

"There were more men inside than I had ever seen there before," he said. "Of course the room became silent when I entered, and they stared at me with venom. I expected that, but there was, in addition, some kind of peculiar poison in the air. I asked Gator if perhaps I could speak with Monsieur Delacroix outside. He said the man was not there but would return eventually. I said I would wait outside. He said I could waste my time however I wanted, but Delacroix wouldn't have truck with a dirty Mexican. That brought jeers, and a couple of men even stood and moved toward me. I retreated to a concealed place behind the building."

"I should never have asked you to go there, Luis. I didn't realize—"

"Monita, I remind you that this was a plan we made together. We agreed it would be more convincing for me to tell him about the map in LeClerc's barn than for you to tell him second hand." It was his turn to squeeze my hands. Even at a time like this, my heart leapt. What intemperate creatures our emotions are.

I took a breath. We wouldn't even be in New Orleans if not for me and my stubbornness.

"What happened next?"

"I waited. Monsieur Delacroix did not appear."

I thought of myself inside Pierre's enjoying gumbo and wine and conversation while he huddled in the shadows.

"Then there was shouting and cursing inside. Then a shot. Then another. Somebody screamed. Men came running out. They said Gator needed a doctor and someone should get the sheriff."

"Merciful heavens, Luis, you should have gotten out of there."

"I was hidden. My leg still bothers me too much to run well. Besides, I figured the more I learned the better. In due time both the doctor and Sheriff Carew arrived. They pronounced Gator dead, and several men said they had seen me shoot him. They formed a posse, Monita. Carew and his men are hunting for me even now."

I took Luis's hands in mine. "We will find a safe place for you, *amigo querido*. Then I will talk to Carew. He is a fair man."

Luis shook his head violently. "You didn't see those savage men, Monita. Fair or not, Carew has no choice but to jail me in the face of the testimony of those witnesses, and he cannot protect me from that mob, even if I'm locked in a cell."

"You may be right. But there is no doubt you need a safe place to hide while we work all this out. Follow me."

"Where, Monita?"

"To our only true friend in this mysterious city where I fear we do not belong."

Chapter Nineteen

Refuge

We followed random streets and alleys, little knowing where we were. All we could think of was to keep moving in Angelique's general direction until we happened on familiar landmarks. I generally went first, Luis following, limping enough to worry me, but insisting he was fine. Our way became more and more treacherous. Men were scouring the city, torches lit, guns ready. You'd have thought Adelita's was city hall and Gator the mayor, considering the zeal with which they galloped the streets, hollering to bring Luis to the noose. Or the firing squad. We at last reached our haven, but the vigilantes had beaten us there. Two of them, torches lit, stood on the veranda, Angelique huddled between them in her night wrap. Luis stood and shook his head.

"So much for our refuge," he said.

One was dressed in coveralls and BVD's. He wore heavy boots laced nearly to the knee. The other was in a vividly red shirt and pants of heavy canvas. His suspenders were black and wide. For footwear he sported low-heeled riding boots. Both seemed heavily outfitted for a July in New Orleans.

"Stay here in the bushes, Luis. I'll take care of this."

"Monita, no." I felt a tug on my sleeve as I walked toward the front steps, but I paid it no mind. I also paid no mind to the torch bearers, but headed straight to Angelique and embraced her.

"My goodness, Angelique. You didn't tell me you were expecting suitors."

A heavy hand fell on my shoulder.

"You're that Kelly woman, ain'tcha?"

"Angelique. I expected a better class of gentlemen from you."

Angelique looked dismayed. I grabbed the pinky finger of the hand on my shoulder, turned on my heel, and bent it backward. I was rewarded with a satisfying yell of pain, and the hand disappeared.

"Would you care to perform a proper introduction, Angelique?" I said.

"I'm sorry, my dear, but their names they did not tell me."

"Then perhaps. . ." I gestured toward the man who was still shaking the hurt out of his hand.

"Only names you need are that we're the law, and right now we are out looking for a killer."

"Dangerous work, and you are doing an admirable job without harming innocent citizens such as myself and Madame Chevalier. I would like to commend you to my friend, Sheriff Carew, but without your names, I will be unable to do so."

The two shuffled a moment, looked at one another. Invoking Carew's name had been a good move.

"I'm Mike. Mike Kramer. This here's Luke."

"What did you say your last name was?"

"I never said, but it is Moreau."

It was easy to deduce from the way he swallowed his "r's" that French, not English, was Luke's first language. Also, that these two had never met before tonight.

"Well, Luke and Mike, thank you for your help. Sylvia, have all your boarders returned now?" I squeezed her hand.

"*Oui,* Bonita. All of them."

"So, you see, you can resume your search elsewhere. We are safe here."

Again they shuffled, traded glances. "I don't know. We was supposed to guard this place till they told us different."

"That probably was a wise strategy at the time the order was given. How long ago was that, by the way?"

Luke pulled a rather handsome watch. "I calculate more than two hours."

"Ah. So you see things are moving so fast, they've doubtless forgotten you. You do have a horse nearby do you not, Mike?"

"How did you know?"

Without mentioning his boots, I said, "It seemed to me you carry yourself like a horseman. There's a certain confidence about you." More men have fallen to vanity, I believe, than to all the cannons of war. "And Luke, you strike me as someone who likes to keep at a job, stay on a schedule, not waste time waiting for things to happen. So, rather than sit here guarding a place that needs no guarding, you'd do better to pursue your quarry in the streets where it is undoubtedly fleeing like a terrified fox."

"By God, lady," Mike said. "You make sense. What do you say, Luke? Should we get out on that Mexican's trail?" Luke hesitated. Mike continued. "Well I'm going whether you do or not. Any more standing around, I'll jump out of my skin."

He fairly leapt off the porch. Luke followed, a few steps behind.

"*Merci* for keeping us safe, friends," Angelique called, then turned to us and lowered her voice. "Now, Bonita, what in the world—"

"Shhh." I interrupted her and put a finger to her lips. "Listen." Before long, we heard hoof beats, the sound receding quickly. Mike and Luke had departed.

"The way you tricked those men. You are *absolument merveilleuse,* Bonita."

"We must act quickly." I scampered down the steps and called to Luis. "Quit playing in the flowers, Luis. Come inside. Hurry."

He parted the cabbage-sized hydrangea blossoms with his hands, stepped out, and immediately sprinted toward the house. I was right behind him.

And, sad to say, Mike and Luke were right behind me.

"Hold it right there, greaser," Mike said.

My tactics with the two thugs had not been nearly as marvelous as Angelique thought.

Chapter Twenty

Lynching

His captors had Luis tied hand and foot to a saddle in no time at all. With pistols brandished in our direction, Angelique and I had no way to stop them. We were in the same dilemma we'd been in at Magnolia, and I felt the same fear and frustration I had then.

"We got to bring the women as well," Luke declared.

"The Mexican will be enough for now. Let someone else come back for the females if the sheriff wants them," Mike answered.

Luke rode double on Mike's horse while they led their prisoner, my beloved Luis, bound and lashed to Luke's. When they disappeared, Angelique began to wail.

"Never in the Ville de Saint Francis did we suffer so. Would I had never come here."

"Come, Angelique. We have no time to waste."

"Come where? What are we to do?"

"Do? We are going to the jail to free Luis."

"*Non, non, non.* Bonita. It is not a thing for me and not safe for you as well."

"We are beyond safe, Angelique. We are in the midst of action at all costs." I picked up my skirts and began trotting out the gate.

"*Bon chance*, Bonita. I am sorry I cannot." Angelique's voice trailed after me.

I knew I had no chance of reaching the jail before Luis. Had I known the city well enough, I could perhaps have cut through one of the cemeteries, but I could only use the streets I knew. What I'd do when I got there would depend on whatever inspiration heaven sent me, for I had no ideas of my own.

***

The need for improvisation arose well before I reached the jail. I had been forced to stop and catch my breath, my hands on my knees, when a clamor erupted not far ahead of me. Of a sudden, my breathlessness mattered not at all. I sprinted toward the noise and toward the growing flames as more and more torches arrived on a scene that filled me with horror.

I believed Mike and Luke had intended to deliver Luis to Sheriff Carew, but the crowd had become a monster with its own body and mind, and the monster had no intentions of allowing Luis to be incarcerated. The scene was a small square with a huge magnolia tree at its center, and from one of its branches hung a noose. I could not see Luis, but I had no doubt he was headed for the rope, if he had not already arrived. In most cases, my small stature would have been a disadvantage, but for the moment, it would serve me well.

What would not serve so well was the undersized derringer beneath my skirts. Not for the purpose I had in mind. However, nearly everyone in the mob carried a pistol, and it was a simple matter to lift one from its holster without the owner detecting the theft. Thus armed with a hefty .44 revolver, I crawled through the forest of legs and boots like a child struggling her way through a crowd at a fair.

Mike and Luke had not yet given up trying to prevent the hanging, but their efforts had become half-hearted. Hands grabbed the bridles of their horses, pulling them away from Luis. Others yanked Luis toward the magnolia.

"This is not legal, gentlemen, but it's on your heads. I can't do no more," Mike yelled.

"Hang him, hang him, hang him," became a chant as the crowd forced Mike and Luke to abandon Luis. A man with a full beard and tobacco-stained teeth lifted the noose and dropped it over Luis's head.

Not for nothing, though, had I grown up a tomboy on Rancho Sausalito and fought my way through the gold rush in frontier San Francisco. Before anyone knew I was there, I ran forward, grabbed the saddle horn on Luis's horse, leapt aboard and fired my pistol in the air.

"No hanging today, boys," I yelled.

I pointed the gun at the bearded ruffian beside me. "Remove that noose." He dithered for a moment, looking to the crowd, which was dithering as well. I had them off balance for the moment, but I knew I had only a brief time before they regained their savagery. "The next one won't go in the air," I said. He hesitated still. I fired, aiming for the shoulder, but in truth cared not if I was off target.

The man yelled, bent over in pain, clutching at his wound. I grabbed the rope, used it to haul myself to my feet, and lifted it over Luis's head.

"Go, go, go," I yelled.

Luis did what he could with his feet and hands bound to urge the horse forward. I dropped back down and slapped my animal on its haunches. I fired once more over the heads of the crowd. I reached around Luis and managed to grab the reins of his horse. Miraculously, everyone was so shocked they parted before us like the Red Sea before Moses. In moments, we were clear of the crowd, but I knew the confusion wouldn't last long. I could go neither to Angelique's nor to Carew's jail, which would provide no more refuge from this hydra-like beast than a house made of sticks and straw. At home, I knew a hundred destinations for situations like this. Here, I knew none.

"The race track," Luis yelled. "Straight ahead, bear right."

I followed his directions, wondering how he knew of this track. I wove through some side streets in hopes of confusing our pursuers. Behind us, hoof beats thundered, cursing voices roared, and torches fired the darkness. Any minute, I expected someone would appear before us to cut off our flight. But no one did, and presently we found ourselves behind some grandstands of what must have been the race track Luis had described.

"Keep going, Monita. If we reach the stables, we can find something to cut these ropes and figure out how to escape."

The stables were a maze of sheds and corrals, redolent with the heady smells of animals and manure. The aromas brought to mind the Rancho Sausalito barns I recalled so fondly. The place was deserted. Not a stable hand in sight. Most likely the lure of the manhunt had drawn everyone away.

It wasn't difficult to find a well-equipped tack room, and the ropes that had bound Luis soon lay in pieces at our feet.

"How did you know about this place?" I asked.

"My time waiting for you outside Adelita's, Monita, proves profitable once more. Men love to talk of coming here to Metairie and betting on horses. They encouraged me to join them and offered directions. Now let's grab fresh mounts, and go."

But we didn't move toward the horses. We stood still for a moment. I embraced him, pressed my head to his chest. He stroked my hair. It had been years since my only other romance, the one with Carter Maxwell, a man who preferred mountains to cities and wilderness to me. The emotion I felt in Luis's arms was akin to the intensity I'd experienced with Carter, and it nearly choked me.

He murmured, "This. . .this. . .it is impossible, Monita."

"Ah, *querido,*" I whispered. I lifted my eyes toward his.

He looked in my eyes but a moment, then looked away and shook his head, whether in denial or confusion, I couldn't tell.

I snapped myself back into the urgency of the moment.

"Where should we go, do you think?"

"Back to San Francisco," he said. "We are nothing but criminals here."

"Perhaps that would be wise, *amigo,* but I have a better idea. Let's head back to Adelita's."

Chapter Twenty-One

Lion's Den

With everyone out searching east for Luis, it was not difficult to avoid our pursuers by heading in the opposite direction. Now we were implicated not only in murder, but in horse stealing. Carew would have fun writing up a list of charges. I considered that invention fitting since it was alleged horse-rustling that had gotten my parents killed.

I left Luis with the horses near a warehouse on the dock and continued on to Adelita's alone. Much against his wishes, I carried the .44 in plain sight, tucked into a belt I'd improvised at the stables. I'd decided I needed to play the role of warrior to the hilt if we had any hope of prevailing against the forces arrayed against us. I wasn't sure how Delacroix could help us, but he seemed a man who would be able to find some opportunity amid the present chaos, and I had made a start at an alliance with him during our last conversation.

I had never been inside the place at night, but Adelita's appeared essentially unchanged by all the turmoil of a few hours earlier. The lighting was much the same as in the day, when little sunlight oozed through in any case. There were a few more candles and a lantern on the bar, which was shrouded in black. In Gator's honor, I presumed. Sales continued with a new barkeep, a short, dapper young man with red hair, sporting all the mustache he could manage and garbed in a fresh starched-and-pressed shirt. He wore a black armband on his right arm, a blue and yellow striped sleeve garter on the other. Something else was off. I couldn't tell what it was for a few moments. Then I realized the large mirror was gone. Only the frame remained.

"I'm looking for Monsieur Delacroix," I said.

"I'm a bartender, not a secretary. What'll you have?"

"I apologize for my lack of manners. My name is Bonita Kelly. What is yours?"

"'Bartender' will do me fine, *Bonita*." He rested his elbows on the bar and leaned toward me. "Now, are you going to have something to drink or not?"

"Well, *bartender*, I see my display of propriety has had no effect on you."

I turned away from the bar and headed toward the curtain leading to the back rooms.

"Hey, you can't—"

I drew the revolver, turned, and pointed it in his direction. "It would be a shame for Adelita's to lose two bartenders in one day." I would have fired a warning shot, but I had only four bullets remaining. However, my brandishing the gun turned out to be a sufficient threat, sending the patrons and the bartender alike diving for cover. It was nice to feel powerful instead of fearful and helpless.

I parted the curtains and called as I crept down the dark hallway, lit only by two guttering candles. "Monsieur Delacroix? Daniel? Addie? Helmina?" Silence. Then a noise, a footstep, behind a door to my right. I turned the knob and pushed it slowly open with my left hand as I brandished the pistol with my right. "Is somebody—" I never finished that sentence, for someone grabbed my left arm, pulled me inside, and closed the door behind me. Whoever it was also clapped a hand over my mouth.

"Quiet, or you must die by my hand." Xavier. What was he doing at Adelita's?

Chapter Twenty-Two

Riverbank

My surprise at hearing the loathsome voice vanished immediately, and I realized he had come to search for that famous five thousand dollars, taking advantage of all the confusion. Perhaps he and his accomplices, for he was certainly not alone, had created the chaos themselves. I had been about to speak when the hand came into play, fortunately at a moment when my mouth was partly open. I bit down hard on Xavier's palm and stepped back against the door, my gun leveled. Xavier was shaking the pain from his hand and looking at me with a hatred that might have frozen fire.

As I'd guessed, he had companions, and one of them stepped forward at that moment. I didn't know him, a swarthy man with a forehead whose width could be measured in millimeters. But obviously LeClerc had someone ready at hand to replace Jonathan, the man who had attacked Luis and had not lived to tell about it.

"Drop the gun, lady," he commanded.

Instead, I pulled the trigger twice. He dropped to the floor, groaning and holding his midsection. I quickly covered Xavier. I would have to spend a great deal more time in the confessional and do a severe penance for this act, as well as for the shooting I had done to free Luis. Surely, though, the Almighty would understand my dilemma. Or had I missed an opportunity to pursue a more gentle and forgiving way? I couldn't think of any such so decided to ponder the matter in prayer at a more leisurely time.

"Hands high and walk to the back wall," I said. "Ah-ah. Slowly."

Only as Xavier neared the wall where I intended to secure him to a post did I hear the groaning and thumps from the next room. There was no connecting door that I could see, so I'd have to return to the hallway to gain access and investigate. A risky business, since people were sure to come from the barroom at any minute. I ordered Xavier to the floor and backed away as quickly as I could. I grabbed the wounded thug's gun. Would he die? I hoped not. I saw that it was fully loaded, and I exchanged it for my own. Xavier turned his head.

"On your feet, Xavier. Slowly."

I grabbed his belt and pulled him close, gun barrel to his back, as we proceeded out the door and down the hall.

The scene next door was something I'd never have predicted. Helmina, Adelita, and Delacroix tied to separate chairs with rawhide cords and gagged by strips of cloth apparently torn from the rust-colored muslin of Adelita's skirt. The chairs were tied to pillars so they couldn't be turned over and somehow used as escape vehicles.

I ordered Xavier back to the floor, then removed the gags.

I looked toward Adelita. "I have no knife to cut the ropes."

"Look among the herbs they scattered around looking for the money," Adelita said.

Sure enough. And the freed prisoners were in a short time standing, rubbing their wrists and ankles, and thanking me.

"Better use some of those ties on Xavier," I said.

"How did you disarm all three of them alone?" Delacroix said as he wrapped a length of rawhide around Xavier's wrists.

"Three?" I said.

"Yes, three," came a voice from the doorway. The pink-cheeked bartender. Two people, and you figure it's a robbery. Here there were three bandits, and their numbers triggered the realization that LeClerc's minions were seeking more than that elusive five thousand dollars. They were looking to take over Adelita's itself, perhaps all of Delacroix's enterprises. He pulled out a knife and sliced Xavier's bonds, then handed him a pistol. I'd been told slaves were not allowed to touch a firearm, but I supposed these were deemed exceptional circumstances.

I had laid down my pistol to free the prisoners and was now at the mercy of Xavier and the bartender and the guns they had leveled at us.

"We didn't want it to come to this," the bartender said. "In fact, Monsieur LeClerc is bound to be upset that it has. But you've given us no choice. Turn around."

"Why?" Delacroix said. "So you can shoot us in the back?"

"If you'd prefer the front. . ."

"I'd prefer not at all," Delacroix said. "I'll go straight ahead, you ladies spread out and come from the left and right. They can't get us all at once." He stepped directly toward the guns. A man with more courage than I'd ever have guessed.

His bold move froze our attackers for a moment. Enough time for me to retrieve my derringer from under my skirt. Once again, I didn't waste time threatening them, but fired immediately. This time I aimed for legs, trusting that the weaker bullet would disable even if it might prove only momentarily ineffective on the torsos.

I missed both my targets, but I did manage to send them scurrying down the hallway, seeking cover and perhaps reinforcements in the bar.

"Out the back," Delacroix said. He led, and we all followed him into the night. Straight into the barrel of another gun, this one leveled by a man of stature and countenance that made him nearly the double of our old nemesis, Jonathan. The obstacles the Creator was throwing in our way had grown almost comical in number. I wasn't laughing yet, though.

"Monsieur LeClerc thought it would be a good idea to cover the back way," he said. "Now where's that Mexican that killed my brother?"

"Right behind you," Luis said. The voice of the Lord himself couldn't have sounded sweeter. "Lay the gun on the ground."

"Like hell I will."

"Like hell you won't," came another voice from the darkness. A leather rope snaked forward, wrapped around the miscreant's wrist, and sent his gun to the dirt.

Catamount strode on to the scene, dressed in fresh buckskins and coiling his bullwhip as he walked.

"Hope you don't mind my crashing the party," he said.

Chapter Twenty-Three

Bullwhip

"The front door," I yelled. "They mustn't escape."

Luis did a stiff-legged imitation of a sprint into the night. Delacroix followed.

Cat by this time had drawn his own pistol and instructed Jonathan's double to lie face down on the ground. The man complied grudgingly. Next, he motioned to Helmina and Adelita.

"Now if you two ladies would hold down his arms, and if you, Miss Kelly, would hold this, please?" He handed me his bullwhip. "I need both hands to tie him up."

Carter Maxwell had taught me how to use a bullwhip both as a tool and a weapon. He'd been intent on building a cattle empire at a spot he'd discovered in the High Sierra when prospecting for gold. We had known one another only a few months, but he decided he wanted me at his side, and the notion was tempting indeed. I truly loved the man, and I'd have been a cattle baron's wife, would have shared in building what Carter envisioned as a small kingdom among emerald meadows at the foot of the majestic Sawtooth Peaks. A golden future.

But I could not give up my life in San Francisco. Not once I'd discovered Bonita, and Carter himself was inadvertently responsible for that. He and his whip had been instrumental in the success of my search for Bonita. However, unable to resolve our geographical conflict, we'd ended our romance with mutual regret, and pain. Now, though, I felt Carter's spirit enliven me as I wielded Cat's whip.

"Stop him," Luis called. The sound of his voice was followed by the pounding of running footsteps. I hurried toward the sound and beheld Xavier headed toward the river. Gleefully, I unfurled the whip and sent it winging toward him. The braided rawhide wrapped around his ankles, and I pulled back as if I was setting the hook on a big trout, just as Carter had taught me.

"Ha," I yelled, as my captive dived face first into the mud. "If you're going to belly flop at least find some water." I dragged Xavier toward our other prisoner. He clawed at the dirt the whole way, as if he was truly swimming. Cat had been using the lace from one boot to bind our first captive.

"Can you afford another bootlace?" I said.

"You astound me, Miss Kelly," he said. "Where did you learn that?"

"A story for another time. I can hold my fish till you're ready."

Luis and Delacroix hurried toward us, breathless. "At least we caught one of them," Delacroix said. It took him a moment to realize that Cat, busy with binding the fake Jonathan, could not have been the one who captured Xavier. "But how did this happen?"

Luis sidled up to Delacroix and spoke with false confidentiality. "I warn you, Señor, you do not want Bonita Kelly for an enemy."

"Ladies and gentlemen," I said, anxious to change the subject, "now that we have these vermin, what are we to do with them? We can't take them to jail. There's a mob waiting for Luis and me."

Cat finished with his bindings and took his whip back. As he coiled it up, he said, "I came to town hoping to surprise Miss Kelly, but I'm the one who got the surprise. Now that I'm more or less in the middle of this thing, I might as well keep going. On your feet, gentlemen, we're going for a little ride on the river."

***

It was a tight fit in Cat's small dugout vessel, but Cat, Luis, myself, and our two prisoners managed. Delacroix, Adelita, and Helmina returned to the bar to reclaim their business. Delacroix assured us that he could quickly summon reinforcements to secure the place.

It was unnerving to set out on the huge river in such a small craft, but Cat handled it with ease, kneeling at the bow and guiding with his paddle. We were headed downstream, and I wondered how he had managed to propel himself upstream from wherever we were headed. However, I was intent on obeying his admonition to keep the boat steady and didn't bring up the subject. He'd warned the prisoners as well, telling them it would be to their advantage to keep the boat upright because it would be hard to swim with their hands tied.

Once we were under way, our progress was remarkably peaceful. We soon left the lights of New Orleans behind, and the night enveloped us like a mothering quilt. I took the opportunity to breathe and managed to quiet my soul after the rush of violent events we had just navigated. The Mississippi on a calm night is a fine and wondrous thing. Were we near Magnolia, or the Laurents' Belcoeur? The thought of the Laurents reminded me of Venus and Diane, which inevitably brought my mind and heart back to my own Bonita. I'd never imagined this quest would get so involved and so dangerous. Countless now were the number of times I thought I'd have been better off to stay at home. Countless the number of times I pushed the thought aside as useless fancy.

Eventually, Cat manipulated the paddle and we changed direction and slowed.

"We're off the river now," Cat said. "At least the main body of it. Around here, it's all the river even when it isn't exactly."

"Are we off into those famous bayous of yours then?" I inquired.

"Presently. You'll find us threading our way through the trees, roots, and vines, and so on."

"And alligators?" I said.

"Sure."

"Snakes," Luis said. He was seated in the stern, and I'd almost forgotten he was there.

"I see you two have been reading the travel journals," Cat said. "A lot of them are balderdash, but what you said so far is right on target."

While we talked, we found ourselves among huge trees of indeterminate species looming over us and hemming us in on both sides. Occasional splashes and growls signaled, I supposed, the activities of those alligators. I kept my fingers in the boat, mindful of the tales of the famous swimming cottonmouths, which were purported to be more poisonous than the biggest rattlesnakes of our Sierra Nevada.

We resumed our silence. The smells changed markedly as we proceeded, from that of clean, open water to a rich miasma of simultaneous decay and fecundity even more intense than what I'd experienced so far. I reasoned we were deep into the swampland.

"Not long now," Cat said. His voice was soft, almost reverential.

No one answered him. We were completely at his command, after all. But he did not deceive, for presently we glided up to a small dock where he leaped from the boat and lashed us to the pilings.

"Welcome to Frobisher Isle," he said. "Everyone out."

It had been a night filled with fire, water, and violence. Not to mention incipient romance. I was far from all my money and property and, though I was not without friends and allies, I had essentially been cast ashore in a strange land with few resources to hand. How any of it had gotten me closer to answers about my parents, I had little notion. However, I had to trust in Providence. He holds all the answers. I had none of my own.

Chapter Twenty-Four

Back to Magnolia

Morning light revealed that Frobisher Isle was more than just the small pile of mud in the midst of a bayou I'd been, for some reason, expecting. Cat told us it would take hours to walk it properly, depending on the tides, which swallowed some of it during high waters. The main building before which we'd docked the night before was more than a cabin, if somewhat less than a true house. Built of rough-hewn cypress, it consisted of three rooms plus a loft, where I had slept, and it was well furnished for all of its isolation. It contained enough tables and chairs for one or two people to exist comfortably on a permanent basis.

The outside was rustic, but the interior carpentry revealed a fine hand. The floors were tongue-in-groove. The wall paneling was finished and varnished. The molding edges were joined instead of butted end to end. Even the furniture and cabinets were hand-made and expertly finished. It would have been crowded for five of us, but Cat had chained the prisoners to the wall of a small boathouse near the dock.

I slipped out for a short stroll while the men still slumbered. Already the air was warm, delightfully so. The water was absolutely still, gleaming in the fresh sunlight. It seemed as if one could step out and walk on it. Our dilemma was redolent of danger and uncertainty, but somehow my heart was smiling. I suppose our Lord gives us these moments to remind us of His ever-present love.

"Beautiful, isn't it?" Cat appeared beside me, silent as an apparition out of a fairy tale, to startle me from my reverie.

"Yes," I said, "and peaceful enough to make one believe all this conflict is only a bad dream."

"Unfortunately, it is with us all the time, this struggle. Just part of the human condition, it seems. Would you like to see more of my little haven?"

I gazed at the green fecundity around us. "Absolutely. New Orleans is different from San Francisco, but it is still a city. This place is entirely foreign and infinitely intriguing."

We walked a trail that paralleled the water, he pointing to different plants, some with medicinal qualities, others merely tasty on the supper plate.

"But you can't eat everything and live to tell about it," he warned.

"That's true at home as well," I said, thinking of a child who recently died from munching on the decorative oleander in his mother's garden. "Mother Nature is a benevolent lady, but unforgiving of errors."

"Yes, indeed. And—oh, there's a poor man's beaver."

"Muskrat." I was glad to see something familiar.

"Yep. Lucky for him his coat's not worth much. He'll probably be around forever. Can't say as much for the beavers."

"What won't last? Beavers?"

"They're near to trapped out now." He said it matter-of-factly.

"I know their value dropped off when the carriage trade turned to silk hats a while back, so surely they won't disappear now that they aren't worth so much."

He shrugged. "There are still enough people who want to buy a coat or a cheaper hat to keep us trappers going after them, so I don't give the poor little guys too much more time."

"Yet you continue?"

He shrugged. "Nature's way. We devour one another. One thing disappears, something else will replace it."

I stopped and looked up at him. "Rather a heartless view."

"You said yourself that Mother Nature is unforgiving."

Hoist on my own petard, even though I hadn't meant my remark exactly that way.

"Speaking of unforgiving, how did you get the current of the mighty Mississippi to forgive you long enough to paddle that little boat upstream from here all the way to the docks?"

He flexed his arms. "Astonishing muscle power," he declared, flexing his arms. We both laughed. "No. I have boats stashed here and there, ready to go when I need them, is all. That one was hung in the back of one of the boathouses near Pierre's most of the time."

"Clever and resourceful of you. I can't thank you enough for all your help. Lord knows where we would be right now without you."

"Knowing you, I suspect that you would have prevailed in any case. But I'm proud and happy to do what I can."

I stopped and turned. "Knowing me? You know me hardly at all."

His voice softened. "What I don't know, my imagination creates, and it's a vision to be longed for."

I was surprised to find that his forwardness did not offend. I gave him a sidelong glance that conveyed I know not what. Over the years, I'd stubbornly refused to refine my flirting skills, preferring the persona of a hard-nosed businesswoman. At that moment I was sorry for my mulishness in the matter. I took a breath and turned away.

"A vision to be longed for *and* pursued," he said.

I let the breath out slowly. I turned back toward him. He was still there, his eyes warm with desire.

"You have something of the poet in you, don't you, Cat?"

"When I have the inspiration," he said.

"How can I. . . amidst all this. . . " I gestured vaguely toward the heavens.

"Understandable. Is there someone else?" he said.

"There is no room in my heart just now for other than securing custody of my daughter and clearing my parents' reputation. A romantic entanglement would only complicate and delay matters. Perhaps Luis and I should continue on our own."

He lifted my hand and gently pressed his lips to it. "While it is in my power, you will never be on your own," he whispered.

I drew my hand away and headed back to the cabin.

***

Breakfast was a feast of fresh-caught perch, coffee, rice and boiled nettles Cat gathered from the grounds surrounding the house. While we ate, Luis and I brought Cat up to date on our situation. Only highlights, though. We didn't yet quite trust him with the whole story.

I did explain that my dining alone at Pierre's had been an attempt to put myself in the spotlight and force or at least encourage someone to action because we felt our search had stalled. Our progress in finding the truth about my parents had been slow and confusing and complicated by unforeseen events.

"And now, Bonita?" Cat said.

"It seems all I've done is increase the confusion and put us in more danger than ever."

"On the other hand," Luis said, "we seem to have gained a friend." He gestured toward Cat. "Or at least an ally."

"Count me as both," Cat said. "And maybe something more."

I cast my eyes downward, hoping not to lead him on exactly but to at least keep our relationship ambiguous. We would need his help, and I wasn't entirely averse to his attentions. I could feel Luis's eyes on me. Was he feeling relief? Jealousy? Fear?

I grew suddenly angry at myself. It was not up to me to monitor Luis's feelings. He was a grown man, after all. As for myself, even though I had no business indulging any emotions of my own except those connected with my parents and my child, the Lord put no prohibition on finding a morsel of enjoyment in perilous circumstances.

"I thank you beyond measure for your help," I said. "But I wonder why you are risking so much for us. Do you have a mysterious secret persona?" I was whispering now, looking left and right as if fearing eavesdroppers. "Perhaps this is a game for you, wandering around like some sort of paladin doing good deeds for folks in danger. Reveal yourself, I pray you."

Cat jumped right into the drama, covered his face and groaned. "Ah, you've caught me out, Bonita. I'm actually more of a pirate than a paladin. For years I sailed under the Jolly Roger preying on the weak and innocent." He drew himself up to full height, lifted his arms, shaped his hands into talons, uttered an evil laugh.

"Now, I'm trying to make up for my past wrongs by doing good deeds. You're the first beneficiaries. Congratulations. In olden days, I might have waylaid you and left you alone with your purse empty and your heart broken."

"Ha, ha," Luis said. "Funny. We don't have time for this."

"I know this is no time for frivolity, Luis," I said. "I apologize for starting it. It's just that sometimes I feel our world will never again be a light and happy place unless we make it so."

Cat's apology did not turn Luis at all. "What is the real story, then, Cat?" he said.

"It's pretty simple. I'll try to keep the telling as light and happy as I can.

"My parents died within a week of one another during a cholera outbreak. I was away, having a decidedly frivolous time at Yale, attending class occasionally, but spending most of my time in taverns singing drinking songs. I went to Yale because I wanted to be on my own, which I could never have been at Harvard with my parents close by.

"But then, with my parents gone, I truly *was* on my own. Without them, the very people I'd fled, the world suddenly felt entirely unlike that light and happy place Bonita just described. It was empty and dark.

"They left me some money. Not a fortune, but a significant amount. I had no desire to stay in Boston, nor to return to New Haven. So I wandered, involved myself in some escapades better left untold. I studied on my own and picked up a law degree. Not for any purpose. I simply wanted it. Frivolous, eh?

"I eventually used some of my inheritance to buy this place. There was considerably less to the house when I started fiddling with my hammer and saw. But I've brought it to a point where it suits me well. As I told Bonita earlier, I can roam the plains and return to the swamps or even the city when I need to feel more or less permanent for a spell. I'm a lucky man now. Between the traplines, construction, and lawyering, I make enough to maintain and even indulge myself from time to time."

"As at Pierre's," I said.

"Yes, indeed. And you, Bonita, are a perfect example of how lucky I am."

"Lucky to be consorting with fugitives?" I said.

Everyone laughed a bit nervously.

"It pleases me to do what I like and what feels right. So. Here we are." He gestured toward us with open hands. "That's my tale. Pretty much all of it. Now. Your turn."

Luis and I looked at one another.

"I sense you have held back," Cat said.

We squirmed. There was no question that Cat had saved us. And he had saved Delacroix as well, no doubt because Adelita's owner was with us. But dared we tell him everything? Suppose he was already friends with someone? LeClerc, for example? Or with an enemy of, say, Angelique? We might land in the same frying pan with our breakfast perch. But, almost simultaneously, we nodded at one another.

"Go ahead, Luis," I said. "It's your turn."

Luis told everything more succinctly than I could have. I watched Cat carefully during the telling, looking for smiles, frowns, anything that would reveal where we or the other characters in the drama stood with him. He wore the same bland face throughout.

"And so," Luis said, "what is your legal advice? The law is after me, and all our sources of information have dried up. I'm wondering if we ought to just head back home and fight for Bonita's daughter there."

"What?" Cat exclaimed as he stood suddenly. "Just when you're on the verge of winning everything?"

I stood as well. Astonished. "On the verge of winning?" I said. "Are we back to joking?"

"I'm as serious as a cottonmouth on the strike," he said. "Come on. Let's go."

"Go where?" I said.

"Magnolia," he said. "Where else? Oh, but wait a minute. Bonita, on second thought we might get into some activities where skirts could put you at a disadvantage. Back up in the loft behind the curtain, there should be something more appropriate."

And, indeed, I found quite an array of female garments there. I wasn't the first lady who had spent the night at Frobisher Isle. Perhaps Cat intended something more than helping a lady in distress.

At any rate, one of the women had left behind a pair of very serviceable canvas trousers that fit me tolerably well. They were decidedly unfeminine and would be unacceptable in a society salon, but their utility was undeniable. There were even some sewing tools, which I used to scissor the skirt off my bodice. I stepped in front of the mirror, another Frobisher miracle, and studied the effect of my new outfit. A rakish look, I thought. Perhaps I would even start a style trend. I had launched enterprises in real estate, haberdashery, mining equipment, livestock, and a dozen others. But it would be nice to pursue something a bit more feminine.

I jerked my thoughts back to reality. I needed better footwear, but I found nothing better than the delicate shoes I'd chosen for Pierre's. They would have to do, though I feared they were not long for this rugged world.

I hurried down the stairs and out toward the boathouse.

Xavier and Jonathan's brother, whom we now knew as James, shuffled toward the pirogue, mute and sullen. A dispassionate observer might have guessed they were resigned to their fate. I guessed differently. Cat had told them where we were going, and I felt certain they'd make their move once we got to Magnolia. One by one we eased ourselves from the dock into the small craft, Luis boarding last.

"All aboard," called Cat. And we shoved off.

***

We approached Magnolia in late afternoon, this time from the water side of the indigo field, where we disembarked without benefit of a dock. Cat let us off, then swam away, towing the boat behind him, to a small inlet where he hoisted it high and tucked it among some cypress tree roots several yards from the bank.

"It won't do to leave our getaway vehicle in plain sight," he explained. He was wet from the short swim when we set off for the house. The barn and other outbuildings were, I judged, at least a mile in the distance.

Cat had discussed his plan on the way, and we trudged through the indigo without a path to guide us. It was not the flowering season, so he figured we would not get covered with dye, but we still picked up an abundance of dark stains along the way. A pungent, earthy odor hovered over the field like an aura.

Xavier and James seemed a bit more vigorous as they approached home, doubtless planning an escape, or hoping for a rescue. I thought Cat's plan, which our captives hadn't been privileged to overhear, would forestall their aspirations. I estimated it was approaching five or six in the evening when we reached the edge of the field, where we planned to wait for dusk. The waiting would be the hardest part for me.

The gags on our prisoners were doubtless uncomfortable after all this time. I didn't care about that, but their complaints about the need to relieve themselves became so strident that we finally relented. Cat took Xavier off a ways into the field. I turned my back. Luis guarded James, and I held my pistol at ready.

Presently, we heard a curse and the sounds of a struggle. We turned in alarm and saw Cat and Xavier fighting. Xavier went down. While our attention was distracted, James made a run for freedom. People think once someone is your prisoner he is in your thrall. The truth is not so simple. Things seemed to suddenly be falling apart. I should have been fearful, I supposed, but I turned determined instead.

Luis overtook James in no time, but his legs were unbound, and the big man was able to put up quite a battle even with his hands tied. I dashed over and poked the barrel of my six-shooter between his eyes. That quieted him, but our problems were not over. Luis had sliced open a nasty wound in the man's thigh. When Cat arrived, Xavier slung over his shoulders, we saw that Cat, too, was bleeding from a cut on his arm. I couldn't imagine where Xavier had managed to conceal a knife.

"It was lashed to the inside of his thigh," Cat's voice was ripe with exasperation as he explained. "My fault. I should have searched him better."

Now we had one prisoner unconscious and the other bleeding and scarcely ambulatory. Cat was injured as well.

"A scratch," Cat said. "We have bigger problems."

Our original plan had called for two able-bodied hostages and the use of the secret passageway through the kitchen and up the stairs. The idea was that once everyone was hidden and secured, I would make a surprise appearance either in the dining room or parlor. There I would confront LeClerc about the failure of his attempt to take over Adelita's and the rest of Delacroix's enterprises. I'd reveal the presence of the others as it became appropriate to the conversation. Very slick idea, but a bit complicated, and no longer viable.

No matter, I thought with a smile. I had another idea ready to hand.

Chapter Twenty-Five

Pursuing LeClerc

ight from lanterns and candles appeared in the windows of the house as darkness settled around the plantation. James was groaning in perhaps false pain. We checked his tourniquet and bandage periodically to make sure he was neither bleeding nor gangrenous. Further ministrations, if they were actually needed, would have to wait. Xavier was regaining consciousness, but he remained woozy.

"Time to go," Luis announced.

First stop is the barn," I added. I was happy the waiting was over.

Luis threw James' hand over his own shoulder and propelled him forward. Cat moved Xavier along by his belt. We listened at the barn's wall and heard only the snorts and shuffling of horses in their stalls. No suggestion of human activity. We entered quietly through the tack room, hoping not to stumble on someone napping or drunk. It appeared the place had been left to the animals for the time being. We all slung a length of rope or rawhide over our shoulders, anticipating that future activities might soon require them.

From there, we advanced to the building's main door, a huge swinging affair big enough to admit a hay wagon. It stood open. Across the thicket and greensward stood the veranda and parlor of the main house, where I'd spent the afternoon and evening that had ended in such a fearsome manner.

Luis propped James against the wall. This hadn't been part of the plan, and I was confused until I saw how tight his teeth were clenched and understood that he was recalling the whipping he'd suffered in this place on that awful night. He stepped over to Xavier and slugged him hard, first in the stomach with his right hand, then in the face with his left. Xavier's nose gushed blood. I'd never seen Luis so ferocious. Xavier moaned loud enough that we could hear him through his gag.

Cat admonished him. "Hey, partner. Not fair. Man's tied up."

Luis said nothing, just walked over and picked up James.

I spoke to Cat. "He's entitled. I'll explain later. Now, let's move."

Our new plan was riskier than the old one, but simpler. Complexity is often the enemy of success, and we hoped our new and simpler tactic would prove a boon. We advanced across the lawn, up the steps, and across the veranda.

"Time for the big challenge," I whispered. "Is everyone ready?"

Luis and Cat nodded eagerly. I threw open the French doors and yelled, "Monsieur LeClerc, we have a surprise for you."

We pushed our way into the parlor. Cat sat Xavier in a chair, making no effort to stanch the flow of blood from the broken nose. It would ruin the velvet fabric of the maroon upholstery. Fine with me. Luis tossed James in a leather chair on the other side of the door. He loosed the bullwhip he'd carried on his belt. I stood in the center of our little formation.

A sweetish aroma of burning whale oil emanating from the lanterns filled the room, tinged with odors of rosemary and honeysuckle from the bouquets scattered here and there. The mynah hopped around in its cage, sounding its shrill whistle. The sound was sure to arouse alarm, which was exactly what we wanted. I knew we'd present a bedraggled spectacle with our clothes so stained with indigo and blood. But I was more than ready to confront our tormentor whatever our appearance. How much more powerful this felt than the covert approach we had planned earlier.

We heard a commotion from the dining room. Did LeClerc have guests or was this a night for him to dine alone? I hoped for the latter, but was more than prepared for the former.

"LeClerc," I called again. "In here, if you please."

He came bearing arms and protected by a man on either side of him, similarly outfitted. LeClerc himself carried a shotgun. The others carried revolvers. They paused to assess the situation, but we were done with assessing. I shot the man to the right of LeClerc in the leg. Luis threw his knife into the shoulder of the man on LeClerc's left. Cat sent his leather twining around LeClerc's ankles and pulled back hard, sending him flying on his back. His shotgun discharged into the ceiling, bringing down shards of plaster and exposing beams. Luis and I ran forward to disarm all three. Cat stayed back to make sure we weren't ambushed. Our attack was unplanned in its details, but its execution was a choreographer's dream. As a bonus, the explosions seem to have silenced the mynah bird.

"Napoleon would have approved, gentlemen," I said.

"*Sí*, Monita," Luis said. "But now what?"

Of a sudden, I saw that the household slaves had lined up on the stairs behind LeClerc and his thugs.

"You will pay dearly for this, Miss Kelly," LeClerc said.

"Ah, you call me 'Miss Kelly,' Monsieur. You remember your manners even amid adversity, A sign of great breeding. But it is only the old story of a soft velvet glove concealing savage iron, isn't it?"

I instructed all three men to lie face down on the floor. I thought of them as calves being readied for branding, a task I'd performed many times on Rancho Sausalito. Using the rawhide we'd procured in the barn, I bound ankles and wrists first each to each then each pair to the other. I didn't quit tightening the ropes on any of them until I'd extracted a yelp. When I'd finished, not only could they barely move, but their every effort only tightened my knots the more.

"Bonita, you are a caution and a bundle of surprises," Cat said.

"She has had much practice," Luis said.

"And a great teacher," I said, nodding toward Luis. "However, as much fun as this has been, we are going to have to modify LeClerc's bindings to question him properly. Cat, I'll watch Xavier while you perform the ceremony."

Cat cut the connector between the Magnolia owner's ankles and wrists, then wrestled him over to the couch.

Thus, it was that we had LeClerc seated on a sofa before us with his armed minions trussed up on the floor at his feet. Luis, Cat and I arranged three chairs fanned out in front of him so that we could all see him. Plus, among the three of us, we could watch the other doorways. I thought we hadn't much to fear from the house servants, but I didn't know for certain.

The bird resumed its shrieking. "Help. Help." So, it knew how to speak after all. I felt like shooting it, but forebore.

"Rose," I called. She appeared, wringing her hands. "Could you please bring some water for your master? And help him drink it since he won't be able to hold a glass."

LeClerc never took his eyes from me as he said, "You'll not move an inch on her orders, Rose. Remain where you are. The same goes for the rest of you."

This was rich, almost as if LeClerc was trying to maintain control from the grave. "Suffer the angry master rather than see his property controlled by another. Is that it, LeClerc?"

He glowered. I smiled.

"Your empire is crumbling, Monsieur. For proof, you need only look across the room." Xavier and James slumped and squirmed under his scrutiny.

LeClerc seemed undaunted. "Xavier and James obviously failed in their mission tonight, but it is only a minor skirmish in a much bigger war, Miss Kelly. One in which you will heartily regret becoming involved."

"You involved me the minute you did whatever you did with my parents, LeClerc, those many years ago. I traveled a couple of thousand miles to search for the truth about them. My search has led me to you. What have you to say?"

"To you? Who have tonight committed several hanging offenses against me and my household as well as against the citizens of New Orleans? You and your Mexican accomplice are felons and fugitives." He turned to Cat. "And you, my buckskin friend, are in league with them. It will be an attractive gallows, with three hooded corpses swinging. One of the bigger parties New Orleans has seen in some time."

Luis stepped forward, leaned over almost nose-to-nose with LeClerc. "Yes, we have seen how fond your good citizens of New Orleans are of lynchings."

Cat chuckled. "It saves the public expense of a trial and is more fun besides, eh, LeClerc?"

"Not to mention," I added, "avoiding the pesky business of juries and proper evidence." LeClerc said nothing, but he did smile.

"Returning to the subject at hand," I said, "we know these things: Under your orders, Xavier and James, along with others, tried to take over Adelita's. They had kidnapped Delacroix and were perhaps about to murder him as well as Adelita herself, and her colleague, Helmina. As part of their plot, they framed Luis for the murder of the bartender Gator and would doubtless have framed him for whatever happened to Delacroix and his people. That would have cleared the way for you to take over all of Delacroix's operations and gain revenge on him for whatever long-running feud you have with him. Luis, do you have anything to add?"

Luis shook his head. He still stood threateningly close to LeClerc, who kept trying to inch away from him. Luis allowed none of his wriggles and twists to increase the distance between them.

Cat turned from LeClerc to me. "You've been here only a couple of weeks, Bonita, and you've ferreted out more information than most people would have discovered in a year."

I kept my eyes on LeClerc. "Any comment from you so far, Monsieur?"

"I could have moved in on Daniel any time in the last decade," he said. "Why would I wait till now?"

Luis chimed in. "Because you have never, Señor, had such convenient scapegoats as Bonita and myself. My race alone makes me a criminal, and Bonita is a foreigner who dares to ask uncomfortable questions of people with matters to hide."

LeClerc merely shook his head and smiled.

"But," I continued with Luis's theme, "I'm prepared to let you go and leave you and Delacroix to fight it out in return for some answers about my parents."

LeClerc sighed. "Your parents were commissioned to deliver five thousand dollars from Daniel Delacroix to me. The money never arrived, and your parents disappeared. The conclusion is obvious. But whatever the circumstances, Daniel still owes me the money."

"And what was the money for?" I said.

"Services rendered."

I nodded to Cat, who unlimbered his bullwhip and waved Luis aside.

I said, "Perhaps, Sir, you'd like a taste of the treatment you ordered up for Luis."

"When I gave Xavier my false confession," Luis said.

"Well?" I said.

LeClerc's face was a mask.

"This is going to be fun," Cat said. He stepped back, whirled the whip above his head and propelled it in LeClerc's direction. When he flicked his wrist, the end snapped like a gunshot close to LeClerc's ear. LeClerc froze, except that his eyes widened. Cat repeated the maneuver, this time near the other ear.

"Well?" I asked him.

Silence. The third shot of the whip snapped in front of LeClerc's nose. This one startled him, broke his mask, and sent him leaning back and away.

"Next," Cat said, "I could lift a chunk out of each ear. A little blood might move things along."

I prayed that LeClerc would finally talk. Threats were one thing, but to actually resort to the kind of torture Jonathan and Xavier had inflicted on Luis was more than I could stomach.

"Perhaps now?" I asked.

"All right," he said. "You'll probably find out anyway, and it's too late for you to do anything about it."

At last, I thought, I will get to the heart of this mystery. Then came the sound of hoofbeats. Many of them. And shouts as well.

I ran to the front of the house, stepped out on the veranda and beheld a troupe of twenty or so horsemen galloping down the long magnolia colonnade toward the house. I ran back to the parlor.

"It seems your dinner guests have arrived, LeClerc. Rose, you will explain that Monsieur LeClerc left suddenly, and that you have no idea when he will return."

I allowed no time for LeClerc to countermand my orders to Rose. Along with Luis and Cat and our now sizeable contingent of prisoners—LeClerc, his two henchmen, Xavier, and James—I headed out the French doors in the direction from which we'd come.

The boat had been scarcely big enough for the four of us. I had no idea how we'd accommodate a fifth person, but the water was our only escape route now. We headed across the greensward toward the barn, slowed by the fact that LeClerc was resisting Luis every step of the way. Luis finally stopped and delivered a fist to the Magnolia patriarch's jaw, a blow that knocked him unconscious. Paradoxically, he was a much lighter burden slung across Luis's shoulders than he had been on foot.

We had nearly reached the barn when they caught us. Nearly a dozen of them, half of them carrying pine-knot torches. They circled us as if we were runaway cattle who needed to be returned to the herd. It seemed either that Rose hadn't obeyed my orders or that she'd been overruled by other slaves. Understandable. How were they to suppose their master wouldn't return and deal most harshly with them if he thought they'd abetted his captors?

Sheriff Carew was in charge. With a lawman directing things, this had become more than a renegade lynch mob with no legal authority. Perhaps his badge gave us some extra protection or they might already have fired the guns they pointed at us. Or perhaps Carew's presence lent even greater power to LeClerc's villainy. I spotted the old drunk Bodine in the group, swaying as much in the saddle as he had on his feet when we'd first met him emerging from the cellblock. I nudged Luis and pointed. He nodded.

"Big trouble, Monita," he muttered.

Carew called, "Miller, you and Carey grab the Mex and tie him up good to one of your saddles. McKnight, you and Pitzer do the same for the big guy in buckskins. Bailey, cut Monsieur LeClerc's ropes, and do what you can to bring him to. While the men jumped to obey, I gave a surreptitious wave of my fingers in Cat's direction and strode directly toward Carew, stopping face-to-nose with his mount. Startled, he backed his horse a step or two.

"Sheriff," I said. "You've misconstrued what's happening here. If you'd give me a moment—"

"This is not the time for discussion, Miss Kelly," he said.

"I guess not," I said.

Two horses away from Carew, a saddle lay empty and unattended, left by one of the men the sheriff had dispatched to help LeClerc. I dashed for it, leapt aboard, and galloped into the darkness. I trusted that the distraction would give Cat and Luis the chance to escape, but I couldn't wait around to find out. I had thought my days as a lone runaway were over after my masquerade as a boy cattle herder when I was but fourteen. I had thought after that to fight life's battles with a shrewdness, integrity, and intellect instead of physical prowess or sly cunning. Now, as I headed through the indigo fields toward the water, those earlier days and the Lord's mysterious ways were on me once more.

I uttered a fervent, if hurried, "Hail, Mary" as I rode, praying the Lord would be not only with the Holy Mother, but with both of us. I understood that the life of my soul and of my daughter's depended more on grace and wisdom than on my own foolish and weak efforts. Still, I knew I must fight on in my blind human way. Thus is our lot on this earth.

It wasn't long before the hounds of hell dashed after me. I thought if I could stay ahead of my pursuers and their torches till I reached the water, I'd find a way to safety. I had to assume that Xavier and James had told them I had a boat waiting. I had no idea whether I could locate it in the dark. I did manage to reach the bayou ahead of the mob, leaped from my mount, dived in, and swam for all I was worth.

This was not the big river, which meant the current was minimal and wouldn't carry me far from our boat. It also meant that I was now bait for alligators and snakes. I would rather take my chances with them than with the beasts who now dashed up and down at the water's edge, brandishing torches and guns. I swam as silently as I could, diving under and coming up for air intermittently.

I felt my way among the cypress roots and branches and hummocks, searching for the boat, listening to them debate strategy.

"Wait for daylight."

"Won't matter. She can't get far."

"She don't have a chance nohow."

"Don't know the swamps."

This last comment was right on target. Even if I touched the boat, how could I tell? I might mistake it for just another cypress root. Or might put my hand on an alligator's nose instead of a log. A snake slipped past me going in the other direction. Cottonmouth? How would I know? He didn't seem interested in me, but the next one might be. It is fine to put oneself in the hands of the Lord, but it is often better to use the power of the brains with which the Lord has blessed us. I climbed up on a cypress root and found myself a seat a few inches above the water. I prepared to spend the night. Should my roost prove safe through the darkness, sunrise would light me either to safety or to the next peril God had arranged.

Chapter Twenty-Six

Back to the Playhouse

Dawn again. Mist rose from the water, enveloping everything like a thick San Francisco fog. It almost felt like home except for the cloying heat and that underlying aromas of decay that had now become so familiar. I unbuckled my belt from where I'd cinched it around a branch to keep from sliding into the water if I fell asleep, as I surely did more than once during the long night. In the sense that LeClerc, Carew and the posse would be searching for me, the mist was my friend. On the other hand, I couldn't see any better than they, so to search for the boat would be a waste of time. Better to go with the known.

It didn't take long to reach the streambank, or bayoubank, or whatever they called it. But my way ashore was blocked by a tangle of blackberry vines. I started to work my way along the bank searching for a path through the thicket when I heard intermittent cries and hoofbeats. Good. I'd be able to keep track of my potential captors even while I was hidden from them.

But my optimism tempered considerably when a shadow loomed above me. What would Carew do if he did catch me? Would he, could he, protect me? I submerged as far as I could and still breathe. My heart pounded, but my hands remained steady. Fear had become my constant companion.

"Cain't see a damned thing, Charley. How about you?"

"Same, Ike. Still, we got no choice but to keep patrolling the bank till Carew calls us off, or we find her, one."

"I got the choice of getting back home to my chores. Ain't no pay connected to this deputizing business."

"Yeah, and the next time you show yourself in town, Carew will find some reason to clap the irons on you."

"I suppose you're right. I'm getting to hate that little bitch more every second."

"No more than I hate that tub of guts of a sheriff. Why don't you ride south? I'll go north, and we'll meet up here again in thirty minutes. Unless you find her, then holler like crazy."

"You always did know how to have a good time, Ike."

"Nothing but a party everywhere I go. See you soon."

In case the whole conversation had been a ruse, I waited until I could stand it no more. I dog-paddled my way through the muck looking for a path to dry land. I reasoned that whatever current coursed through the swamp would have carried me south. I worked my way upstream. What a treat it would be to find a tub and a warm bath, but that was a distant fantasy at this point. Finally I discovered a rudimentary boat landing and succeeded in scaling the bank. You'd think a long soak in such warmish water wouldn't chill a body, but it surely did mine. Emerging from it was like being wrapped in a snug quilt.

Once on dry land, I alternately ran and crouched in what I hoped was the direction of the mansion. The further I got from the water, the thinner the mist, and at last I could see the indigo field. It would provide good cover till I reached the barn. The swamp odor was a good deal thinner up here as well, replaced by the sweet pungency of the indigo plants. My stomach tightened with trepidation at approaching the big house again, but it was either that or the snakes and alligators. So forward I went.

The search party seemed to have been confined to the bank, for I spotted no one in or around the indigo. I got through the field in no time, and the barn presented few problems. Men and animals milled around the place, but there were plenty of nooks and crannies, and no one was expecting me to appear anywhere near there. The house would be different. I was tempted to purloin a horse and try for Angelique's, but I couldn't leave without finding out what had happened to Luis and Cat.

From the veranda, it appeared that the household was up and bustling as if all were normal. Then I saw the first of the patrols. A pair of men rode past the house and disappeared up the drive, their horses at a trot. Each held a rifle in one hand, stock resting on a thigh, reins in the other. As I'd suspected, this wasn't going to be as easy as it seemed at first. Alternating between dashing as fast as I could, then crawling on my hands and knees, I made my way to the kitchen door. Two more pairs of lookouts passed by on the drive, but their attention seemed not to be on the house.

The playhouse little Venus and Diane had showed me offered a way into the heart of the LeClerc household, and it was there I hoped to find both information about Luis and Cat and a means of escape. The playhouse was unguarded as usual, and once inside, it smelled musty enough to assure it had been unoccupied for some time.

I negotiated the short tunnel from the playhouse to the pantry without trouble. Information and escape were important, but at that moment sustenance became even more essential than both of them. I could hear voices, movement, clanging in the nearby kitchen, so whatever I did, it had to be done in a hurry. I found little available for ready consumption. Indeed, for a while I despaired of finding anything at all among the canned peaches and beans and oysters. All delicious, but I had no means of opening the cans. Similarly, I couldn't chew on uncooked rice or beans. Finally, I had to settle for a few handfuls of hardtack biscuits from among the fifty or so pounds of them in a burlap sack. My Uncle Richardson, being a seaman for many years, liked to keep hardtack around for munching. No one else could stomach the stuff, if only because it was a hazard to even the healthiest tooth, let alone about as tasty as a handful of hard clay. Thanks to him now, though, I recognized the tough biscuits and stuffed as many as possible into the pockets of my trousers and headed for the secret door at the back of the room.

The door led to the stairway I'd descended with the Laurent's girl, Venus, an event that seemed like weeks instead of days earlier. I ascended, slipped into the closet, and knelt by the door into the bedroom. If no one was visiting Magnolia, it should be unoccupied now, but there was no way of knowing for sure. I remained still, listening. I didn't dare even nibble on my tasteless provender, though my mouth watered as if I were a dog loose in a butcher shop.

I counted five hundred breaths. Then five hundred more. And still another five hundred. Near a half an hour and not a sound. I dared to munch my way through several crackers. Then, the edge off my hunger, I reached up to turn the knob. I slowly opened the door, crept into the room, and closed it behind me. I crawled around the bed, saw the door into the hallway before me and headed that way. Then the door moved and I slid under the bed.

Two pair of bare Negro feet strode in my direction. One pair went to one side of the bed, the other stayed on the side nearer the hall.

"Master don't never use this room but for company. You hear anything about someone coming?"

"Hmph. No one tells me nothing. Only time I know something's going on is when I see it happen."

Lily and Sherry, the household slaves I'd interacted with the night of my confrontation with LeClerc. I contemplated crawling out and asking them a question or two, but decided to stay put and listen. Lily snatched a sheet, and it cracked like Cat's bullwhip when she shook it. Dust flew.

"Easy, now. If we don't get the dust off before whoever it be gets here, we be paying a big price," Sherry said.

Lily grunted. "I tell you one thing, I wish they'd done took that Mexican and the other one back to town instead of locking them up in the smokehouse."

"You get no argument from me. They gets loose they'll be shooting each other and whipping us for whatever goes wrong."

A voice called from downstairs. "Sherry, Lily, what you two girls doing up there? We need you in the parlor." Rose's voice.

"Upstairs, downstairs, acting like we hummingbirds can fly everywhere," Lily said.

If Sherry said anything, I didn't hear it. All four feet walked out the door in short order, and I now knew where to find Luis and Cat.

Chapter Twenty-Seven

Where To Now?

There were a number of outbuildings on the estate grounds, but the smokehouse was easy enough to spot. As logic might dictate, it was not far from the kitchen, a bat-and-board affair with a tall metal stack protruding from the roof. Two men armed with rifles stood guard, a shiny new lock and chain graced the door. Those last two elements gave me more than pause.

I could see the situation from the window of the playhouse, but for the moment I had no idea how to solve it. The guards and locked padlock assured me that Cat and Luis were inside. I decided to sit quietly, think, and pray for guidance. I consumed a couple of more pieces of hardtack and prayed some more. The Lord sent me no ideas, at least none that seemed workable. Presently, I prayed myself into a nap. Shouts from outside woke me.

"Jasper and Willy was supposed to relieve us, wasn't they, Stilton?"

"An hour ago, Baron. My cows are going to be wailing it's been so long since they been milked."

"To hell with it, then. I'm leaving anyway. Carew thinks this is the damned army way he orders us around."

"You know, that sounds all right by me."

I got to the window just in time to see the two guards' outlines grow fuzzy in the twilight. I'd slept the afternoon away. But once again, Providence had answered me now by removing the sentries. There was still the matter of the padlock, but I had to trust to darkness and to His guidance for that. The guidance came presently.

I hurried back to the pantry, this time sneaking into the kitchen instead of down the trap door. Keeping low, I drew near to a woman who was carving steaks from a roast. Before long, she laid down the knife and lifted her apron to her brow to wipe perspiration from her forehead. It was all the opportunity I needed to snatch her knife from the counter and hurry myself back to the tunnel. Once there, my fear returned. Stealing the knife called for more close-on daring than I was used to. I figured I'd better accustom myself, though, if I was to get out of this fix.

I was still in my crouch as I dashed over the twenty yards or so to the smoke house. Darkness was approaching quickly now. The battens were the standard one-inch thick and two-inch wide boards used to hold together and seal the cracks between the sideboards of the structure. Hoping the deserting guards wouldn't be replaced right away, I cozied up to the back wall and whispered loud as I could.

"Luis, Cat. You in there?"

"Monita?" It was Luis.

"I've got a knife to pry off a bat and make an opening. Knock where it would be best."

"About here," Cat said. "No shelves or anything in the way."

I jammed the knifepoint under the board and pulled. The blade snapped.

"Damn," I said. Too loud and decidedly too profane.

"Monita?" Luis said.

I said nothing. The thicker part of the blade would be better for the task at hand anyhow. I worked it under the bat more slowly, right near a nail. Back and forth, back and forth. Before long, I had it out far enough that I thought I could try to pull the nail. Out it came. With a bit of a screech, but it came. I tried to do the rest of the job with my fingers, but just as my haste with the point of the knife had slowed rather than speeded my progress, I made no headway.

I returned to the previous successful method. Back and forth and back and forth and back and forth. Then came a second nail. Now I had some leverage. I was able to get both hands behind the bat and pull with my whole weight, ignoring the splinters I was collecting along the way.

"Bonita," Cat said. "Where are the guards?"

"None here right now."

"Stand back," Luis said.

I did as ordered, and a moment later both men began kicking at the weak place I'd created in the wall. In a couple of minutes more, they shouldered their way through just as if Ali Baba had called, "Open, Sesame." We had time for a quick congratulatory hug, and I felt as if a void had been filled to have us together once more.

I led them toward the playhouse, where I thought we might figure out our next move. We turned to find ourselves staring right into a lantern not more than ten yards away.

"There she is," cried one voice.

"All three of them," yelled another.

The lantern dropped, and darkness enveloped everything. Perhaps the man had been so anxious to reach his gun that he'd forgotten he was holding a lantern. Somehow, all three of us decided on our direction at once and without discussion. We needed to get out of Magnolia, and there were too many obstacles between here and the water. We dashed into the cotton field bordering the magnolia tree colonnade.

Chapter Twenty-Eight

Return to Frobisher

Cotton is soft once it's been put through the gin, but out in the field, the protective shells around the ripe bolls are not kind to human skin. Nor is it easy to flee undetected through a field of plants only three feet or so in height. But Cat knew the country, and Carew's army had lost its discipline. Our pursuers had become a ragged, disorganized, and discontented posse. To my untrained eye, the field was table-flat terrain. In truth, it was full of hidden swales and gullies that not only served to hide us from nearby searchers, but became virtual highways through the landscape. It wasn't long before we'd left our pursuers behind. We could hear men on horse and foot charging around the cotton field even as we walked down a clear path through groves of trees. I was filthy and scratched, but out of danger. At least for the moment.

Cat brought us back to the water. He said that come daylight he could probably find the boat we'd used to come to Magnolia, but it was unnecessary. He groped around the base of a number of trees on the banks of the bayou, finally selected a cypress, shinnied up, and lowered another pirogue, complete with a paddle lashed to it, from a limb where it had been tied and concealed.

Luis and I looked at one another and laughed. "How many of those do you have?" Luis asked.

Cat shrugged. "A dozen or so here and there. Maybe more. You have to know where to look for the blaze on the trees to find them."

"Fast getaways must be a regular need for you, then?" I said.

He didn't answer the question. "Look, it'll take us a while to get back to Frobisher Island. You can already tell this boat is smaller than the one we came in. It won't hold all three of us at once. You two get in, and I'll push. The water won't be more than chest high most of the way. I can just sort of swim when it gets too deep. You can trade off with the paddle."

"If you say so," Luis said, "but can you keep that up the whole way? Maybe we can spell one another."

"No more talk, now. Just get in and let's go."

***

The sun was well above the horizon and the morning mist gone for another day when we finally sighted Cat's home. Even then the journey wasn't over.

"I been careful to keep this place a secret," he said, "but Carew and them could have tracked me down by now." He guided the boat to a small piece of high ground. "Just wait here while I scout."

It took him a good half hour to determine that we weren't floating into a trap. In the meantime, Luis and I sat wet and bedraggled. I held a strand of my hair in front of me. It looked and smelled like the moss streaming out from the cypress roots.

"We came on a hunt, Monita. Now we are the ones being hunted."

"We are still hunters as well, aren't we?" I remarked. "Hunting and hunted at the same time. It's a full life the Lord has granted us, is it not?"

Luis laughed, his arms wrapped around himself to ameliorate the chill. "Your optimism, Monita. I love it. It is foolish and endearing at the same time."

I reached out a hand to him, and he grasped it in his own, which was damp and cool. Our eyes connected for a moment. It was a repeat of our moment at Angelique's, except it was even more intense. A thrill passed through me, and I dropped my gaze. I gave his hand a last squeeze and released it.

"Ah, Luis, my knight. What are we to do?" I was aghast. The question was really for myself, not for Luis. And Cat was part of the "what am I to do?" I had simultaneously revealed and concealed too much. I raised my eyes to his again. He was smiling and shaking his head.

"It is up to you, Monita. All this is too mysterious to me. Like the mist on the water, it is one moment everywhere, then it is gone, and who knows where?"

I sighed again, said nothing. I could have described my own emotions just as Luis had described his.

"All clear, folks. Come on in," yelled Cat.

Luis and I pushed out of our emotional bubble as he used the paddle to propel us away from the bank.

"On our way," I yelled.

***

I was exhausted, and it was a tough decision whether to wash or sleep first. Cat had rigged a little cold water shower that required climbing a ladder to load a small tank with three buckets of well water from a hand pump. From there, it was open a valve and let gravity do the rest. The two men were gracious enough to carry the water and allow me to bathe first, to stay inside and allow me privacy. There was no soap, but it was to this day the most wonderful shower I've ever experienced.

I wrapped myself in a soft blanket, climbed into Cat's loft, and let thoughts of LeClerc and Delacroix and Carew float away in favor of visions of my reunion with little Bonita, my lost and found and lost again daughter. The fantasy surrounded me like that mist Luis and I had just talked about. I gladly floated into its warm embrace.

Chapter Twenty-Nine

Sneaking In

I suppose it was hunger that awakened me as much as Cat's banging around in the kitchen. Luis was helping with the breakfast preparations, and I had been slumbering the day away. I stood at the railing that looked out over the kitchen and living room.

"What time is it?"

"Pushing on two o'clock, Milady," Cat said. "We thought maybe you'd expired up there." The smell of frying meat filled the air. Luis was cutting yams.

"I wouldn't be foolish enough to die with only you two heathens to attend to my last rites."

"Whatever we did, Monita," Luis said, "it would be heartfelt even if not what the priest would do."

"I bet God wouldn't care, either," Cat said.

"How comforting. I suppose I'd just as well keel over now. It would be a good way to get out of this mess."

"Get dressed and come down. We must discuss our destiny."

"My destiny is to gobble down some of that salt pork." I said. "I will be right there."

I found a dress in Cat's little store that nearly fit me, but the mirror showed my hair to be in a horror of a tangle.

"I don't suppose any of these paramours of yours left a hairbrush," I said to Cat.

"Clothes, yes. Hairbrush, too precious."

I wrapped a scarf around my head to hide the distressed coiffure and headed down the ship's ladder that provided egress from my haven. I was as rested and robed as I was going to get. As we sat and addressed the feast Cat and Luis had prepared, I opened the subject of our next move.

It was heaven itself to relax around that table. These men and I had endured much together, and even though we all knew there was more to come, we savored this moment of peace. We ate and drank and smiled and laughed.

"You ought to give up trapping," I said, "and open a restaurant. Pierre would have to watch out."

"Don't you think it might lack somewhat in location?" Cat said.

"With the proper publicity, it could succeed," I said.

"Yams." Luis's mouth was so full he was hard to understand. "I'd never have imagined."

"And these greens. As good as I'd find from any greengrocer back home," I added.

"Anything will grow in this soil," Cat declared proudly. "I've barely tended this garden at all for several years, and it still keeps producing as if I cared for it every day. And the pork does fine for quite a while if you salt it properly and seal it from critters."

"You've got the food part all figured out, Cat," I said. "Maybe Delacroix would help you with some capital for the rest."

Cat and Luis laughed, but my mention of Delacroix returned us to the world we'd escaped for those few precious minutes.

"We have only one ally in this, folks," Luis said, "and he is the man we are supposed to revile. However, I believe I have a way to approach him."

"Without getting your neck stretched in the process?" Cat said. "I'd like to hear that."

"I will use a hat."

"A hat?" I said.

"*Sí.* It is a fact that to most white people, Mexicans look alike, just as do black people. The same is true in reverse, of course. In the clothing I wore before, someone would identify me immediately. With a hat, such as the one hanging on the wall over there I wouldn't get a second glance. And do you have a shirt with perhaps a ruffle? It would be not much disguise if one looked closely, but it would be enough to keep me out of jail."

"Brilliant," I said. "Perhaps I could do the same kind of thing. I've spent no little time masquerading as a man. Maybe all three of us?" For the first time since we'd left San Francisco, I got the sense that our serious project might have some room for a bit of fun.

"Are you proposing that I don a skirt, milady?"

"Don't be silly, Cat. No. Wait. On second thought, that's not a bad idea."

"Yes it is," he said. "A very bad idea. However, I do have a pair of overalls and a shirt that would go with it."

"If we go into Adelita's separately, and from the back, we should be quite safe," Luis said. He then excused himself to follow nature's call and left me alone with Cat.

"Are you sure you want to get even more deeply involved in this?" I said. "It doesn't promise to get any easier or less dangerous."

"Your fight has become mine, Bonita. I couldn't stop if I tried, and I am not going to try."

"Even though I—"

"Even though. And put your guilt aside. What I do is for my benefit as much as for yours or anyone else's."

"My guilt?" I said.

"I may know you better than you think, milady."

I was struck silent and began clearing the table while Luis put his costume together.

"Luis, you look about as innocent as a fugitive bank robber in that outfit," I said, laughing.

We were holding a bit of a review of our costumes in front of the main house. Not only had Luis traded in his normal *vaquero* headgear for the felt slouch hat he'd spotted on Cat's wall, but he'd added a greatcoat and some flat-heeled boots.

"As long as I don't look like me," he said.

"I suppose so," I said. "Cat, on the other hand looks like he's just off work in a saw mill somewhere with that red-checked shirt and coveralls."

"Oh," Cat said. "Wait a minute." He hurried back inside and emerged in a beat-up straw hat of indefinite design or provenance.

"Excellent job," Luis said. "As for you, Monita, I am not so sure."

"Not so sure? How can you say that? I thought the trousers would be difficult. But all I had to do was take in the side seams and voilà, I narrowed the legs and transformed those blousy combat pants into something fit for a male fashion plate, no?" They didn't look entirely convinced. "In the dark, perhaps?" They laughed. "Then away we go."

***

Thus attired, we strolled down the dock near sundown, separating from one another by fifteen-minute intervals as we approached the back door of Adelita's. We were leery of the front door because we didn't know what changes Delacroix might have made. We hoped that the back door might give us a private moment or two to assess the situation. We'd decided I should go first, my stature making me perhaps the least threatening of the three of us. I tried the door. Locked as we expected. I knocked softly.

Helmina called from within. I identified myself, and she opened the door. Thank goodness she recognized my voice and that they hadn't developed a code. My explanations prepared the way for Cat and Luis. Delacroix was in residence, and we were before long seated as if we were at a normal business meeting.

Adelita was tending bar. It seemed strange not to see Gator there. It also seemed strange to see Luis sitting beside us as an equal. We all had full beer mugs before us.

I allowed Cat to explain what had happened at Magnolia during our latest visit. I was not surprised to learn that Delacroix already knew about it. When Cat finished, I told the part Delacroix perhaps did not know.

"LeClerc said you gave my parents five thousand dollars which they were to deliver to him. Neither my parents nor the money ever appeared. When I asked what the money was for, he wouldn't tell me." I let my incomplete story hang in the air. Delacroix called to Adelita.

143

"Come sit with us, Addie." She raised her brow in surprise. "And lock the front door, and bring Helmina as well. Things are about to change around here, and you all need to know what's what."

The darkness I had originally sensed in the man's aura lightened. I felt once again my parents' presence—more strongly than ever. My level of anticipation rose higher than Nob Hill, the highest point in downtown San Francisco. My feelings were an equal mix of dread and joy. Perhaps I was to know at last the tale I had come so far in time and distance to unearth.

Tables were pulled together, chairs gathered. We finally settled down, the lanterns glowing dimly in the darkness of this rotting bar, the seat of a crime empire, waiting for the king of that empire to speak.

"Well, Monsieur Delacroix," I said. "What have you to tell us?"

Chapter Thirty

Revelations

"LeClerc was telling the truth, at least part of it, as he knows it," Delacroix said. "He gave me forty-five hundred to invest in a steamboat, money which was to earn interest while the boat was being completed. I was supposed to be the broker, gathering money from various investors for the project. The boat never existed, of course, though I showed him one being built and told him it was his. To complete the charade, I even arranged for him to talk to a couple of other supposed investors. The five thousand was supposed to represent his money plus the interest. I pulled the extra five hundred from some of my other enterprises. I told him that your parents, Bonita, would bring him the five thousand.

"My idea was that there would be a robbery, a fake one, of course, which your parents would report afterwards. The money would be delivered to a confederate of mine. LeClerc would lose his money, and everything would go on as usual."

There was still something behind his words I didn't understand. Something about my folks he wasn't revealing. "What was 'as usual'?" I asked.

"Adelita's was as you see it now. My various enterprises prospered."

"And my parents?"

"They were to continue as before, doing odd jobs of various kinds. Things like taking the cash to LeClerc."

Adelita said, "You ain't telling nothing, Danny. What's the changes you're talking about?"

"Get me a bottle, will you Addie? No need for a glass."

When the whisky arrived, he took a long, strong pull.

"I never saw a need to tell you or anyone else any of this. My secret. Hells bells, you aren't even supposed to be here."

I waited.

"Your parents. . ." He paused. His eyes actually puddled for a moment. "I loved those two. They were brave and loyal. The fake robbery turned real. No, no, I'm jumping ahead. You ever heard of the underground railroad?"

"Sure," Cat said. "Who hasn't?"

I told what I knew. "Slaves get delivered from captivity and go by secret ways till they get to the North and freedom."

"That's what we've been doing for years," Delacroix said. "That's where the five thousand was supposed to go."

I couldn't breathe. I looked from Cat to Luis to Delacroix. "My parents were agents of some kind for the underground railroad?"

"They were the best," Addie said. "They'd pretend sometimes they was a young couple on a journey with a slave or two waiting on them. Or they drove horses from one point to another to help make sure transportation would be waiting when the fugitives got there. One time they even took a little swaddled up nigger baby to a place where its parents was headed. Those folks were on foot, you see, and couldn't handle that part of the trail carrying a child."

By the time Addie finished, I was choked and teary. I rose from my chair and walked randomly around the room, trying to recover. I stopped moving when I felt my mother's arms around me. My father embraced me as well. The Lord had at last delivered us to one another again. And, true to His mysterious ways, in a time and place I could never have imagined. I had no notion of what the others were doing or saying. I was transported, swaying and crying. Through my tears I saw my parents, both of them, smiling at me. Smiling. Well, if they could, so could I. I motioned for them to come with me as I returned to the table. And, do you know, they followed? They stood close by for everything else that transpired.

I sat down, took a draw on my beer. "And what went wrong with the robbery?"

"It was Carew," he spoke with fury in his voice. "Daniel and Fiona were to meet a fellow near the crossroads going toward Magnolia, give him the money, then return and report the robbery to Carew. Instead, Carew himself waylaid them, took the money, and told them if he ever saw them again in Orleans Parish or anywhere in Louisiana, he would toss them in jail and throw away the proverbial key. To back it up, he had that flyer you saw in San Francisco faked up with my name on it and made outlaws of them."

"And what's all this about things changing around here?" Helmina said.

"You know LeClerc and I have been enemies for a long time. Our families were on opposite sides in the French revolution back in the 1790's. His folks took my folks' land and killed everyone they could find. They gave LeClerc's grandfather some money to come here and set up a family outpost in the new world. All that baloney he gives out about his grandfather starting from scratch to claw his way out of the swamps is as much fiction as *Robinson Crusoe.*

"My people, the few that managed to survive, were set loose on the land with nothing. They got here a generation later than LeClerc's on a debtor's boat as servants indentured to a man who died of the fever two years after he landed. My grandfather ran off into the swamps, where my father was raised, selling fish on the wharf. But they never forgot their history. I managed to claw my way out of the bayous, but Magnolia has been a target of my vengeance since childhood."

He gulped from the bottle, looked at it. The level was about a quarter down. He started to lift it to his lips, then set it down.

"I've been going at it slowly. Most of the slaves we've freed have been from Magnolia. There was a mysterious fire in one of the cotton fields last year. The steamship plot was a new tactic. The plantation is bleeding. This latest business with Gator's murder and Xavier and Jonathan shows how desperate LeClerc is."

Luis said, "And I am the perfect culprit, giving him an excuse to eliminate you and take over your income."

Cat laid a hand on Luis's shoulder. "We're all in the same stewpot with you now, friend."

Delacroix went on. "It has become a battle to the death between me and LeClerc, and you three have the choice to join me or to get out. I can help if you choose the latter."

"I must return to San Francisco with a clear record," I said. "And vindication for my parents."

"Even with the truth revealed," Delacroix said, "your parents would still be criminals. Helping a slave escape is a hanging offense in Louisiana."

"That, I can carry as a badge of honor. But they must not be branded as thieves nor Luis as a killer."

"Then, apparently, LeClerc and Carew must be dealt with," Cat said.

"Indeed," Delacroix smiled as he spoke. "And I believe we can start with our friend, the sheriff."

Chapter Thirty-One

The Turning Worm

It was nearing midnight. The jail was guarded, but lightly. Two men braced the door. How many might be inside we didn't know, but Delacroix's plan didn't require that information. We needed only to know whether Sheriff Carew was in residence, and we had seen him enter the building an hour before.

We had discarded our disguises, preferring to confront Carew as our true selves. For armaments, we carried our own wits and a few pieces from Delacroix's armory. Delacroix assured us that the need for firepower would be minimal. He felt sure that two of Carew's bodyguards would readily turn on their boss and join us. The sheriff had recruited Bert Hannity and Larue Bon by transforming their jail sentences into light duty as part of his protection detail. The move saved the parish money, which Carew duly pocketed for himself. Both of them would jump at the chance to have their sentences commuted, whatever the method, but they had no loyalty to Carew. I would recognize Hannity, Declaroix said, by his broad shoulders and tall stature. Bon was an unremarkable sort except for a vivid scar across his forehead, the mark of a knife that had been aimed at his throat but missed its target.

Second, I had revisited my old friend Rebekkah, the San Francisco prostitute who had procured Luis' knife. This time she was glad to see me, and I her. As usual, she appreciated the drinks I bought her in one of Delacroix's riverfront dives. An hour or so into our reunion, I broached the subject of our difficulties with the sheriff and Magnolia. She already knew most of the story, of course. Our activities had been the talk of the underworld. I went on to describe in a general way our wish to thwart Carew, revealing no details she might be forced to divulge later. And, lo! Just as I had hoped, Rebekkah said Carew had a favorite among her clan. One Mary Lou Gibbs. Mary Lou had a scandalous letter most everyone knew about, a letter that she would be glad to lend us if it would help rid her of the badge-toting ton of lard that came falling on top of her every few days.

I felt quite optimistic that our strategy, our inside allies, and the incriminating letter would be all we needed to unseat our obese opponent. But optimism wins nothing without action, and we forged ahead.

Adelita approached the jail, feigning intoxication. The guards at the door, neither of them the allies Delacroix described, set down their rifles to keep her upright. Cat took care of one, Luis the other. Knocking them unconscious, dragging them into the shadows and binding them. I tried opening the door, found it locked, and proceeded to knock and yell for Carew.

"I'm tired of running, Sheriff," I yelled. "I'm here to give myself up."

It wasn't Carew who opened the door, but one of his thugs. A big man in overalls, leather vest, and high-laced, heavy-soled boots. Bert Hannity, doubtless. Encouraged, I pushed inside at the same time he pulled at me. Four men, including Bert, were stationed around the room. Larue Bon, lank brown hair dripping down from his slouch hat, stood behind Carew, who sat at his desk. His brow was raised in curiosity, but he did not seem alarmed. The room stank of ripening sweat.

"Well, Miss Kelly." He spread his arms as if to embrace me, an event I would for certain avoid. "You are welcome. Though I must say it seems unlike you to simply surrender like this."

My parents' spirits were not so strong here as at Adelita's, but they still hovered close, giving me strength. "Oh, I'm not giving up, Carew. I've just quit running. I'm giving you the chance to surrender peacefully or be bound and escorted to the commander at Fort Macomb and turned over to the federal army for trial."

He laughed, along with the other men. "Trial? Me? Young lady, you are surely deluded." He was still laughing as he stood. I was encouraged that my words had moved him, if even a bit. "On what possible charge?"

I stepped closer to him, almost ebullient now, smelling victory. "The armed robbery from my parents, Fiona and Michael Kelly, of five thousand dollars, as well as the unlawful order banishing them from your jurisdiction and beyond."

He waddled from behind his desk, pulled at the waistband of his mud-stained denim trousers, which fell back below his massive belly the moment he let go his grip. He folded his arms, and leaned against the desk. He cocked his head and flashed a grin around the room. We were perhaps a step away from one another. It was obvious he was no more given to personal hygiene than when we first met.

"Am I to be privileged to see your evidence before I'm incarcerated?"

"That will appear at the trial."

"It will appear in a fairy tale, for I committed no such crime. Thus, there can be no evidence. You, on the other hand, are guilty of aiding and abetting a fugitive wanted for murder, obstructing justice, and a number of other felonies. Bert, lock her up."

He reached behind him and retrieved a ring of keys from the desk, which he tossed in the direction of the huge man I had confronted at the door. Our confederate. I smiled inwardly. Things moved fast after that.

Bert caught the keys, but turned his pistol on the sheriff. Bon pulled down on the other two bodyguards and confiscated their pistols.

I'd been carrying two pistols. In case they searched me and found the one in my pocket, I had a derringer Adelita had given me concealed under the kerchief I was using to hide my rumpled hair. But they hadn't searched me, so I pulled out the .44 revolver and fired it at the ceiling. The shot was the signal to Cat and Luis to proceed with the next step in our plan, which was designed to get Carew and the other bodyguards out of this office quickly and, most important, voluntarily.

Bert flipped the key ring back to Carew.

"It's been a pleasure serving you, Sheriff, but I hereby declare my employment at an end."

The odor of smoke followed soon after. A blaze appeared at the window that opened on to the boardwalk. I yelled, "Fire." Then just to add to the chaos I pulled the trigger on the .44 once more as I dashed toward the street. Bert flung the door open, and all five of us plunged into the darkness. I stayed behind for a moment, rummaged through a couple of Carew's desk drawers, found what I wanted, and followed the men outside. Our two accomplices had immobilized their former compatriots, using their pistols as clubs. We saved a different fate for Carew.

The plan had been for Cat to wrap the fat man's ankles in the tentacle of his bullwhip, trip him prone, then tie him up while he lay on the ground. At the last minute, I yelled, "Trade you," and tossed my pistol to Cat while he threw me the bullwhip. Thus I had the pleasure of employing the skills my Carter Maxwell had taught me in the not-so-distant past. The best part came when I yanked on the whip handle with all my might and was rewarded with the sight of Carew tumbling on his face to the boardwalk.

"I hope you got slivers in your nose," I yelled.

Luis stepped on his neck and held a gun to his head while Adelita and Helmina lashed his hands and feet together. We hadn't set the building on fire, of course. Pitch pine kindling made excellent flames and smoke, so there was nothing to extinguish but the torches while we completed our project.

When constructing our plan, we'd pondered the challenge of transferring Carew's bulk from the sidewalk to horseback. Luis, as was so often the case, solved the problem in a most ingenious way. Aided by Bert, he rigged a block and tackle to a hitching post and slipped the hook end around the ropes that bound the sheriff's feet. It took both Bert and Luis drawing on the pulley to drag Carew horizontally across the sidewalk, lift him to saddle height, and sling him prone, belly-down, across the back of a stout horse. We cinched his hands and feet under the belly of his mount. It was a splendid show, made all the more delicious when he began his caterwauling.

"You're outlaws, the lot of you. I'll see you hang before this is over," he yelled. Cat wrapped a bandana around his mouth, and that was the last we heard of him for a while.

Luis and I mounted and rode near the head of Carew's horse, Luis leading the animal by the reins. Cat rode behind us. We thanked Bert and his partner and told them they were free men as far as we were concerned. They delivered a couple of mighty whoops and galloped away on a couple of horses doubtless purloined from the Orleans Parish stables. Delacroix and his ladies, we'd decided, would follow us, but at a discreet distance where they might be able to detect and forestall trouble before it developed.

A small crowd had gathered, most of them late-night drunks from the saloons. A few of them were sober citizens in nightcaps. One Bible-waving man in a frock coat stepped in front of Carew's horse.

"I have been saving heathen in the barrooms, and I can save you usurpers of the public order as well," he declared. "I pray you accept our Lord and deliver yourselves to justice."

"There is no one in any parish who is closer to God than I am," I said. "Now move or be run over." My parents faded from my presence like a gentle breeze kissing my cheek. I bade them a comfortable farewell, knowing they would return.

The Bible man stepped toward us. We urged our horses forward. He stepped aside. We were actually on our way to hand Carew over to the troops of the U.S. Army. We had no idea whether they would accept him.

Chapter Thirty-Two

The Colonel Speaks

Both from experience and my own temperament, I have learned that sitting back and waiting is the worst strategy for achieving anything. I suspect, even, that it is against the Lord's will, He who commanded us to go forth rather than merely linger and hope. Witness the parable of the talents, in which Jesus prescribes harsh consequences for the man who buries his money and shows no return. Though it seemed chancy to expect the army, with the scant evidence in our hands, to give credence to our tale of Carew's perfidy, we forged ahead. Leaving the fat man bound securely to the poor horse that carried him to the post, we entered the commander's office.

Colonel Purdy was a short, stocky man, clean-shaven, if decidedly swarthy. His uniform, even at this late hour, when he had undoubtedly been called from his slumber, was all military. Knife-edge creases and gleaming brass. He was also short of breath, having to draw deeply for air every few breaths. We had decided that Delacroix and I should be the ones to present our case. The Adelita proprietor's dubious reputation aside, he was a prominent citizen of the parish. Though I was an outsider, I could offer a respectable and possibly softening female influence.

"So, you have made some sort of citizen's arrest of a sheriff, a civilian, duly elected for decades, whom you expect me to incarcerate, indict and try in a military tribunal. Even if I wanted to, I have no authority, Miss Kelly and Monsieur Delacroix. It would be a matter for the state courts."

"We came to you, Colonel," Delacroix said, "because we're not equipped to spend three or four days transporting this tub of lard to Baton Rouge."

"Could you not," I said, "on the basis of this letter to Monsieur Delacroix's employee—"

"Employee." Purdy smirked. "One of his string of whores, you mean."

"A woman of integrity, whatever else you may think of her," Delacroix said, "whose word can be trusted."

Purdy smiled and shook his head. I persisted.

"You could certainly hold Carew here, telegraph the authorities in Baton Rouge, and bind him over to them when they arrived, could you not? Let them decide what measures to take after."

"This is so unorthodox it's almost laughable. I could also hold you and Delacroix and your partners outside for kidnapping."

"Could you at least read the letter?" I shoved it across the desk toward him. He shot us a hard stare, gasped for breath, then finally bent to it.

M. Lou, my sweet of sweets,

I sense a waning of your affections lately. I have come into possession of a considerable sum. But why be vague? I can enrich you to the full extent of the $5,000 I recently procured from a couple of blundering Irish criminals. Only make known to me your heart's desires, and the money will be yours in return for a renewal of the warm fondness with which you have rewarded me over the last while.

Purdy frowned. "The date on this is twenty-four years ago?"

"A year after my birth," I replied.

"That's a long time for a woman to be working at this, uh, trade," Purdy said.

"Proof of her constancy and trustworthiness, Colonel," asserted Delacroix .

We had decided to alternate our comments with one another to keep the Colonel in a verbal crossfire.

"And why would he date such a sketch so precisely?"

"He told her he wanted his gift to signify her independence day, when she could give up her profession. However, she knew a life with him would be a bondage even more onerous than the one in which she was already ensnared."

"And," Delacroix continued, "you should know that the date is one week after Miss Kelly's parents, who were undoubtedly the 'blundering Irish' he mentions, and who were my employees at the time, were robbed of five thousand dollars they were conveying from me to Monsieur LeClerc of Magnolia plantation. LeClerc can testify to the truth of what I say."

Purdy nodded, sucked in some extra air. "Nevertheless, the letter means nothing by itself. 'A.C.' could mean 'Arlin Cooter' or 'Amos Cantor' or the names of any of a thousand men who have had congress with this Mary Lou."

"But not written on this date or penned in this hand." I laid before him samples of letters in Carew's handwriting I had grabbed from his desk. Purdy compared the note with the letters. The match was undeniable. Purdy ballooned his cheeks, slowly exhaled.

"Well, if this can all be corroborated, it's quite damning. You understand the risk you're taking, I hope."

It was Delacroix's turn. "Certainly. If the State people don't agree, Carew may be released before long, and could easily bring charges against all of us."

My turn. "We're prepared for that. Such a felon should not be allowed to continue in office."

"He's not a felon, Miss Kelly, until he's been convicted. Now, I'm concerned about public order with no sheriff in charge, so I will declare martial law for the week or so it will take, should Carew be arrested, to establish some sort of alternative system of justice."

Delacroix and I shared a smile at Purdy's sudden decision to accede to our request.

"But don't feel too smug. I am not going to incarcerate you immediately, but I expect you to remain available until I say otherwise."

"Understood and accepted," I said.

Delacroix declared, "I have a business to run. I am going nowhere."

Purdy grimaced. "More than one business, the way I understand it, Monsieur. But let that be." He turned to the soldier who had been standing at ease behind the desk.

"Corporal." The soldier, no more than a boy now that I examined him more closely, snapped to attention.

"Yes, sir."

"Organize a detail to escort Sheriff Carew to the guard house. Monsieur Delacroix, will you show the way to the prisoner?"

"My pleasure," Delacroix answered.

Presently I was alone with the Colonel, a situation for which I had been hoping.

"You have been most generous with us, Colonel. I thank you."

"I have been generous beyond my good judgment. I hope I don't live to regret it."

"And yet, I presume to encroach on your generosity even further."

"You are a most insistent young lady."

"I am confident that you will sympathize with my plight," I said. I explained my situation as succinctly as I could, took a breath and made my request. "If you would testify in writing to what has occurred here this evening, it would go a long way toward lifting the shroud of guilt from my parents." "What's happened here this evening is proof of nothing."

"Not court-of-law proof, no. But at least it would show that someone in authority is willing to delve into the charge that Carew and his minions stole that money."

He ballooned his cheeks once again, drumming his fingers as well this time. While he was pondering his decision, I snatched a loose sheet of foolscap from a thin pile on the desk, dipped a pen into an inkwell, and wrote the note Cat had drafted with his lawyering skills and that I had memorized to make this moment seem spontaneous:

July 18, 1855

I, Colonel Purdy, United States Army, do hereby affirm that I have taken into custody Sheriff Andrew Carew of Orleans Parish, Louisiana, on suspicion of the theft of $5,000 from Fiona and Michael Kelly on or about July 1, 1831. Indictment and any further measures in his case are pending.

Signed. . .

"Well, since it claims no more than the present facts, I suppose there's no harm," he said. He signed and dusted it with sand. I reached for it, but he pulled back.

"Stop by around midday tomorrow. I'll have a fair copy made by then. Army regulations."

"Of course, sir," I said, trying to hide my disappointment. We shook hands. I attempted a salute. He gave me a strained smile, returned my clumsy effort, and I left. I was exhausted, but happy that at least Luis and I—and, I hoped, Cat—would be able to proceed safely to Angelique's for some measure of sleep before we launched into the next chapter of this story we were writing for ourselves.

Chapter Thirty-Three

Luis

We slept the day away, did Cat, Luis, and I, having arrived at Angelique's just as dawn etched the swamp forest against the lightening sky. I thanked my Lord for Angelique, a woman of such great heart and generous nature. I wished I could take her back home with me. And I gave thanks as well for our safe haven. With Carew in the guardhouse, we were once again in her embrace.

Earlier, a messenger had delivered a statement from Delacroix declaring that both my parents and Luis were guiltless. Another arrow in our quiver of weapons against Flora Torres, the false mother from whom I must wrest my daughter once we returned home. But that battle was in the future. We had much to do right away.

Late in the afternoon, Luis and I hurried to the post to retrieve the copy of the testament that Colonel Purdy had signed. Traveling through the city, it was apparent that martial law was in place, with soldiers stationed around Carew's office and at several other key buildings such as banks and the cathedral.

Purdy, it turned out, was away from the post. On his way to Baton Rouge, we were told. And the document we needed would not be available until his return. We did ascertain that Carew was still behind bars, but it was troubling that Purdy had gone to the capital without communicating with us. We wondered why he could not have delegated the errand. But, alas, there seemed to be nothing else we could do in the interim, so we returned to Angelique's to partake of what she had promised would be a memorable meal.

Her delicious supper was also our breakfast, and we sat on the veranda, unmolested by mobs or phony lawmen, enjoying crayfish *étouffée* and a bottle of exquisite French Bordeaux she had uncorked for the occasion. The *étouffée* was even better than the one I'd tasted at Magnolia. The fragrance of her flowering garden honeyed the air with scents of honeysuckle and roses and more. Not to mention the spicy tang of the food. Why the smells and even the tastes seemed more intense and pervasive in this warm humidity than at home, I didn't know, but why question such splendid gifts?

Halfway through the meal, Cat stood and tapped his wine glass with a spoon. "Let us toast the charity of this wonderful lady, whose kindness is deeper and wider than the mighty river that flows near."

We all stood, tapped our glasses, one against the other. Their crystalline ring sounded as mighty to us as the bells of Saint Louis Cathedral on a Sunday morning. Angelique blushed.

"You drink to me, but my embarrassment is large, so I will drink as well to make the pain less so."

"*Santé,*" Luis said.

"Ah, the Spanish gentlemen is learning my language," Angelique said. This remark occasioned another round of tinkling glasses and drinking, after which the bottle was empty and one of her servants was dispatched to fetch another. And so it went, past the *étouffée,* and the brandy and napoleons until I became rather light-headed. I was about to suggest an end to the festivities when Luis intervened.

"Madame Angelique, as wonderful as the—how does one say '*la fiesta*' *en Français?*"

Angelique clapped her hands. Ah, and I am learning the language of the *gentilhomme* Espanol, for well I know *fiesta,* which *en Paris,* Señor, we call *la fête.*"

"*Très bon,*" Luis said. "*Mais je regrette la fête* must end, for now we three. . ." He gestured to Cat and me ". . .must discuss matters which for your own safety it is better you not overhear. I hope you are not offended."

"Oh, not in the least. It is beyond time when I should have seen to the kitchen and retired. It is such joy to me you have returned safely." She embraced each of us separately, then blew us a kiss as she passed through the doorway and into the house. Cat, Luis, and I drew our chairs together.

"I don't want to leave this place, ever," Cat said. "Think you could arrange that, powerful lady?"

I sighed. "I fear that's considerably beyond my purview, Cat Man. And I dread the perils that lie immediately ahead. Even when—if—I get Purdy's document in my hands, I would like more solid proof of my parents' innocence. Luis still stands accused in some quarters of Gator's murder, and we have promised to help Delacroix tear Magnolia from LeClerc's control."

"He has helped us immensely, so I will gladly join him," Cat said.

"And I," Luis said.

"And how could we not?" I added, "Given what we've suffered from LeClerc and the knowledge of what he and his family have visited upon Delacroix's people for so many decades? But even if we get the proof we need, then what? Don't forget that much as he has helped us, we did Delacroix a huge favor. He's been paying Carew protection money all this time, and we assisted him in lifting that burden from his shoulders."

"Shoot," Cat said. "He could have rid himself of the fat man years ago." He made a pistol out of his forefinger and thumb. "Bang, bang."

"Certainly," I said. "Perhaps he held off because he was averse to assassination. However, think of it this way: The extortion money was less expensive than the investigation from the State that was sure to follow, so his motives may not have been so pure. Now we have taken Carew out of the way, and he was involved only indirectly, almost lawfully, so he escapes penalty. Furthermore, our Adelita friend is quite selective with the truth he tells. I noticed that when he told Colonel Purdy of Carew's theft from my parents, he neglected to mention the fake holdup he had planned for my parents that same night."

"But, Monita, to tell that would have destroyed our whole plan."

"My point, Luis, is that duplicity seems a habit with him. We have only his word that the money was destined for a good cause or that my parents' participation in the scheme was voluntary. Perhaps all he says is golden, but I am suspicious. He was vague about his designs for the future of Magnolia, or the future of LeClerc himself, for that matter. Perhaps his ultimate design is to take over the plantation for himself."

Cat said, "I think, my dear Bonita, that you have an endearing need to draw a clear line between good and evil. Tidy to the mind, but not always a match for reality. It's quite possible, isn't it, that Delacroix is both criminal and savior?"

"I admit it. His letter absolving my parents and testifying to their character will be a powerful weapon against Flora Torres." I raised the letter Delacroix had volunteered to write and sign.

"Perhaps," Cat said, "he's doing the right thing for what you consider the wrong reason, but doing the right thing nevertheless."

"I believe that is a sure path to damnation."

"Is it your responsibility to care for Delacroix's soul? And what about your own? However pure you think your motives and goals are, you've enlisted the help of whores and thieves to get them done. Can you truly say you stand above Delacroix in virtue?"

"Even our Lord was not above consorting with the lowest among us."

"I've heard that argument a million times," Cat said. "I don't think—"

Luis held up his hand. "Let's return to the matter at hand. Our task is simple, Monita. Now that we have the letter from Delacroix and the one from Purdy, your parents' innocence is established. Once we get LeClerc to sign the paper admitting that he paid to kill Gator and frame me, then my innocence is proven as well. We have the paper written for him. All he must do is sign, which he will do to save his neck."

I said, "He will likely figure he can squirm out of the confession later, claiming coercion."

Luis said, "Yet, you will have that paper as well as Purdy's to take back to San Francisco and free young Bonita from Flora Torres. And your parents are proved innocent. Were those not our purposes here? What happens here after we leave is not our affair."

"You are persuasive, Luis," I said. "And yet there is the matter of Delacroix's plan to free the Magnolia slaves and help them travel north. If he does plan to take over Magnolia, I suppose he plans to manage it with paid labor somehow. But are the freed ones not part of our responsibility? Cat, you have lived here a long while. What do you think?"

"It will not be easy. Once you own a slave in Louisiana, he is yours to buy and sell, but it is a felony to set him free. Plus, the road north is a tough one, and the slaves know it. Swarms of men with hounds and horses will be hunting them. There's the old, the sick, the children to think of."

"You say they may not want to go?" Luis said.

"Some will. Many, I guess. But not all by any means."

"Again, that is not our affair, is it, Monita?"

I smiled at Luis. "You are right, of course. It is a fault in me to intrude in affairs that are not mine. What we will do or should do is uncertain. We know only that we cannot remain still. We must trust to His grace to guide us into the unknown. Good night to you, my Catamount." I embraced him. "And to you my sweet knight." I embraced Luis also, and planted a soft kiss on his cheek as well. "After Angelique's breakfast, we will meet Delacroix, Adelita, and Helmina at the bar to finalize our Magnolia strategies."

"I may not sleep, thinking of what Angelique's going to come up with for breakfast," Cat said.

We entered the house and were turning up the stairs to our rooms when Luis said, "After sleeping all day, I think I will sit in the parlor for a while."

"In the dark?" I said.

"I will light a lantern if I need to," he said.

"Well, *bonne nuit,* Monsieur, " I said. And thus we shared what I thought would be our final words of the evening.

***

I was in my gown, my hand on the counterpane, when a surge of emotion, a mix of fear and joy, impelled me downstairs. Luis stood when I entered the parlor.

"Monita," he said.

I stepped past him and sat at one end of the couch with my bare feet tucked under me. He sat at the other end, looking alternately at me and staring straight ahead. Finally, he spoke.

"Cat is very attracted to you."

So the romantic conflict was out between us. Luis had more courage than I to bring up the subject. I still was too cowardly to delve into it. "He is a fine man who has done much for us both. Saved our lives."

"Yes. We owe him a great deal." He waited a couple of uncomfortable beats before continuing. "You deserve more than me, a man so much older."

"Don't say that."

"A brown man with a white woman. They would never accept us."

"Who wouldn't?"

"The judges, for one, would not, if they are to allow Bonita to join you."

"And if there were no judges?"

"But there are."

"*Love sought is good, but given unsought is better.*"

"What?" he said.

"It's Shakespeare, from one of his plays. You could say I sought love with Carter Maxwell, and it was wonderful, but he is gone. It endures only in memory. Which, sweet as it is, is insubstantial and unsatisfactory."

"And neither of us sought this love," Luis said. "If it is indeed the sort of love that leads to an altar."

"Luis." I leaned toward him and smiled. "It is that sort if we make it so."

"We have a bond of years much stronger than many with only amorous ties. And we have much more than our memories of one another. If we choose to enter into romance, will we ever have more than you and Carter?"

"What if we can't help it?" I said.

He took a breath. We were silent for a time.

"Do you have such a memory, Luis? A memory like mine of Carter Maxwell?"

He drew a great breath. "Graciela. She died before I met you."

I started to ask how, but I realized I didn't want to know more. I had enough pain of my own.

We moved together on the couch, lips nearly touching. Despite the recent baths Angelique had provided, he bore faint male aroma of musk. I felt a stirring in my nether regions, feelings that I had always before associated with Carter Maxwell. But not this time. Now my body, like my heart, was visiting upon me sensations unsought. Unsought, yes, but I welcomed the passion the feelings boded. Why this now, Lord? I thought, Why this at all? I kissed my two fingers and pressed them to his lips. "*Mi amor*," I whispered, and fled to my room.

Chapter Thirty-Four

Assault

The conflict between Delacroix and LeClerc having escalated to open warfare, we had agreed to help not only out of obligation to Delacroix and to seek retribution for LeClerc's brutality toward us, but in hopes of obtaining the slavemaster's signature on the two documents we'd prepared. So far so good, but now that we found ourselves preparing for battle, I wondered at the wisdom of our decision.

Delacroix's motley band gathered in the mid-afternoon heat at the crossroads where Luis and I had encountered our Magnolia pursuers after our first escape. Broad daylight seemed like strange timing to us, but Delacroix said he hoped to catch the plantation in a swelter-induced lassitude. He chose the location because this far outside the city, we were beyond the demarcation line of Purdy's martial law. There was none of the flowery scent of Angelique's garden here. Cotton fields stretched away on all sides, some low-lying green and budding, others waist high and full-bolled. Breathing became difficult as the crowds of men and animals stirred the thick dust. The heavy aroma of manure floated underneath the rich mix of odors generated by overheated human and animal bodies.

Delacroix arrived astride a handsome black stallion. He affected no military uniform, but dressed in the same ruffled shirt and swallowtail coat that he wore inside Adelita's. As for his followers, they ranged from two men in top hats and frock coats to an ancient-looking character dressed in rags with only twine to hold up his flour-sack trousers. A number wore remnants of army uniforms that doubtless had seen service in the Mexican war nearly a decade before. The erstwhile soldiers had readied themselves for battle with a variety of armaments, ranging from shiny rifles to primitive weapons gleaned from attics and cellars, sheds and barns. As many as carried firearms carried only knives or swords. One even hoisted a scythe over his shoulder. Five black men clustered near the borders of the crowd. They did not mix with the whites, but apparently were tolerated in our company at least for the duration of this conflict. As near as I could tell, I was the only female, yet I did not feel out of place. I wore the trousers I'd acquired at Frobisher Island, and I was accustomed to the role of warrior by this point. I was less comfortable with becoming part of a mass assault. My mission to New Orleans had been personal and private. Though I had welcomed help here and there, I'd had no thought of joining anything resembling the small army around us.

"Luis, what are we doing here?" I spoke *sotto voce* because I didn't want Cat to hear. "Is this really part of our fight?"

"Every day, I have been hoping and pleading you would agree to start for home," he said.

I thought of the many Old Testament heroes. Saul and Joshua and David and the rest, of the battles they had fought. I thought of our Lord and Savior and of his military pursuits. Of course, there were none. Jesus fought his war with words and weapons of the spirit. Was I honor-bound to keep a promise like the one I'd made to Delacroix, one in which I no longer fully believed?

Luis continued. "But we cannot, I believe, break our promise and abandon the people that LeClerc and demons like Xavier have harmed and will continue to harm if they are not stopped."

I nodded and reached toward him. Our hands clasped. We would go forward.

"You two coming?" There was an edge to Cat's voice as he trotted past us. Luis and I shared an embarrassed glance and heeled our horses forward.

Down the road we progressed, perhaps twenty of us. In addition to our doubtful force, Delacroix had assured us that others would be approaching the estate from the water, as we had so recently done. Luis, Cat, and I chose to ride near the front, but rearward a bit from what would be the point of attack. We wanted to keep ready to move in whatever direction seemed the most advantageous.

When we came in sight of the main drive's colonnade of magnolias, Delacroix stopped us. He rode to the rear, designating groups and individuals to head to the left into the cotton fields so as to flank the mansion. When we reached the entrance, he made similar arrangements for the other side of the house. It was amusing to see this saloon profligate acting like a bonafide general.

The rest of us moved straight down the drive. So far we had been unopposed. Perhaps Delacroix's timing strategy had worked. But Cat assessed the lack of resistance as a bad sign. Surely LeClerc had not decided to hunker down in the house and leave us to wander at will through the rest of his grounds and fields. And indeed, the silence came to a sudden end as shots and clamor arose behind us.

Where they had been concealed, we never knew, but the group that came on us from the rear was a relatively small one, a mixture of black and white, slaves and, most probably, sharecroppers. But they did considerable damage before they withdrew. I estimated a half-dozen of us incapacitated by death or injury and three or four more taken out of action to care for them.

"Move on," called Delacroix. We heard a scatter of gunshots from other parts of the plantation. "The house. The house."

Some of the crowd ran up the front steps, only to be turned back by gunfire. Cat, Luis, and I spurred our mounts toward the playhouse, which we hoped would lead us through that tunnel to the pantry, then from there through the second tunnel to the secret stairway to the closet in the girls' room. We thought we'd then be positioned for a surprise attack from inside the house itself.

We had told no one of our plan because the tunnels and small stairway would accommodate so few. We tethered our horses some distance away so as to avoid drawing attention to the building. We got through the playhouse into to the pantry with no trouble. But the pantry itself presented difficulties. The defenders were using the kitchen as a munitions center. Arms and gunpowder and cartridges were spread everywhere, and slaves were engaged in loading and reloading firearms, delivering them to various defense points in the house and returning with just-fired weapons to reload. There was no question of us three taking over the kitchen ourselves. Even if we succeeded, it would take an ugly firefight to get out, with just as much chance of an exploding powder keg blowing us to kingdom come as of defeating the enemy. The wisest course of action would have been to return through the playhouse and find a new attack route. However, exigency, not wisdom, was the order of the day. My fears were beginning to dissolve amid the action.

The only route to the trap door in the pantry floor and thence to the door that gave access to the crucial stairway leading to the inside of the house involved crossing a good six feet in full view of the kitchen. Our only advantage was that the slaves' attention was drawn to the door on the opposite side of the kitchen where weapons were being carried in and out. I bellied across the floor, lifted the trap door, closed it behind me, and slid down the ladder as if it were a pole. Once again, I was trapped into the miserable pursuit of crouching and waiting. I yearned for action, but was paralyzed for the moment. I reminded myself that, without the planting and the waiting there is no harvest, so I remained still, silent and hoping. Eventually, the trap door lifted, and Luis squirmed through and dropped down the ladder. We hunkered down together until at last Cat followed. I smiled and pointed us forward like a cavalry commander.

At the end of the short tunnel, I turned the doorknob and pulled. The door was locked from the inside.

"This has never happened," I whispered.

Luis and Cat simultaneously pulled knives from their belt sheaths. They grinned and went to work on the hinges while I guarded their rear, pistol in hand. It seemed like forever, but I'm sure it was no time at all before the door was swinging free, hanging by the hasp and padlock that now provided no barrier at all. As we made our way up the stairs, we tried to prop the door to evade detection, but I'm quite sure the state of affairs was obvious at even a casual glance.

I was afraid the door at the top might be padlocked as well, but we made it into the bedroom closet without difficulty. I was about to open the door into the bedroom when the sound of a gunshot exploded from within. Then another. An echo of running footsteps followed the gunfire. Cat, Luis, and I needed no conversation except that of shared glances to communicate our understanding of what was happening. The bedroom windows opened on to the front of the house and offered a good firing position. The footsteps indicated that empty rifles were being rushed to the kitchen for reloading. This was an end to the planning and tactical maneuvering. We were about to enter the battle.

Chapter Thirty-Five

Guerilla Tactics

I knew the attention of whoever was at the window would stay with the front of the house. Also, unless they'd moved the furniture, the bed would keep us concealed for our first few feet into the room. After that, we'd have to take things as they came.

Luis and Cat drew their knives again, hoping for a silent attack. I drew my pistol in case their blades were not enough, and we crept forward. The bed was still in place, but, though no one could see us from the windows, neither could we see what was happening there. We reached the end of the bed and rose to our knees. Xavier was at one window. That was not a surprise. But to my astonishment, a woman knelt at the other, rifle resting on the sill. We planned our attack in silence, using gestures, then we leapt.

The woman turned from her post when I was a step away. It was Rose. I was holding my pistol by the barrel, intending to use it as a club, but she dropped her rifle, fell back, and screamed. So much for silence. From Luis's direction I heard a grunt and a clatter. Rose was crabbing away from me. I dropped to my knees and finger to my lips, made a shushing noise. She dropped into her pooled skirts, sobbing.

Two rifle barrels poked through the partially-closed door. Cat yanked on one of them and pulled the other slave I knew, Sherry, stumbling into the room. I grabbed the rifles away from her, tossed them aside, and pointed my pistol at her. Cat closed the door.

Sherry, on her knees now, held her hands up. "Lord, oh, Lord, please don't take me, Miss Bonita. I'se not ready in the least."

"Just stay there, Sherry." I turned toward Luis, who was wiping blood from his knife blade on to his pants. Xavier lay in a red puddle. Even from several feet away, the overripe smell of blood dominated the air. I cast my eyes heavenward and crossed myself. Empty gestures, I know, Lord. I felt no sorrow in my heart for this cruel man, however oppressed he might have been.

But we had no time for congratulations or conversation. Encouraged by the lack of firing from the windows, the attackers doubled their attack and poured a fusillade through the windows. We lay prone once again. It mattered not that the firing came from our allies. Bullets hit and kill whoever or whatever is in their path, friend or foe. Doubtless the attackers would follow the volley with a charge on foot any moment. Sherry scrambled into Rose's arms, and the terrified women sounded a fresh torrent of screams and sobs.

I knelt beside them.

"We didn't want to, Miss Bonita," Sherry said between sobs. "We wasn't going to kill nobody."

"I'm sure not, ladies," I said. "Please try to calm down." The crying subsided somewhat.

Cat said, "The hallway you talked about that opens into some other rooms, Bonita. You think we should go room by room or straight down the stairway into the parlor?"

"If I were LeClerc, I would have people at the windows in every room," Luis said.

"He probably does," I said. "But the parlor is the heart of this place." I had a providential flash, turned to Rose. "What would you do?"

She looked startled. Not surprising, considering that I may have been the first white person who had addressed her as if she had a brain. "Me? I don't know anything about all that."

"You don't have to play stupid with me," I said. "You know this house, and you know LeClerc."

Sherry said, "Miss Bonita, days to come, we gots to live here with the master."

Sympathetic as I was with their feelings, I couldn't afford to coax them out of their timidity. "All right, Mr. Catamount. I say we rush straight to the parlor. You and Luis take that room and announce your victory to Delacroix and the rest. I will take my pistol and play Hannibal in the Alps at the bottom of the stairway against anyone who might come out of the bedrooms."

"Don't need to worry none about them, Miss Bonita," Rose said. Had she finally discovered a drop of courage?

"Why?" I said.

"Sherry here has the keys to all them doors." She looked at Sherry, whose eyes were cast to the ground. Finally she took a breath and nodded.

"I sure do. I'll follow right behind you all and lock every door we pass. Just you all say you done it yourselves or we we'll feel the whip for certain sure."

"Can we trust them, Monita?" Luis said.

I looked Rose in the eyes. "Can we?"

She nodded. Enough for me.

"But they got some powerful men down there with guns aplenty. I'se afraid for you all."

"And for us, too," Sherry added.

"But we have surprise aplenty fighting for us," Cat said. "Let's go."

I might have argued for a bit more sober deliberation, but he opened the door and we ran, crouching, toward the head of the stairs. I decided to trust Rose and Sherry enough to not even look behind me. Luis, Cat, and I virtually dived down the stairs and clustered, guns drawn, on the landing that rose three steps from the parlor and fed directly into it. What confronted us was considerably more than a couple of frightened slave women. LeClerc had apparently called together a sizeable contingent of fellow plantation owners. Some of them wore army uniforms, doubtless mementos of their service in the war against Mexico, just as some of our own contingent did. It was as if the U.S. Army had split and was fighting against itself. I recognized Laurent of the Belcoeur Plantation, with whom I had shared supper my first evening here.

Just as Rose had promised, we were outnumbered and outgunned. But just as Cat had promised, surprise was with us. So intent was the combatants' concentration on the situation outside, so thick the fog of noise and gunsmoke, that they didn't even hear us thud down on the landing. I choked on the bitterness of the smoldering gunpowder, realized I'd have to give up drawing full breaths for a while. The mynah's cage was destroyed, as was the bird, I supposed. I didn't miss him. Luis and Cat had traded their knives for pistols, and we opened fire immediately, adding our own flashes to the pyrotechnics already in progress. I had never fired directly into a human body before, but the haze and furor of explosions were so intense that the enemy I assaulted seemed barely human, and the task was much less fraught.

We ran as we fired, heading for the dining room, which gave access to the kitchen. If we could stop the flow of arms and ammunition from the kitchen, the beast in the parlor would starve and die. The dining room had no outside windows, so no defenders were stationed there. However, a constant parade of armed defenders and servants moved in and out of the kitchen. Also, as we had noted earlier, firing toward the kitchen carried the extra risk of sparking explosions among the munitions.

I saw one man topple backwards as I fired in his direction. Had I killed someone? One step later I felt a bullet slam into my thigh. It hurt no more at the moment of impact than if I had bumped heavily into a door or piece of furniture, and it didn't prevent me from joining Luis and Cat as we dove under the massive walnut table and upended it, our backs to the wall, giving us fields of fire both into the parlor and toward, but not into, the kitchen. Our positions were untenable in the long term. The table would soon become a pile of splinters under the rain of gunfire. We hoped, however, that we would not have to stay there long, just long enough to prevent fresh arms from reaching the parlor for the time being, and to split the attention of the defenders between the yard and the dining room. Surely our tactics would enable Delacroix's scruffy crew to prevail before our defenses collapsed. I had emptied my pistol on the way in. I turned to reload, but reaching for more cartridges sent a pain shooting down my leg. A huge pain, doubtless delayed by the original trauma. I yelled.

I pulled up my loose pants leg far enough to see that the bullet had torn through the muscle on the outside of my calf and passed through without hitting the bone. Part of my brain assessed the wound as not so serious. But the hurt and blood attracted much more of my attention than the objective analysis. I gasped and whimpered, and the pool of blood on the floor reminded me of the gruesome sight upstairs where Xavier lay.

"Here, Bonita." Cat was at my side. In a trice, he sliced the sleeve from his shirt and had the wound bandaged. He stomped a strut from one of the dining room chairs and used it and a piece of twisted cloth to improvise a tourniquet. "Tighten and release it often," he said. "It is all we can do for now."

I nodded, smiled, and with a glance at Luis, who was concentrating on the enemy, kissed his cheek. "Thank you," I said.

He smiled back, then hurried to his station. I reloaded, then found a way to position myself and keep firing.

Chapter Thirty-Six

Please Sign Here

It wasn't long in measured time before we succeeded in choking off the supply of ammunition that made the parlor bunker operative and enabling part of Delacroix's army to pour through the front door. I seemed like forever, though, with my leg hurting as it did. A few of those who came through the front door went on to take command of the kitchen. Cat moved the table to give us a path to the parlor. Luis helped me up. He tried to carry me, but I resisted.

"Just help me to the sofa," I said. "I refuse to be helpless." I put one arm around his shoulder and kept the tourniquet tight with the other.

We had taken only a couple of halting steps before we were greeted by one of the most amazing spectacles I've beheld. Up the veranda steps and straight through the French doors rode Daniel Delacroix on his black stallion. No general in the history of warfare, I'll wager, has made a more decisive declaration of victory. He leaped down from his saddle and handed his reins to a lackey, who led the animal outside.

"Where's LeClerc?" he demanded, looking over the defeated combatants, kneeling at gunpoint on the floor, their hands clasped behind their heads. "Ah, Gilles, *mon ami*. There you are." He gestured to his followers. "Which of you will volunteer to take the rest of these miscreants to the stables?" Hands shot up. "*Trés bon*. I know there are chains and ropes and manacles in the barn as well as punishment cells for the master's errant servants. Make sure these gentlemen are secured. Monsieur LeClerc will remain here."

Luis and I stayed in place while all this was happening, but my pain was too great for me to cease my moaning.

"Monita," Luis said. And this time, I didn't object when he swept me up and laid me carefully on the sofa.

"Bonita?" Delacroix said. "What happened?"

Everyone was distracted for a moment, and LeClerc decided to make a break. Before he reached the French doors, though, Cat had him in a bear hug, lifting him from the floor as one might restrain a child throwing a temper tantrum. He carried him across the room and threw him down in one of the wing chairs.

"Naughty, naughty, Gilles. Can't have any of that."

I can smile now at this in memory, but at the time, the pain in my leg had consumed the attention of my whole body and mind. I found nothing at all amusing. I couldn't recall being wrapped in more hurt and tears since the night my baby Bonita had been torn from me at her birth. With Delacroix's help, Luis managed to find an unbroken bottle of whisky amid the carnage. He fed me some, then bathed my wound. The antiseptic burned as much as the bullet.

Finally, with the wound packed and wrapped tightly, the blood flow was stanched without the help of the tourniquet, and the pain became bearable, though it was on the point of drowning nearly all my other senses. Satisfied that I was all right for the time being, Luis and Delacroix turned their attention to LeClerc.

The plantation master had been silent, but now he began to speak a torrent. "You will hang, Daniel. Whether I live to see it or not, you have violated the laws of man and God today as you have for these many years. You cannot escape justice. Magnolia is mine. You cannot simply appropriate it and—"

Delacroix backhanded him. Which, judging from the smile that followed the initial shock, was exactly what LeClerc wanted. My clairvoyant vision came into play, encouraged by the crisis and by the whisky, I suppose, and both Delacroix and LeClerc were surrounded in darkness. There was no hint of the light I had witnessed around Delcroix off and on. His vengeant spirit masked all hint of virtue.

Luis stepped forward. "Before we proceed here, we have an urgent piece of business." He pulled from his pocket the two documents we wanted LeClerc to sign. "The first," he said, holding the document high, "testifies to the fact that you know that Fiona and Michael Kelly participated in the underground railroad and were in no way involved in the theft of the $5,000 that Carew stole. And this," he said, presenting the other paper, "absolves me of all guilt in the murder of my bartender, Gator."

I wondered if Delacroix had ever known Gator's real name.

"Of course," LeClerc said. "I am a fair man. Bring me pen and ink." Delacroix motioned to one of the slaves in the room. Presently, LeClerc had the tools he'd requested. He signed each paper with a flourish. When Luis looked at the signatures, he frowned.

"Monita," he held the paper up for all to see. "He writes "*Signed under coercion.*"

I had an urge to protest, but the pain overwhelmed me. "I believe that is the best we can do," I said. "Do you have more whisky?"

Never again will I hear of any bullet wound as being "slight" or "not serious." A great deal of conversation took place in that room between LeClerc and Delacroix, but I heard none of it. Undoubtedly, much of it affected me, but I cared not at all. I was consumed with my attempts to drown my pain in whisky. And I succeeded at last.

Chapter Thirty-Seven

Another Surprise

Once again Angelique Chevalier provided a haven for us. It was as if she and her domicile were the very table our Lord had prepared for us in the presence of our enemies. I spent the next while in fitful slumber while she, Luis, and "Le Docteur Beauchamp," who had so ably cared for Luis, attended to me. It turned out that the "while" was the better part of three days. It also turned out that I remembered very little of what had happened after I was wounded. Delacroix's dramatic ride into the parlor was a clear image, as was his slap across LeClerc's face. Only when Luis and Cat showed me LeClerc's signature declaring that he had signed under coercion did I recall something of that part of the action.

"What has happened since?" I asked.

"Delacroix has taken control of Magnolia. Adelita will be its mistress," Cat said. I smiled and shook my head at the very notion.

Luis added, "LeClerc is a prisoner in his own barn."

"What of his cohorts?"

"It is strange," Cat said. "Delacroix released them after they pledged to recognize him as the new owner of Magnolia."

"Why would they agree to that?"

"Clearly, their pledge means nothing," Luis said.

"I'm sure they want to buy time until they can organize another attack," Cat said.

"And there is more," Cat said. "Colonel Purdy is dead. Shot down by a sniper on his way back from Baton Rouge."

Fear thrilled through me, bringing fresh pain to my leg. "Jesus, Mary, and Joseph." I crossed myself. "And our letter?" It was a question whose answer I knew before I asked it.

"No one at the fort will admit anything," Luis said. "There is a Captain Fredericks in charge. We now fear that Carew will be released at any moment."

"We must leave," I said. I started to squirm my way out of bed.

"You cannot travel yet, Monita," Luis said, grasping my shoulder.

"We have no choice." I threw his arm off. "Delacroix's position is tenuous. Ours is moreso. With Carew on the loose, we will be jailed or shot or hanged in no time."

"But—" Luis objected.

"Tonight," I interrupted. "I'm right, am I not, Mr. Catamount?"

"Much as I hate to admit it, she is," Cat agreed. "We'd better pack up."

"Only if Doctor Beauchamp says it is all right," Luis said.

I objected again. "He must not know, Luis. We can't hide it from Angelique, but we must keep our departure as secret as we can or risk the same fate as Colonel Purdy."

Luis raised his hands in surrender, then clasped and shook his head in exasperation. "I have no arguments to offer, only my fear for you, Monita."

"My fear for staying is twice that for leaving," I said.

"But Flora—"

"We can fight Flora. The mystery of who my parents truly were has tormented me since I discovered their horrid fate on Rancho Sausalito. We don't have the paper we wanted, and perhaps the courts will demand it before freeing my Bonita. But we have other weapons we can use. What's most important is that *I* know and that Bonita *will* know at last what happened here. What Fiona and Michael Kelly did, and what they did not do. My heart is joyful with that knowledge and filled with pride for their courage and good works."

"That, if you'll forgive my French, is one hell of a speech, Mademoiselle Bonita Kelly," Cat said.

I sat up and gave Cat, then Luis, as tight a hug as I could manage. "Now, my knights, can we get moving before Carew appears?"

Chapter Thirty-Eight

Flight to Egypt

I still cannot explain why our ride out of New Orleans arose in my mind as parallel to Joseph and Mary's flight to Egypt to escape the slaughter of innocents. Carew fit the role of our Herod, certainly, but there was no killing of children nor warning from an angel. And we did not carry a holy baby in our arms, unless one counted my Bonita and our intent to rescue her from Flora Torres, who for all her harshness was no murderer of children or anyone else. But spirit often overwhelms logic, and the idea that Joseph, Mary, and Jesus rode with us lifted my soul.

Cat led us through back streets and back trails, and we cleared the city safely. We rigged a makeshift brace to keep my leg somewhat elevated and to shield it from the bumps and rigors of the ride. Still, it took occasional draughts of the brandy Angelique had provided to make the process bearable. Cat called a halt around two in the morning. We had been on the road nearly six hours, and the horses were exhausted. Not to mention the riders.

"We can rest in this glade," he said, "then use the fresh mounts in the morning." He had prevailed on his friends at the race track to lend us three extra horses even though he couldn't promise them a quick return.

Luis helped me down, and Cat took care of the animals. The men stood watch while I slept the deepest of exhausted and drugged sleeps.

***

Deep as my slumber was, it was brief. We resumed our journey at sunrise, dining while we rode on water and beef jerky and the last of the buttery croissants Angelique had baked as a farewell gift. Unique and exquisite fare for a trek over through the swampy Louisiana wilds. Texas, let alone California, was still far ahead of us, and the quality of our fare would doubtless suffer the farther we traveled. I figured that once we were out of town, our adversaries would wish us good riddance, forget about us, and resume their quarrels with one another. My calculations were mistaken once again. We'd been riding for a couple of hours when we topped a rise and looked behind us.

"We have company," Cat said.

The three men on horseback were dots on the far edge of the plain below.

"Could it be coincidence?" I asked. "Just travelers like ourselves?"

Cat shook his head. "Doubtful. This is not a common trail."

Luis nodded. "It is wisest to assume they are pursuing us, then, correct?"

Cat said, "We are easy to follow, given our extra horses, and we are not nimble, thanks to Bonita's leg."

Luis pointed to a grove of trees downhill from where we stood. "They won't be able to see us turn off," he declared. "We could hide ourselves and wait."

Cat agreed. I dismounted and lay down, resisting the urge to sip more brandy. The pain was constant, but not excruciating, and I had no intention of becoming a slobbering drunk in the face of our enemies.

My respite was short-lived. When they were close enough to identify, I had another surprise to add to the long list I'd collected on this journey. Luis and I confronted them, pistols drawn, where they'd halted, eyes to the ground, trying interpret the sudden off-trail turn of the hoof prints they'd been following.

"Monsieur Laurent," I said. "Surely your commitments at Plantation Belcoeur are more important than the time it is taking to follow me across country."

He startled, but recovered quickly. "Hardly, Miss Kelly. In attacking Magnolia and freeing slaves, you attacked the fundamental concept of our entire southern agricultural and social system. What's more, I was forced to spend two days and nights in chains, imprisoned in a dark hole as if I were some insolent field nigger. You cannot be allowed to walk away unpunished. Jerome." Laurent tossed his head. One of the men spurred his horse down the hill to our left. Laurent himself spun his mount in the other direction. The third man made as if to follow his boss.

By that time, Cat had circled behind them. He wielded his bullwhip again, and in an instant the aforesaid and astonished Jerome sat in the dust, bound in leather. Luis and I both fired. I, at Laurent, Luis at the other man. I missed my target, but hit his horse. Luis did not miss.

In a few seconds, then, the situation had reversed. Luis jumped down from his horse, disarmed Laurent, and commanded him to kneel with his hands clasped behind his head, just as he had been ordered to do when Delacroix's forces had defeated LeClerc's at Magnolia. Luis's gunshot victim lay face down on the ground. Cat toed him onto his back, looked him over, and shook his head. He gestured a similar pronouncement over Laurent's horse.

It didn't take much discussion to decide what to do next. In short order, Laurent and his henchman, Jerome, stood bootless next to where the blood of man and animal stained the earth. We dragged the dead horse off the trail and into the trees. Vultures would take care of it presently. The dead man was lashed to his horse, whose head we now turned back toward New Orleans. Luis, Cat, and I prepared to resume our journey, leading four horses instead of three.

"Have a nice walk, gentlemen," Cat said.

I said, "Tell Venus and Diane, Laurent, that if they are ever in San Francisco, they are welcome in my house. I'm sure they will get along beautifully with my Bonita. You need not accompany them."

Laurent spat at me, though not on me.

I chuckled. "I won't hold that assault against them. Now, on your way."

Cat flicked his whip and nipped the flank of the corpse-burdened horse. The animal whinnied and trotted a few steps east. Laurent and

Jerome, anxious not to lose their only potential transportation, trotted after him. We watched them until they were well out into the flat of the land, then we turned west. My future lay on the other side of this plain which spread before us so bleak and unpromising. I took heart and hope in knowing that home lay not so far away. My hope, however, was blemished by fears of all that remained unknown. I decided to approach one of those fears directly in that moment.

"It appears you intend to come with us, Cat," I said. "Are you sure?"

"As we sometimes say in the courtroom, Bonita, 'asked and answered.' So let's move on."

"It will be a very different kind of fight Señor," Luis said.

"And what of that?" Cat said.

Had I avoided a conflict, begun one, or merely brought one to the surface? I turned to Shakespeare once again. *Time must untangle this, not I,* I thought. *'Tis too hard a knot for me to untie.* It was the battle to enfold my Bonita in my embrace that mattered most. I needed to lay everything else aside.

"No more lollygagging, then, gentlemen," I said. "*Adelante.*" And thus we headed toward my homeland.

Chapter Thirty-Nine

Opium Dreams

I thought we'd have clear sailing once we'd dispatched our pursuers. In my joy over our series of triumphs, I fancied we were nearly home, but my memory of the distances we'd crossed proved faulty in the extreme. Long miles and other trials still awaited. The usual privations of desert travel—thirst, hunger, wolves and the like—we weathered well. Twice, patrols of Indians rode a watchful parallel to our course, but they never paid us a visit. I supposed they were not currently at war with our kind, and the small loads we carried gave them little incentive to attack. Our route took us over a portion of the Santa Fe trail, frequented by freight wagons with richer bounty than ours, giving us incidental protection, perhaps, from brigands with designs on the property and lives of travelers.

Santa Fe itself, the halfway point in our journey was the same bustling place it had been when Luis and I visited on our way to New Orleans. The big difference this time was that we'd been strangers then. Now Cat was with us, and he seemed to know everyone, having traveled through the city many times on his fur-trading expeditions. The pain in my leg had diminished. But it was still severe enough to force more rest stops than we desired, adding unwanted time to our journey.

A doctor Cat knew said I was healing nicely and gave me a small bottle of laudanum for the pain, cautioning me to use it sparingly. I thanked him and immediately turned the container over to Luis and Cat with instructions not to administer it unless I screamed bloody murder.

We left Santa Fe well-provisioned and optimistic. It was back in the murderous Tehachapi Mountains, where we'd lost our poor mule, Camille, that the trip turned sour. And it was all due to me.

My leg began throbbing in the night, and by noon the next day was swollen enough to render the skin tight as an inflated balloon.

"Infection," Cat said.

"Yes," Luis agreed. "Only one thing to do."

Cat nodded and begin gathering firewood. I knew what was coming and started to grit my teeth. "Laudanum," I yelled.

"What?" Cat said.

I yelled it again.

Then it was Luis's turn. "Did you say something, Monita?"

I finally caught on to what they were doing, and I knew it was funny, but I hurt too much to laugh. My next yell was a curse. An expression fit for the brothel where I'd learned it, but which had never passed my own lips before.

It was Luis who administered the medicine and Cat who wielded the knife, its blade white hot from the flames. What poured out from the suppurating wound I learned only later from their description. I was more than happy never to have seen, or smelled it, for myself.

Most of the remaining part of the trip was a floating madness of pain and hallucinations, many of them quite wonderful. Bonita was there. She seemed quite real. Just as real was the sound of her delicious laughter. But such happy images weren't my only visitors. A demon of a Flora Torres leaped from hellfire and scorched her way through my fantasy, sending poor Bonita fleeing in agony and fear. By the time I returned to sanity, we were at Mission San Jose. Almost home for true this time. My fever had passed, and, at least as far as the dreams of Bonita were concerned, I fully appreciated what drew those sleepers and dreamers to the opium dens of Chinatown.

Chapter Forty

Homecoming

I sat on the satin-upholstered sofa watching my partner and dear friend Sylvia Gonsalves at the sideboard, filling our snifters with brandy. It was wonderfully sweet to be back home in our suite at San Francisco's Brown Hotel, where our business ventures had begun and flowered. It was at least the third celebration of my return from New Orleans. My leg had improved to the point where I manifested only a slight limp. The yearning for laudanum was still with me, though waning. A glass of brandy or two dulled the craving enough to make it bearable.

I had trekked to the Mission and made finally a true confession of all the sins I'd committed during our journey. I had left in tears, but also in what I felt was a state of grace, feeling absolved and reconciled that I had engaged in violent acts only to save myself and my compatriots. The penance the good father had prescribed would take some time, but it would be an easy burden compared to the guilt I'd been carrying.

Sylvia handed me a glass of the golden liquid, sat beside me on the sofa, and we clinked our glasses before taking the first sip. It would be bad luck to neglect the toast.

"So, my mentor," I said. "How would you advise me?"

"Are you sure you're rested enough, Bonita, to proceed with all this?"

"It's October, Sylvia. I want Bonita living with me by Christmas at the latest. Earlier if we can manage."

"What are you thinking? She can't live here in the hotel," Sylvia said.

"An eight-year-old child? Certainly not. That wonderful house we own out near the Mission would be perfect. There is enough room for all three of us."

"You would evict the Hansens then?"

"'Eviction' is a cruel word. We can find another place for them. Buy one if we have to."

"I would miss the hotel," she said.

My stomach started to twist. I couldn't imagine not sharing quarters with Sylvia. It would be a rending of my life's fabric. Why was she resisting me in this, the thing my heart most yearned for?

"Surely you would come with us, Sylvia. It would be impossible without you." I took a sip of brandy. More than a sip, if I am to be honest about it.

"Well, we can ponder that," she answered. "First, there is the matter of tearing your daughter—"

"*Bonita*," I corrected her.

"—tearing *Bonita* from the arms of the Torres—"

"I think we are well supplied with weapons to counter the objections Flora raised to my relationship with her," I said.

"Surely you realize those objections were only an excuse to cover her real intentions. She will never willingly surrender custody to you."

"I am her mother. I know it. Flora knows it. Bonita knows it. She belongs with me," I said.

"So what?" Sylvia said.

I stood, aghast, drank the rest of my brandy and stepped across the room to refill my glass. "You are not on my side? You, of all people?"

"Always," she said. "But to bring to the negotiating table, you have only documents of uncertain origin, one of which was signed under threat. Flora Torres has raised the child from infancy. Legally, my love, you are virtually powerless."

"You forget the testimony of Rosalia, the midwife. A sister of Mariano Vallejo himself."

"She would be convincing, I suppose. But when the hour arrives, will she actually take the stand? She is a Vallejo, after all, and the very fact of her court appearance will reflect on the family. There are those who will pressure her to remain silent. It's a thin reed to lean on, Bonita. We will consult our lawyer, but I will be surprised if his opinion is not the same."

I said nothing about my conversation with Cat, in which he had told me virtually the same thing. When I asked him why he didn't voice his objections in New Orleans he said we were all in such danger we needed to get out. It hadn't been the time for fine legal points.

"That is not to say these papers are useless," he had said. "Only that they are not likely to help us much should the matter end up in court."

I asked Sylvia the same question I had asked him.

"If these letters are of no legal value, I have risked life and limb, not just my own, but Luis's as well, for nothing."

"Not for nothing. Come here." She spread her arms wide, pressed me to her, then returned us to our places on the sofa. She took the brandy snifters, set them on the floor, then grasped my hand. "Your parents. You know of them now. Perhaps no court will recognize the proof, but you know in your heart, and you can be—indeed are—proud of who they were and what they did."

"But if all that won't win me my child, what good is it?"

"Bonita, if there is anything our experience together has taught us, it is that there are many disputes that are settled beyond the walls of the courthouse."

I recalled how we had destroyed the network that was vandalizing and sabotaging our business in the early days, hamstringing our horses, vandalizing our wagons, burning our buildings.

"We were able to plant spies in the houses of our conspirators. Servants who were never noticed and could hear their plans. We cannot do that with the Torres family," I said.

She smiled and raised an eyebrow. "Can we not do something similar now?"

"What? Tell me."

"Before we move ahead, love, we need to make sure that what we are doing is for the welfare of that little girl."

"What girl is not better off with her natural mother?"

"Have you talked to her?"

"She has been asking questions. She's suspicious. I told you that's why Flora blocked me."

"But have you asked Margarita—" She raised her hand before I could make my automatic correction. "—Bonita herself? Have you made it clear to her that you are her mother and invited her to leave the home where she's grown up and to come with you instead?"

I opened my mouth. Then closed it. I had nothing to say. Always when I imagined the scene Sylvia described, I had the image of Bonita rushing into my arms while Flora stood angrily by. I had never taken the step of imagining it word for painful word. Sylvia had now forced me to realize that it was not enough for me to want custody of Bonita. Before all else, before the papers and proofs and whatever other struggles might follow, Bonita must understand the stakes as fully as her eight-year-old self could comprehend them. And, most important, she must agree herself to come with me. Otherwise I would be committing the exact sin that I had tried to avoid by pretending to be her aunt. The sin of tearing a child from the only home she had ever known. The very sin that Flora's father, Benito Alvarez, had visited upon me when he had torn Bonita from my womb. Was I coveting Bonita for my own benefit and not for hers at all? And yet, what choice did I have, since I could never accept being denied her presence, even as her false *tía*. Her pretend aunt.

I reached toward Sylvia and took her hand. "What do you propose, my dearest? I am ready to listen."

Chapter Forty-One

Secret Ways

Sylvia usually liked to keep a clear head when discussing important matters, but in this case, she decided brandy provided the best decision-making fuel. She refilled our glasses, and I resolved to sip only the smallest measure. I was pained to my very soul, since I had deluded myself that I had returned from New Orleans with all the proof I needed to barge in and reclaim my daughter.

"First of all, we must act quickly," Sylvia declared. "The Torres are preparing to leave."

"Leave?"

"For Mexico City."

"To hide Bonita from me?"

"If it were only that, they would have left when you departed for New Orleans six or seven months ago. I believe she hoped you'd give up your quest and would not return. But coincidentally, now that you're back, there has arisen some problem with her father's property. It is a real dilemma for her, but I believe it also provides a convenient excuse."

"Property, indeed," I scoffed. "She is kidnapping Bonita and running away." I put my hands on my hips. "Sylvia Gonsalves. How do you know all this? You do have spies in the Torres household, don't you? What else have you found out?"

"Let's just say I've been watching the situation closely. I feared for you and Luis the entire time you were gone. Ask anyone. I was distracted, crying at the drop of a disturbing word. I was completely unlike that imperturbable madam who for years contended with the most contemptible elements of our world. But I knew if and when you returned, information would, as always, be our most important tool."

She put the glass to her lips, drained half of it in a draught. First Luis, now Sylvia. They were vulnerable human beings, not the invincible Titans I had manufactured in my fancy as fortresses against my own insecurity.

"They are leaving within a week. Miguel has already gone."

"So soon?"

"Do not despair. Their haste is to our advantage. The household will be in some chaos with the preparations. Flora and Miguel and the servants should be so distracted that they will present a weaker front than they did before you left."

"If things are as they were before," I said, "it is that María who will be our main obstacle, excluding Flora of course."

"You are thinking as I do, Bonita, that a confrontation with Flora should not be our opening gambit. First, we have to persuade the girl they call Margarita that you did not desert her."

"Desert her? Is that what they claimed?"

"She heard some of the commotion when you stormed into the house before your New Orleans expedition. Flora said you had given up and gone away. You didn't care enough about her to make any further efforts to see her."

I took another gulp from the snifter. My eyes teared hotly, and I leaned against the back of the sofa.

"Abandoned her? Ah, I could never dream of such a thing." I half-reclined in anguish.

"Well, you can stay awash in self-pity, or you can do something about it all, Bonita."

If there was anything Sylvia could do, it was to yank me into a world of reality and solutions.

"Well, we will certainly need men. Unfortunately the hour has not yet arrived when humble women will obey the command of a female voice. Fortunately, we have two of the best with us. But that house is like a fortress."

"Ah, but there is a back way."

Would there ever come a day when I could survive without Sylvia Gonsalves? Then I remembered Magnolia and its tunnels and secret staircases. "Oh, yes. There is always a back way isn't there?" I chuckled.

"Constructed just for us, however unwittingly," she said and lifted her glass.

We laughed, drained our glasses, and hugged. I hadn't thought our campaign to bring back my daughter would begin this way, but begin it had, and the excitement lifted me fair to set me dancing.

Chapter Forty-Two

A Scene in the Garden

How the Torres family could have taken up residence in the same house where Flora's father lived and in which he was murdered, I had never been able to fathom. It was rumored they had completely redone the room in which he died, but that wouldn't have been enough for me to bury the spirit of a dead father. Not nearly. Especially a man that evil.

The building presented strong and high walls in the front, and it was rendered even more unassailable by virtue of the rocky cliff that bordered its back wall. The three of us—Luis, Cat, and I—stood at the foot of that cliff, just before dawn two days after my conversation with Sylvia.

Alvarez had been a devious man, and it would have been like him to construct just the sort of surreptitious passageway toward which we had been guided by Sylvia's informant. What surprised me was that the informant was María, the very guardian I had feared would keep me from my child. The old *niñera* the Torres' had brought from Mexico had become so feeble that she was unable to fulfill her duties, and her poor health had now confined her to her room, unable to emerge even for family meals. The family had installed María in her place because she had been part of Alvarez's staff here in San Francisco, and they assumed she would transfer the loyalty she felt for him to the rest of the family. Sylvia had many contacts among the community of grateful women she had helped to find employment outside the brothel she had closed. María herself had not been among those, but a cousin of hers was. It was she who had informed Sylvia of the disdain María held for her former employer. It took some time, but with kind words, promises, and, indeed, monetary encouragement, Sylvia had been able to turn that disdain into a regular supply of information.

The early morning fog wrapped us in a chill. Beside the trail that bordered the cliffside rubble grew a forbidding tangle of blackberry bushes. A single boulder protruded from the growth. One would never guess that boulder to be a doorway to a private entrance into the Torres mansion. Part of its face was a cleverly sculpted and painted piece of oak, which pivoted aside to reveal a steel lever. That, in turn, allowed one to pull the stone aside on the rollers which made its opening a simple matter even for a single person, such as yours truly. I felt a little like one of the women at the tomb of Our Savior.

"After you, gentlemen." I gestured to Luis and Cat to go ahead of me.

We'd brought a kerosene lantern to help us navigate the passageway. It didn't throw a great deal of light, but we didn't dare use the lanterns that lined the walls for fear of revealing our presence.

"Real miners built this," Luis said. "See how expert they were with the timbers? And the stairs are deep and safe."

"Well, there should be plenty of miners around here," Cat said.

"And many of them without work after going bust in the mountains," Luis said. "They would have been glad for the employment."

"I don't want to know how Alvarez kept them from spreading the word about this," I said.

"From what you've told me about that guy, I'd just as soon stay ignorant about that, Cat declared. "Now let's get on with it."

Both the men had a bit more of a tortuous journey than I did, since they had to bend the whole way, almost to their knees here and there. At top of the stairs we found what looked to be a wooden door with a conventional knob. Considering all the elaborate mechanics we'd just encountered, it seemed almost laughable, even though María had warned us to expect it. Luis turned the knob and pushed. It didn't yield. He pushed harder. It still didn't yield. Were we to be thwarted on the verge of success?

"Here," Cat said. "Judging by that fake boulder at the entrance, the builders seem fond of sliding panels. Maybe. . ." He began pushing and pressuring around the door frame with no success. Then he stepped back. "Has to be something simple and obvious," he said. "We're just missing it."

His remark gave me an inspiration, something I remembered from a Chinese lock box Captain Richardson had kept in his parlor. I tried each vertical board in the doorway in turn. It was the middle one that slid up into the doorframe. The doorframe slot that received it was hidden by a narrow piece of lath on a spring. Under the sliding panel was a brass bolt that slid into the doorframe below. A rawhide thong was tied to that. The thong proved to be a latch string that, when lifted, provided access to the other side.

"Good for you, Monita." Luis reached for the doorknob.

I grasped his hand to stop him. "We're not finished yet, I'm afraid. There's never just one key panel." Two boards later I found the one that slid downward into the doorframe and revealed a second brass bolt tied to a similar thong, this one at the top. I pulled it downward. "Now, lift that first one, and turn the knob," I said.

Finally, the door yielded.

"Slow, now," Cat said.

Luis heeded him and opened the door only a couple of inches. Outside, a weak morning light had come on during our labors, and a courtyard garden lay before us. Cat turned down the lantern wick to extinguish its light and hung it on the doorknob by its bale. We listened for a while to make sure no one was within the vicinity, at least no one who was talking. Then we eased our way out of the tunnel. We didn't worry about closing the door behind us. Our presence would soon be no secret, and I planned to exit through the front in any case.

I had to admit it was a splendid garden. A pair of enormous bougainvillea, one purple, the other deep red, framed two stories of the main walls of the house. A central fountain with a muscled figure of Neptune brandishing his trident rose from the center of a surrounding rose garden. Bushes of red and white blossoms alternated around the circle. Varieties of pansies and hollyhocks adorned the beds at the base of the surrounding walls. All this contrasted with the deep green of the lawn that occupied most the area. The flowers and foliage perfumed the air.

I tamped down my elation at navigating our way into the inner sanctum, knowing we'd a ways to go yet. I resisted giving Benito Alvarez any credit for the beauty of the surroundings. I automatically decided he'd left it to his gardeners. Of course Flora might have had some influence. Considering her Christian name and the fact that she had named her daughters—the false one and the natural one—'Margarita' and 'Rosita' might have indicated a taste for cultivating blossoms.

But horticulture wasn't why we were here. We decided to wait for an opportunity to present ourselves and speak with Bonita.

We took a seat on a bench near the rose bed where we could watch the entrances to the garden. There was a ground level door, and, on the second story, a pair of French doors leading on to a balcony. A tiled staircase bordered by an intricately-sculpted wrought iron railing led from the balcony to the yard.

Cat voiced my feelings of the moment. "I have no problem with action, but waiting like this is agony for me," Cat said.

"My grandmother trained me in patience," Luis said. "It was the most difficult skill I ever learned."

"More difficult than breaking horses or shooting or all the other abilities you have?" I said.

"Yes. More difficult by far than any of those."

Cat shook his head. "My father had just the opposite approach." He punched the air with his fist. "'Get in there and make things happen,' he'd say. 'Opportunities won't fall in your lap. You have to generate them yourself.'"

He looked squarely at me. I felt a little like Jane Austen's Elizabeth. Shakespeare's Viola came to mind once more as well. Neither of them had been in quite my situation, but there was a romantic triangle here, and I was at the apex. I wished Cat had stayed in New Orleans. Yet, I was glad he was here. An emotional paradox I could neither explain nor sustain. The tension among us was palpable. Cat was in San Francisco not just to help and support me, though he was certainly ready to do that. Luis was. . . I didn't know. As for myself, I needed to concentrate on my daughter. After that, well, maybe something would happen to make all the rest clear.

I walked around the flowerbeds, pretending to concentrate on the colors and textures and aromas, but in reality seeking to escape the aura that surrounded the three of us. I wondered why my clairvoyance would not come into play and give me an inkling of what I should do. Shortly after I stepped away from Cat and Luis, however, I was thinking of little else but what I would say to Bonita when I got her alone.

I was resolved to separate her from Flora, to tell her everything she surely already knew or suspected. I imagined a moment when she said, 'I knew you were more than my pretend *tía*. Mamá always favors Rosita over me. Can I come stay with you?' A fantasy, of course. But the part about Flora favoring Rosita was not in my imagination. I'd witnessed it many times. She would grasp Rosita's hand when they walked, leaving poor Bonita to trail behind. It was perhaps to be expected that Flora would feel more intensely about her natural daughter, who had been born after years of unhappy childlessness. But it was not Bonita's fault that she was the adopted daughter and had become something of a neglected stepchild. Flora could have at least made an effort. Now she was denying me not out of affection for Bonita, but out of an urge for possession and power. The situation must not stand.

We all three jumped back as the upstairs doors opened and María stepped out on the balcony. She raised a finger to her lips and gestured for us to hide. I was fed up with concealment, but followed her command nonetheless. We crowded next to the bougainvillea, under the balcony. We couldn't see, but we could hear.

"Make sure the girls wear their sweaters," we heard Flora say. She spoke in Spanish, something she would never do with me, though I had grown up speaking the language. Another emblem of her disdain for me. "I would rather they stayed inside with their art and music until it got warm, but Rosita wants to play croquet right now, and when she gets a notion in her head there is no dissuading her."

"Yes, Madam. Rosita is like that. And Margarita also."

"I must attend to some paperwork. Things Miguel would ordinarily do, but which fall on me while he is away. Please do not disturb me until time for lunch."

"I understand, Madam."

A period of silence followed. I looked from Luis to Cat and back to Luis. Luis inhaled and pointed to me. I realized I'd been holding my breath. I smiled and exhaled quietly. How well he knew me. Then came a chorus of children's voices. Or it sounded like a chorus to me, though there were only two.

"I'm going to knock your ball over the wall today," Bonita said.

"My ball will be speeding through the wickets so fast you won't get close," Rosita answered.

"Wait, now," María said. "Each of you carry your mallet and one ball. I'll bring the wickets and the stakes."

And of a sudden, there she was, bundled in a colorful pink sweater, her hair as blond as mine at her age, her nose fetchingly tipped with red from the cold air. Rosita was almost as pretty with her midnight hair and rosebud lips.

"Rosita," María called. "Help me. Please bring your mallet and help pound in this stake."

Rosita followed obediently, leaving Bonita standing alone. My opportunity at last.

"Margarita," I whispered.

"Tía," she said and leaped into my arms. "Tía, Tía, Tía. I have missed you so much. Mother said you didn't want to see me any more and had gone away." She was sobbing. The swelling in my throat nearly choked me into silence, but I had to seize this moment. I swallowed hard. Luis and Cat pulled the thorny branches of the bougainvillea aside and created a little cave. I guided Bonita into it.

"What happened to Margarita?" I heard Rosita say.

"She went inside for a little while," María explained. "Come on. Let's finish with the wickets so we'll be ready to start when she comes back."

Meanwhile I had Bonita to myself. "Why is Luis here? And who is that other man?" She asked.

"I'll explain later. Right now, I have something very important to tell you. Do you believe I love you and would never leave you?"

"But Mamá said—"

"She is mistaken, my sweet. I don't have much time to explain, but what I am going to say is more important than anything I have ever said in my life." I hugged her, kissed her forehead, and grasped her shoulders while I looked into her eyes. "Flora Torres is not your mother, and Margarita is not your real name."

Her brow furrowed. She shook her head. "Why, Tía? I don't understand."

"The truth is this, dearest one." I had to shake my head and clear my throat before I could go on. "I am your true mother. It was I who gave birth to you." She shook her head and looked everywhere as if searching for light in some ominous darkness. "Surely you have suspected something, my darling," I said. "Haven't you?"

"I don't know," she said. "I love you, Tía, but Mamá. . . "

Luis knelt beside us. He placed a gentle hand on her arm. He said, "You know how much we all love you, and we know how confusing this must seem to you. But what Bonita speaks is the truth."

Tears burned my eyes. Years of tension and pain were behind them. Relief at speaking the truth aloud at last. Sorrow for the hurt and confusion I had just visited upon my daughter. An avalanche of emotion surrounded us.

"You haven't seen me recently because I had to go on a journey to another city far away. New Orleans. I gestured toward Cat. This is Cat, a friend who came back with me."

Cat knelt beside Bonita. "Hello, young lady. I'm very glad to meet you." He placed a hand on her arm. I guess we made quite a tableau, the three of us kneeling, virtually surrounding this sweet young girl. My daughter.

"Now," I said, "I want you to go with Luis and visit Tía Sylvia for a for short time while I go speak to Flora Torres." It felt wonderful to avoid calling Flora 'mother'. I stood and grasped her hand. Cat and Luis rose with me. She balked, confusion furrowed her brow.

"Don't worry, sweet one. I'll explain to Flora, and you will return by lunchtime in any case."

She relaxed somewhat, but was still not altogether comfortable. I invoked a game we had often played.

"How brave are you?" She looked at me with a question in her eyes, but an incipient smile on her lips. "Are you brave as a puppy?" I said.

"Puppies aren't brave."

"You're right. How silly of me. Are you brave as a kitty cat?"

"Kitty cats aren't brave."

"You're right again. Tell me something that's brave."

She giggled. She knew the answer to this one. "Lions are brave."

"Aha. Lions. Of course. What sound does a lion make?"

She made a rather puny roar.

"Yes. But we can do better than that, can't we? Come on. Together."

And together we roared.

"Louder," I said. We were both laughing now.

We roared again.

"Make them roar, too," I said, pointing to Cat and Luis.

She turned in their direction. "Come on, you two."

All four of us gave a mighty roar. María and Rosita watched as we ran out of the bushes. Luis and Bonita ran across the lawn and exited the way we had come in. María had been fully briefed on our plan, so she knew what to expect. Rosita on the other hand, seemed understandably amazed and a little frightened. María pulled the girl to her in a comforting hug.

Cat and I sprinted up the steps to the balcony and through the French doors. I was so ready for battle, I could almost smell the gunpowder. Flora Torres had no idea what was headed her way.

Chapter Forty-Three

Dueling Mothers

We strode through the house toward the library. I began to regret bringing Cat with me. This was a matter, after all, to be settled between two women. Strong arms and rough voices should not be required. Or so I thought. The only people we encountered on our way through the house were a couple of maids—one wielding a feather duster, the other carrying a bucket of water. They stepped away from us in shock and even a bit of fear. They knew perfectly well who I was from my previous visits, and they knew I'd been forbidden the house. Given the web of gossip and underground communication in the family, they probably knew who Luis was as well. Catamount, I thought, would have been a mystery. I charged ahead without making eye contact with either of them.

The heavy oaken double-doors into the library were tall and forbidding, stained dark and carved with reliefs of knights in battle. Images that reminded me why Cat was here. I banished my previous doubts about the need for a man, stopped, raised my hand.

"When I drop my hand, please open the doors both together, then close them behind me and see that we're not interrupted unless I call."

"Yes, General," Cat said. He saluted and smiled. I don't know whether I smiled or not, but I dropped my arm. The doors swung open, and we faced Flora Torres, sitting at a polished walnut table, papers, inkwell, and pen before her. Maroon velvet draperies framed both the tall windows that admitted the cheerful morning sun. I stepped in, heard the doors close behind me. Flora stood, leaned on the tabletop with clenched fists. "Another invasion, is it? Well, this one will be much shorter than the last." She stepped to a tapestry bell-pull near the wall.

"Your signal will do you no good, Flora," I said. "Luis and Bonita have gone to visit Sylvia at the Brown Hotel—"

"Sylvia Gonsalves. That whore—"

"My business partner and a woman who would give her sanctified life for Bonita. As would Luis, and well you know it."

She threw her arms high in exasperation. "And another friend who came with us from New Orleans is at the door. "I mean to have an uninterrupted discussion between the two of us."

"So you have brought your giant dressed in rawhide, have you?" So much for Cat being a mystery to anyone. "How about cannon? Do you have a few of those trained on the door as well?" Her lips were tight, her eyes narrow, her arms folded in front of her.

The room smelled of the same odors of tobacco and leather it had carried in the months before I left. The evil stink of Benito Alvarez, which neither time nor distance would ever erase. Masculine smells, singularly inappropriate, I thought, for a standoff between two women. Flora's light jasmine cologne barely registered.

I heard running footsteps from outside the door. Flora smiled, looked in that direction. "Señora." Angry voices and sounds of a scuffle followed.

"Cat is under orders to avoid combat, not provoke it," I declared. "Perhaps you can command the same of your people. I meant what I said about wanting an uninterrupted conversation. "

Reluctantly, Flora strode to the door and slid back a panel. "*Todo está bien,* Alejandro, " she said. "*Pero quedése fuera de la puerta.* "

"Good," I said. "With two guards outside the door, we will remain protected from intrusion. Now, can we please be seated?"

I walked to a leather-upholstered chair pillowed with brass buttons and gestured that Flora should sit on its twin beside it. From a pouch at my waist, I drew the documents I'd brought from New Orleans, handed them to Flora, and sat.

"You objected to my having contact with my daughter." She started at the reference to Bonita as my child, stood and crumpled the papers in her fist.

"Your daughter? You will cease calling her any such thing."

I remained seated, sensing that stillness was the way to control the situation. The maneuver was out of keeping with my normal behavior, but I felt so secure in the rightness of my position that it came as naturally as my customary impulse to overt action.

"One thing at a time," I said. "Please." I motioned for her to reseat herself. She complied, though she perched herself so far forward she was barely on the chair.

"You asserted that I was unfit to have contact with my Bonita—"

"My *Margarita.*"

I took the first of what would be many calming breaths during the conversation. "Your prohibition was based partly on the belief that my parents were criminals. One part of the so-called proof of that calumny was a wanted poster, offering a reward, allegedly from the authorities in New Orleans. The documents in your hands refute that accusation beyond doubt."

"They are lies and forgeries," she hissed.

"At least do me the service of reading them."

She remained stiff as a fencepost. I nodded my insistence. Finally, she straightened them out and gave them a grudging perusal. When she finished, she shook her head and smiled. Luis, Cat and I had considered withholding LeClerc's testimony, but decided that since we were dealing in truth, everything should be open.

I said, "You are no doubt smiling at Monsieur LeClerc's claim that he signed under coercion. However, his statements are nonetheless true. The state of conflict between him and Daniel Delacroix would not allow him to sign an open admission. Missing from that packet is the corroborating testimony of a Colonel Purdy of the United States Army who was murdered after he signed and before he could deliver it to me."

"This would never stand in any bona fide court, Bonita Kelly, and well you know it. And it will not stand in mine." She ripped the papers and tossed them aside. Her aura, dark before, was tinged with blue. Good, I had injected some doubt in her malevolent attitude.

"Those are copies, Flora, so you have destroyed no evidence. You know now that my parents were engaged in righteous work, striving against slavery."

She opened her mouth to object.

"Surely you don't support slavery, Flora, which your native Mexico outlawed decades ago."

She made no gesture of agreement, but I went ahead anyway. "Fiona and Michael Kelly were falsely accused, made scapegoats and fugitives by venal officials and greedy men of influence. My mother fled from New Orleans to Rio de Janeiro with me in her belly, then from Rio to San Francisco with me at her breast."

"They were rustlers."

"No one truly knows what my parents were doing that night. My uncle and Luis both admit they were gunned down before anything could be explained, let alone proved. My uncle went to his grave with a conscience disturbed about the whole incident, despite being absolved many times by many priests. Those documents testify that they were dedicated to a morality of the highest order, a morality entirely inconsistent with any act of thievery."

Flora stood, turned her back to me, and paced to the other side of the table. "Even if this fabrication were true . . ." There was a beat or two of silence. I was surprised to find that I had stood. I waited for what she would say next. She spun on her heel and stepped toward me, leaned on the table. "None of it has any relation to your claim of parenthood to Margarita."

"Clearing my parents' names relieves me of a torment that has pained me since I was twelve. And it removes one of your main objections to my seeing her. But no. None of it proves I am Bonita's mother. That proof lies elsewhere. I hope I will not have to pain all of us by invoking it. Especially in court."

"Proof," Flora said. "Her aura turned dark once again. She crossed from behind the table and stood before me. "I spit on your proof." She did not actually spit, but she might as well have. She turned away, then returned to her chair. She sat and invited me to do the same. The blue in her aura reappeared. Some combination of sympathy and love crept into her voice as she spoke next.

"I cradled and nurtured Margarita since she was small enough for Miguel to hold her in one of his hands. I have loved her and dressed her and fed her. It is true I did not give birth to her as I did to Rosita. I intended to tell her when she was old enough."

"I have already," I said.

"Ahh." She sounded as if she had been stabbed, and fell back in her chair. I almost wanted to go over and comfort her. Some time passed. "It is obvious, as you said, that she resembles you physically, and she has remarked upon it. But what of that? Coincidence. No more. It takes more than flesh and blood and physical similarities to create motherhood. You have brought calamity upon this poor child out of jealousy for your own childlessness, and jealousy is not love."

Calamity I had indeed brought to Bonita's life. And no doubt pain. And more to follow. I questioned in that moment the wisdom, the propriety, the very morality of what I had done. Mistake or not, though, retreat was impossible now.

Flora said softly, "No true mother would do such a thing to her daughter."

For the second time in an hour, my eyes burned. This time tears flooded my cheeks. Still, I managed to keep the whine out of my voice as I whispered, "All three of us have known or strongly suspected who I am. Who Bonita and I are. If you had not forbidden me contact, Flora, we might have continued our pretense of my being her aunt indefinitely. This painful moment might never have happened, at least in this way. Now, though, the pretending is over."

Flora stood and pointed down at me. "You are the pretender, Bonita, with your false documents and your fairy tale talk of *proof*."

I stood and faced her for a second, but I couldn't hold the eye contact. I had to step back into myself to tell the story. I crossed to a window that looked out on a narrow side yard, bounded by a main wall of the property. Its top was strewn with broken glass embedded in mortar to keep intruders from climbing over it. The flowerbed at its base was planted with pink impatiens. Sunlight warmed my face, and the foul odors that so pervaded the room seemed to diminish. I spoke with my back to the room.

"The night she was born, Bonita was taken from my bed before I could see her or hear her cry, let alone bring her to my bosom. The midwife was sent to tell me she was dead, but she made a mistake. She used the words *se ha ido,* 'she is gone' not '*está muerta*' 'she is dead'. I knew, of course, knew in my heart, that she was alive even without such evidence." I turned toward Flora, who had sat down as I spoke. "You would have known of her survival as well, Flora. You would have felt her heart beating from afar. Any mother would." I returned to my chair. "What's more, the midwife of whom I speak still lives, and she will take the stand if necessary, though I would prefer to spare all of us that wrenching experience." I stood and crossed toward Flora's chair. She turned her back.

"I trust that you do not know what happened that night, Flora. I trust you do not know that your scoundrel of a father took my child. Perhaps, to give him benefit of the doubt, he believed his motives were pure. He was, after all, merely trying to provide an infant for you, his childless daughter. Furthermore, he could rationalize that I was without a husband, that Bonita's conception occurred under brutal circumstances, a rape which left the father's identity unknown. As a sort of bonus, it gave him a chance to further disrupt the life and affections of my uncle, who loved me dearly and whom he hated.

"I'm sure he convinced you that it was an act of mercy to deliver this fatherless babe to your arms. And you were living in Mexico City. So far away. What chance that her origins would be discovered? Yet, here we are."

She remained erect, but dropped her eyes. "He sent her with a wet nurse, as if by courier," she said, "with a note, saying he was too busy to come himself, too busy to attend to his granddaughter." It was her turn to shed tears.

"The note said she was a foundling whose mother had died giving birth. Too busy."

"Was he better with Rosita?"

"At least she was always mine," she said. "Too busy. A dead mother come to life. And now, what am I to do?"

She lifted her eyes, her cheeks were now as wet as mine. And, something I never imagined. We embraced.

Chapter Forty-Four

First Meeting Reprised

I found Bonita and Luis and Sylvia in the lobby of the hotel enjoying lemon ices in green crystal bowls. The spoons were gleaming sterling silver. Our best. I looked at Sylvia and pursed my lips. A kiss of thanks for making this occasion so special. They offered Cat and me an ice from a nearby chest in which the confections had been delivered from some place or another. I started to decline, but Sylvia shot me a look that told me I'd better accept.

"Well, well, well, aren't we a happy group?" I declared, when we'd all settled down.

Bonita was about to explode with excitement. "Tío Luis is going to take me to Rancho Sausalito to show me everything. Maybe even a calf being born. And Tía Sylvia is going to help teach me to play piano."

"You couldn't have a better teacher or a better guide," I said. "Tía Sylvia taught me a hundred songs when I was young, and Luis knows everything there is to know about Sausalito or any other rancho."

"Piffle," Sylvia said. "You already knew piano when we met. I only helped you learn a different type of music."

"Piano, eh?" Cat said. "I learn something new about you every second."

"Indeed," Luis said. "There is more to learn than one might imagine." He smiled and gazed at me and held his gaze too long for comfort.

I shifted my eyes to Sylvia, who lifted her brows, a signal of caution. Then she turned the conversation ninety degrees.

"Bonita, did your mother," gesturing toward me, "tell you that we are going to move out of this hotel into a real house?"

This was an announcement to the group, disguised as a tidbit to Bonita. It was also a surprise to me. It meant she had satisfied the housing needs of the Hansen family, the tenants of the place near the Mission I'd intended for us. I tried to hide my surprise and concentrate on my delight that we'd soon have a home where I could live with my daughter and Sylvia as a family.

The chatter went on for some time. There was a plan for us all to go to Sinaloa Norte, the restaurant of our old friend, Alfredo, for an early supper before we returned Bonita to the Torres house. And still they chattered, till I couldn't stand it any longer. I knew everyone was dying to know what had happened between Flora and me, but my first talk had to be with Bonita.

"Daughter, would you come walk with me, please?"

***

We strolled the sidewalks on our way to the destination I had in mind. The streets thronged with activity and smells. Odors of manure, baking bread, and the salty fragrance of the bay waters mingled in the air. We probably heard five languages in the first couple of blocks. The gold rush had made San Francisco a city of the world. I was proud to point out several shops and buildings that Sylvia and I owned, most of them managed by women Sylvia had formerly employed in her brothel. Quite another trade from the millinery and baking and dry goods in which they were now engaged. I of course kept mum about their history as I passed their establishments. I yearned to introduce Bonita to them as my daughter, but that time had not yet come.

"We also have another place, named after you," I said.

"It's called Margarita?"

She wasn't yet calling herself Bonita, which stabbed me a bit, but it was early in this new day of ours. "Not exactly. We call it Casa de M'hija. The house of my daughter. I was thinking of you when I named it even though we hadn't even met. We shelter women there. Women who have fallen on hard circumstances. And we try to help them recover from their difficulties and learn to fend for themselves so they can go forth in the world without fear."

Sylvia and I had been very proud of this project, and I'd looked forward to Bonita's enthusiasm over it. However, as is true of so much in children, her interest lay in another direction from my adult enthusiasms. She emitted a small yelp and moved closer to me.

"Spiders, Tía. Watch out."

She was pointing at a poster outside the American Theater. I laughed, but welcomed the chance to put a protective arm around her. "That's a picture of Lola Montez, sweets, doing her spider dance. She's quite famous for it."

"She dances with spiders?"

"That's what they say. I can't imagine why, and I have no wish to find out. Come along now."

"I didn't know there were so many things to see here, Tía. When we leave the house with Mamá, we always whiz by everything in our carriage." She stopped and looked up to me. "But if it's really true that you are my mother, should I call you *tía* still?"

I hugged her, then crouched down. "You can call me whatever is comfortable, sweetie. I know things have gotten very puzzling for you. What's most important is for us to be happy and together whenever and wherever we can."

"So I can still live with Mamá. And you are my mother also?"

I swallowed. "So you would have two mothers. What a lucky girl you are."

She hugged me in relief and with affection. I recognized it was a logical solution for her. Two names. Two mothers. Even though the thought of sharing her was painful, she had to come first.

In our moment of tenderness, I had persuaded Flora to delay their trip to Mexico City, and she had promised to let me know before they left. But our reconciliation had not proved durable.

"You are very tough, Bonita," she had said not more than a week after our embrace, "but you are not ruthless enough to pursue what you want no matter the consequences. You will not bring this to court because you are too soft to cause my daughter that pain. She would get over it, but you could not bear to do it."

"It may please you to think so, Flora," I shot back, "but do not try me, or you will regret it."

I believed my barbed words when I said them, but I hadn't come far from the house before I knew she was right. The visitation agreement I had wrested from her while she delayed the Mexico City journey was all I would get for the time being.

I returned her hug, and we continued our walk through the city we both called home. A short time later, we reached the place where I'd been headed—Portsmouth Square.

Once a quiet plaza named for the first American military vessel to reach San Francisco during the war with Mexico, the gold rush had turned the square into a center of contradictions. City Hall was there, ensconced in a former concert hall named for the famous singer, Jenny Lind. The Swedish Nightingale, she was called. But the purity of her voice was not at all reflected in the activities that dominated the square now. Opposite the bastion of civic responsibility occupying the building that once bore Jenny Lind's name stood a collection of establishments devoted to gambling and other nefarious activities. Loiterers of various description occupied some of the benches that bordered the plaza.

"Do you remember this place?" I asked.

"I don't think so."

"It looked very different that day, the day of the fiesta following the funeral of Benito Alvarez." I had almost said "the funeral of your grandfather," which is what Flora would have called her predator father, but the word refused to pass my lips. We walked in a sort of circle while I indicated what I was describing. "There were flowers and music and a table where the Torres family and their friends sat. A Maríachi band over there. And you ran around talking to everyone, whether you knew them or not."

"Oh, yes. Everything was much prettier than it looks now. And you came and brought me back to Mamá."

"It was the first day we met, my love. I will never forget it, and I brought you here today because I want you to remember it always as well."

"Don't worry, Tía, I won't forget. Do you want to see how tall I can be? Watch." She ran to a nearby bench, crawled up on the seat, and then on the back and started to walk across like a tightrope walker."

"Bonita," I cried. "Get down right now." And after three or four steps she did jump lightly to the ground.

"I'm going to be in the circus when I grow up," she said.

I laughed and hugged her again. I couldn't stop hugging her, it seemed. I wanted never to relinquish her touch. "Well, you may have to do it on your own. Watching you will be too much for my heart. Come sit on this bench. I have something serious to talk to you about."

"What's going to happen to me, Tía, now that you're my mother?" So we had returned to the same subject we'd discussed only a few minutes earlier. There would be many such conversations, I supposed, before matters became clear. If they ever did.

"Flora Torres and I had a long talk," I said, "and we agreed that we will continue for the time being just as we were before I went to New Orleans. You will live at the Torres house, and I will come visit often. We can go on excursions like this. How does that sound?"

She pursed her lips and looked at the ground. She was considering. How I wished she would insist on reversing the arrangement, staying with me and visiting the Torres' instead of the other way around. Or perhaps, now that she was here with me, I could refuse to allow her to return to the Torres and sue for custody. Possession, after all, was a powerful weapon. Yet, all legalities aside, what happened next would rest not with a judge, but with the child who sat beside me.

"We even talked of your coming to live with me," I continued. "But you should think of all that you would leave behind if you made that decision. I wouldn't want to cause you pain, my sweet."

"I would miss Rosita," she said softly. "And María. And my room and my bed and my dolls."

"I won't try to take you away from any of those things," I said. "That's enough solemn talk for today."

"Are you really and truly my mother?" she said.

"I most certainly am, sweet one. And don't let anyone tell you nay. Come on, now, everyone is waiting for us. And I know you will love the restaurant Sinaloa Norte, and I know that Alfredo will love you, just as we all do."

We walked away, hand in hand, with smiles on our lips and in our hearts, but I couldn't banish the feeling that the shadow of Flora Torres and her dark intentions followed us like a specter.

Chapter Forty-Five

That Which Is Lost

We indeed had a celebratory meal at Sinaloa Norte. After, Bonita and I left the others behind, and I walked her to the Torres house. María, not Flora, met us at the front door. I embraced her, offering thousands of thanks for all she had done.

"*Por nada,*" she said. "I love this child and would do anything for her."

I knelt before my daughter. "*Hasta luego,* M'hija," I whispered. I clasped her precious face in my hands and kissed her forehead. She extended her arms and leaped into mine, holding me tight.

"*Tía,*" she said. Then, "*Mamá.*" She giggled. Maybe she was just trying the word out and the laughter came because its strangeness tickled her. I didn't know or care. She had called me *mamá*, and my heart swelled to breaking. "*Hasta luego,*" she whispered. She released me and ran to María, who escorted her inside and shut the great doors of the house. I stood alone for a moment, gazing in the direction of the bay I could not see but whose savory aroma floated on the slight breeze. The same waters from which it rose had carried my parents to these shores. It had been at the heart of the richness of all those who had dwelt beside them. Captain Richardson, my putative uncle who had raised me. The Miwok people who had saved Rancho Sausalito. The Vallejo family who had nursed me back to health both after my body had been smashed in that terrible fall and after the arduous birth of the daughter who had now been restored to me.

I recalled words from scripture that went something like, "whoever drinks the water I give him will never thirst." The verse might have been speaking of these waters, for, indeed, I owed my life and happiness to a whole series of miracles, all of them owing to the faith and prayer I carried always with me. And all of them in the company of the waters which bordered the earth on which I walked at that moment. Not to mention the waters that had carried us through the battles from which we had so recently emerged. It hurt me to step away from Bonita that night, but the balm of thanksgiving I carried in my heart eased the pain, a hurt that dwindled, but didn't quite disappear.

***

"Sylvia and Cat were enjoying a brandy in our suite when I returned. I started to pour a glass for myself, but Cat interrupted to do the duties himself. We toasted. I reached out and clasped hands with him.

"I can't thank you enough for helping make this perilous day a success," I said.

He kissed my hand. "She is a lovely girl, and only you are worthy to be her mother," he said. His eyes carried that same look they'd had during that confusing moment we'd shared on Frobisher Island. I was a woman who never blushed, but my cheeks grew hot under his gaze. I managed a weak "Thank you," turned away, and sat.

"Where is Luis?" I said.

Sylvia said, "He said he had matters to attend to at Rancho Sausalito."

"At this hour? Surely he could have waited till morning."

"Well he has been gone from there a long while. It's easy to understand that he is needed after such an extended absence." She reached inside her dress and handed me a piece of paper. "He apologized and left this for you."

I looked at the paper, folded neatly with my name printed on the outside in his hand. It carried an aura, something I'd never before seen surrounding an inanimate object. An aura so red and fierce I expected it to explode or burst into flames any second. I tucked it into my own bosom, where it rested like a hot compress.

I finished with my brandy, stood, pleaded exhaustion, and said it was time for me to retire. Sylvia and Cat remained in conversation while I sat on my bed and opened the letter.

Querida Bonita,

Forgive me this letter. I have tried to speak in person but have been not able. Our tender moments on the New Orleans journey will remain always in my heart. Sometimes far away from here, it seemed possible that we might become more than we are. But I know now it is not possible. I hope we can continue as we were before all this happened. I am always your knight. Yours and the little Bonita's also.

Por siempre suyo
Luis

So.

I sat numb, staring into space. All my thanksgivings dimmed. I crumpled the letter, brought it to my lips, and lay back on the bed. I probably made some sort of sound, but I either didn't hear it or didn't recall it when I later relived the moment over and over.

Under the pain of loss flowed a river of confusion. The Luis I had come to know and desire was gone. It wrenched my soul to lose him. Yet, the Luis I had always had, the loving protector, remained. Why couldn't I be satisfied?

Later, I wondered what it was about our souls that we must always, always want more, more, more than we have or deserve? It is this eternal yearning that wounds us over and over and causes us to wound others as well. But those thoughts came later. They were too philosophical to entertain that night, which was given over to regret and self-recrimination until the Lord's blessed darkness enfolded me in sleep.

Chapter Forty-Six

Abduction

I visited Bonita nearly every day, stealing time from my business concerns, which had suffered during my absence. The load had fallen heavily on Sylvia, who had not complained, but who had been working long and hard to perform tasks that normally fell to me. We had vowed never to establish a shop or a rental property and be content to simply collect our payments. We insisted on making regular visitations, on checking to make sure if there was anything we could do to improve the properties or business procedures and to reduce rents or payments if necessary to make sure the tenants or managers could succeed. It had been our signature ever since we had set up K and G—Kelly and Gonsalves—Enterprises. It had enabled us to draw tenants away from bigger firms and establish ourselves in the fiercely competitive business operations of this exploding metropolis.

Our business had now grown to the extent that providing this personal touch consumed our time and energy. We had farmed out as many of the business tasks—accounting and legal matters and the like—to the extent we could, but it was still difficult to keep up. Thus, the time I committed to Bonita was expensive. But, of course, I would spare no expense for her. Our relationship grew apace, and I hoped always that she might say it was time to move away from the Torres household and come to mine, but I tried not to pressure her.

Miguel Torres returned. Sylvia and I had a couple of business partnerships with him, and our relationship had been quite amicable. Now it turned cold, as did my reception at the Torres'. I cared not as long as my reception with Bonita stayed as warm as it did.

I also managed a tearful reunion with Luis at Rancho Sausalito, which stood just a short boat ride to the north of San Francisco. We shared a wonderful meal with my late uncle William's wife, María Antonia. She was a former adversary turned friend. Their two children, Maryanna and Stephen, were both now nearly grown and were taking roles in operating the *hacienda*.

"It grieves me that I caused you pain, Monita," Luis said as I prepared to leave. "It grieves me also that you have been hurt. I remember once or twice in the past when you gave me painful advice I needed to hear. But this. This is different. So very different."

María Antonia, watching from the hacienda porch, must have been puzzled by the way we looked at one another, held our hands in one another's, wrapped our arms tenderly around one another. We were not, after all, lovers. Or were we, in some unfathomable way? It was a question to be asked, but the world would never know the answer, for we carried it in our hearts.

As for Catamount McGhee, he had made his romantic intentions clear ever since our interlude on Frobisher Isle, and he pursued them relentlessly, if indirectly. He threw himself into helping with K and G Enterprises and soon built a reputation for himself as a powerful force on our behalf.

One of our main operations was a drayage business that contracted for both local and long distance hauling. It had expanded to the point where we were short of almost everything—wagons, drivers, and livestock. Despite the fact that he was new to the area, Cat shortly had established a network of acquaintances that led him to skilled and dependable men—and even a few women—who could be trusted to carry loads to Sacramento and San Jose, our main long distance locations. We dived into our capital to pay premium rates to wheelwrights for new wagons and to ranchers for rentals of other wagons that often lay unused except during harvest. Cat rode tirelessly from one ranch to another to find the vehicles. His commanding presence and engaging personality won over nearly everyone he encountered, and his skill with the bullwhip gained the admiration of every worker in the operation.

He was, of course, welcome in our parlor whenever he cared to come, which was often.

Sylvia said one evening, "You know, my dear, that Cat could give two hoots about K and G. His devotion is to you, not the business."

"Surely you know I am not so obtuse as to be unaware of that, Sylvia. But you must admit, the business is reaping great benefits."

"We may reap the whirlwind if you aren't careful, Bonita."

"I haven't deceived him, Sylvia."

She said nothing. Only shook her head, smiled, and poured brandy. But I knew the time for a decision was approaching, and I couldn't for the life of me or despite a thousand prayers, understand what was holding me from embracing this fine man who obviously was ready to build a life with me. Who was actually engaged in doing just that.

"Can you tell me where we are headed, Bonita?" he said one evening.

"I hope in the same direction," I said.

"You hope? You don't know? Can I help with your doubts?"

So many questions. I hesitated. There came a pounding on the door.

I was astonished when I opened it to discover María in tears. "*Se ha ido,*" she sobbed. "She is gone." The same words I had heard from Rosalia Vallejo when Bonita had been robbed from me the night of her birth. I nearly collapsed to hear them. "Miguel has taken her. They are bound for Mexico City."

Chapter Forty-Seven

Flight and Pursuit

Thanks to María once again. Without her, we might not have known about the Torres' escape plan until two days hence, when my next scheduled visit to Bonita came. She paid a great price for bringing us the news, for she could never return to the Torres household now. She would always have a home with us, of course, but she left behind her friends among the other servants. What's more, the fate of her ties with her beloved Rosita, and Bonita was thrown into the unknown. All that aside, the immediate need was to prevent Miguel and Flora from transporting Bonita beyond our reach. María's news was barely out of her mouth before Cat and I launched into action.

There were few southern routes immediately outside the city. The mountains south of San Francisco limit the possible routes the Torres could have taken if they were truly headed for Mexico, and no other destination made sense. Travelers can use the coastal road to the west side of the north-south peaks, or the valley route on the other. María said they were traveling light for speed. All horses, no wagons. Nevertheless, they had a long way to go, which distance would have required prodigious supplies and horses or mules to carry them. They would be moving slowly, and we should be able to overtake them. As we had done when we left New Orleans, Cat and I each took a spare mount. Apart from the anxiety about recovering Bonita, it felt wonderful to ride beside Cat just as we had in our New Orleans adventures. We regained our camaraderie and common focus immediately, and I had to admit to a guilty relief that Luis was not with us.

We reached Mission San Jose in the early morning, but there was no sign of our quarry. We had figured they would stop there. Had we passed and ridden ahead of them? Or were we behind? Perhaps they had taken a side trail and eluded us. Not only had it been too dark to discern trail sign, but the routes were too heavily traveled to detect their tracks amidst dozens of others.

"One thing for sure, Cat," I said. "They will travel through the valley. The coast is too slow, and even if they don't stop at the missions, they will need provisions and rest. They will be seen. Sylvia has sent word to Luis, who will alert our friends among the tribes to the north. Captain Richardson had hired their people for fair wages instead of enslaving them as Alvarez did. It was a move that had not only helped the tribe, but saved his shipping business from Alvarez's sabotage and boycott. Their reach is longer than we Anglos can imagine. Come into the mission and let me introduce you."

Cat's easy ways with people gave him instant entrée to the people of San Jose, the religious and secular, the Anglo and the indigenous. They fed us handsomely, providing us with their traditional hospitality. We needed the refreshment, but our errand was too urgent to linger, and we were soon mounted and on our way.

This time we headed south and inland toward San Juan Bautista. Cat swung out wide to east and west, trying to find out if they had switched off the main trail. It slowed us, which frustrated me, but he quite rationally argued that it would do no good to ride fast in the wrong direction. The ride took us only a couple of hours, but it yielded us nothing. If I was right, their next logical destination would be the Mission at Soledad.

We found a stream, changed mounts, and kept riding. The trail took us west for a short distance. We came over a gentle rise and beheld the sun setting over a calm ocean in the distance, a calm that in no way reflected our mood. We descended the slope and turned back south. Then we saw them. It had to be them. Pitching tents in a pine grove, hobbling horses, preparing to camp for the night.

"How should we handle this?" I said.

"We should just ride in and say hello," Cat said. He was smiling like a man who had just opened a lovely gift.

We heeled our horses into a canter and were within hailing distance within minutes.

"Hello, the camp," I called as we approached.

All eyes were on us as we rode in. Flora, Rosita, three or four servants. No Bonita. No Miguel. Something was wrong. Worst of all was Flora, who sat on a folding stool, knitting. And smiling like an undertaker welcoming a client.

"Hello, Bonita Kelly," she said. "How nice to see you."

Chapter Forty-Eight

Sailing This Time

My daughter clearly wasn't here. But I had to ask anyway.

"'Margarita' you mean? The people you see before you make up our entire party, Bonita. She is not with us."

Besides Rosita and Flora, I saw one maid who probably also acted as the nanny hired to replace María. I saw three men, doubtless wranglers and drivers.

"It looks like we followed a false trail, Bonita," Cat said. "But let's make sure they don't have her hiding someplace."

"We will not allow you inside our tents," Flora said.

"Don't have to," he said.

He unleashed his bullwhip and commenced to yank out a few of the pegs that were holding up the two tents that had been pitched. He succeeded in rousting out only Chuckles, the gray cat I knew so well from my visits. He ran straight to Rosita, who petted and purred her into a calm.

While Cat was coiling his whip, I remarked, "I clearly underestimated you, Flora. You are every bit as ruthless as you claimed." She actually laughed at that, as if in pride.

On impulse, I dismounted and walked to Rosita. "I'm so sorry we frightened Chuckles," I said. I stroked the cat's fur, then the little girl's hair. "I'll bet Margarita misses her."

"It's all right, Tía, she still loves you." Chuckles purred her assent. "Margarita had to go on a boat, but we'll see her—"

"Rosita," Flora yelled.

The girl ran to Flora, sobbing. I'm sorry, Mamá, I didn't mean to tell her, I. . ."

Flora grabbed Rosita by the shoulders, shook her briefly, then pulled her to her hip. That done, she turned to me. "It doesn't matter, Bonita. The ship has sailed by now. Miguel has matters well in hand, and with our many connections south of the border, you will never find her. Never."

Monterey was straight west of us, a busy port that would be a natural embarkation point for Mexico. A fairly short sail to Manzanilla, then an overland journey to Mexico City. She would be in the capital in a week or less. My daughter, captive. She would get over it, Flora had said. But she wouldn't. And neither would I.

"Monterey is close, Cat," I said. "Less than a day's ride I believe."

"We can't take her word that the ship has sailed, so let's get going." He gave his horse a gentle slap on the haunch with his reins, and we headed west.

"You're too late, you fools," Flora yelled after us.

Even after the huge mistake I'd made following Flora, Cat didn't question how I knew Monterey was the place to go rather than some other point. We simply continued to operate as a team despite the adversity. Would Luis have found the tracks where Miguel left the trail with Bonita? We would never know. Perhaps Miguel and Bonita were never with Flora's group at all and had followed the coast to Monterey all the way from San Francisco.

I was once again rather glad Luis was not here. I carried still the tension of his note and of our difficult parting. It was good to have things more or less settled with him, but my feelings were still confused. My feelings for Cat were becoming more and more clear. I watched him riding beside me, sitting easy in the saddle, alert, but not fearful. He looked my way and grinned.

"We'll find her, you know," he said.

I smiled back, then blew him a kiss. Was that moment on Frobisher Isle growing into full-fledged partnership of the heart and soul? The second the thought entered my mind, it transformed itself from a question to a statement.

"Yahoo," I yelled.

He looked at me, startled and puzzled.

"And we'll dance by the light of the moon," I sang. "Come on, Cat, sing along."

And down the trail we rode singing about those buffalo gals. My spirits were high, but that nagging logical part of my brain told me that Flora could be right and that we were far too late to keep the Torres family from hiding Bonita in Mexico in a maze worthy of Daedalus himself.

Chapter Forty-Nine

At The Docks

Twilight in Monterey is a beautiful time. The bay is much bigger than San Francisco Bay, and from the shore, it is so vast it hardly seems a bay at all, but just part of the great Pacific itself. The town was bustling and colorful. I always loved visiting here both for its scenic loveliness and because it had much of the diverse charm of San Francisco without so much noise and dirt.

That day, though, Cat and I had no taste for scenery, and we had left our singing behind on the trail. We rode straight to the harbormaster's office. A harbormaster keeps a record of ships as they enter and leave the harbor, so I trusted he would know if Miguel had indeed sailed away with Bonita. The office was closed.

"Never mind," I said. "John Gastonberry knew my uncle well, and I was introduced when I was young. I think I know where to find him."

The Badger's Lair was aptly named, being dug so far into a hillside it was practically underground. Just the kind of place you might find a badger if you were foolish enough to go looking for one of the most savage animals nature has to offer. Gastonberry had two haunts, but this was the one where he and my uncle did the most business.

My female presence caused some grumbling when I came through the door, but after all I'd been through at Adelita's I barely noticed. Gastonberry was there, all right, hunched over a glass of amber liquid, engaged in an intense conversation with the man on his right. I stepped between them and signaled Cat to take up a station on his left. Our move confused him. He swung his head left and right.

"Greetings, sir," I said. "We know one another."

"Not to my recollection, we don't," he said. "And you aren't allowed in here anyway, lady."

"I'm Captain William Richardson's niece, sir, or was. You probably remember me as a little girl."

His face turned suddenly kind and receptive. "Why, maybe we do know one another after all. You're not little Bonita, are you?"

"Indeed I am. And this is my partner, Mr. Catamount McGhee."

The men shook hands. "What in the world makes you willing to brave this lion's den?" he said.

"I need only a small bit of information," I said. "Then I will get out of your way and out of the bar and things can return to normal for you and the other patrons."

"Well?" he said.

"We were wondering if Señor Miguel Torres set sail from here today."

"Very strange you should ask about that. Señor Torres keeps a sloop here and uses it from time to time. He certainly expressed every intention of embarking for Manzanilla today. We filled out some paperwork. He seemed in a terrible hurry. He left my office on the run. And yet, at the end of the day, I noticed that the *Rosita* was still moored. I walked over to see if I could help, but she was unoccupied. I suppose he ran into some difficulty or another."

Cat said, "Was there anyone with him that you saw?"

"He had two men with him. Big guys. I assumed they were his crew."

"No one else?"

"Nope." He took a sip of his drink.

Cat and I shared a glance. "Thank you Mr. Gastonberry. Nice to see you again."

As we left, at least twenty pair of eyes followed me all the way out the door.

We stood on the sidewalk outside. It was a clear night with crystalline stars and a half moon. A good night for a search.

"They're still here in Monterey," I said.

"Perhaps the *Rosita* plan was a decoy and they left on another boat."

"Gastonberry would know. I would guess there was something else afoot. Miguel is a man who prides himself on staying in control. If he was so visibly upset, something went wrong with his plan."

"You're having a burst of your clairvoyance and you can feel Bonita's presence or something?" Cat said.

"I would wish it were so, but no," I said.

"So what next?" Cat said.

"We walk, and we ask questions," I said.

"Just wander around?"

"Not wander. Walk with a purpose and a pattern. I know a little about Gastonberry. I don't know what places Miguel frequents. But he's a prominent man. He stayed somewhere. He ate somewhere. He and Bonita."

"Makes sense. Someone should remember. And this place isn't so big that word will get around about us searching, too."

"Something will happen, and we will be ready to exploit it when it does."

"The El Toro is right over there. Good place to start?"

"It's as good as any," I said. I reached over and squeezed his hand as we set out. He smiled, and didn't seem surprised or discomfited in the least.

Nobody at El Toro could or would help, but the bartender said he had a note he was supposed to send to a hotel called The Monastery if anyone else came looking for Bonita. So Miguel suspected we were on his trail. There was no help at the King's Palace Restaurant, but at Malaria Mary's, a couple of very tough-looking gents with searching eyes entered just as we were leaving. We ducked behind a pillar to avoid them. At Misty Point Bar and Grill, the bartender told us Miguel himself had come in earlier looking for a young girl. Just like the El Toro bartender, he'd been given a note to pass on to The Monastery in case anyone else came looking. He said there had been a couple of hard cases with Miguel. Something about the whole situation put him on the side of Bonita's avoiding Miguel and his cronies.

"He's lost her," Cat said on the sidewalk outside. "She must have run away."

"If she's alone, she's in trouble," I said.

It was fully dark now, except for the moon. "Where would she go, Cat? She can't go to restaurants and such. He'll find her."

"Is she wilderness savvy at all?"

"She wasn't raised like I was, so she would have a hard time in the woods or on the beach. God in Heaven, please help us." I lifted my arms and eyes to heaven. A couple of passersby stepped faster as they steered around us. And then I spotted Miguel. He was leaving a hotel two or three doors down.

I pulled Cat's arm, and we ducked back into the Misty Point. We concealed ourselves behind the same pillar we'd used a few minutes earlier. Presently, Miguel walked through the doors and joined the other two men at the bar, where they commenced an earnest discussion. It was getting late. Past my child's bedtime. A wave of helplessness washed over me.

"Now, we'll get it out of him," Cat said. He reached for his bullwhip, but I laid a restraining hand on his arm.

"No, Cat. It will be bad between us if we foil his plan to kidnap Bonita that way."

"No 'if' about it, milady," he said, smiling.

"All right, 'when' we foil his plan. But we must be a little careful how we go about this. Sylvia and I have business connections with him. We will have to live with him to some extent when all this is over. And Flora will still be in Bonita's life. And in ours.

"Miguel himself doesn't care so much about Bonita as Flora does, but losing her will still be a loss of face. A public beating down would make even the simplest conversation impossible in the future. What's more, we've agreed it's doubtful he knows more about Bonita's whereabouts than we do."

Cat seemed disappointed. "We should just follow them, then?" he said.

"Maybe we should go straight to that hotel. The Monastery."

Miguel and his men pushed away from the bar and headed out of the building. They were in something of a hurry.

We waited awhile, then followed. We were still unsure about our next move, but when we saw them turn the corner at the end of the block, we decided to follow after all. Then an old man shuffled past.

"This way," he said in a voice so soft I wondered if I'd actually heard anything. He gave just a flick of a wrist to encourage us to follow. He was Indian, one of the poor blanket-garbed men who eked out a living at various odd jobs till they gathered enough money to drink themselves into oblivion. At least that's what one would assume at first glance. A slim lead indeed, but we had little else, so we trailed after him. His shuffle led us to a sort of alley between a hotel and a dry goods store. Once in the alleyway, the light disappeared so completely that we could not see him so much as sense him as a darker-than-the-dark shape ahead of us. He stopped.

"Stay here," he said. He continued down the alley and out of sight.

"Where are we?" Cat asked.

"I wish I could tell you," I answered.

He wrapped an arm around my shoulders. "Seems like we're supposed to wait."

"So we wait," I said. "This could be some sort of arrangement engineered by those Miwoks from the north I mentioned." That didn't seem possible, given the distance and time involved, but I'd learned that they were capable of things far beyond normal expectations.

"From what you say," he said, "they're ready to help out in whatever way they can."

"I haven't been to the village in years. I should have stayed in closer touch."

A noise. A doorlatch. A pencil of light. A voice.

"Here. Quickly."

In a moment we were standing in the dirt-floored basement of the hotel. A lantern hung from a rafter. Before me appeared a man who to my mind was as close to holy as it is possible to be without a habit or a roman collar. "Octavio," I cried, hugging him fiercely. "Thanks and praise be to my loving God. But why are you here?" I had a guess, of course, but I dared not utter it.

The arrangements between the tribe and my uncle would have been impossible without this humane, mission-educated man who had devoted himself to the welfare of his people. "By the way, this is my partner, Catamount McGhee." He acknowledged Cat with only a nod.

"This way."

The next room was dim, lit only by a kerosene lamp turned low. There was a small table. And a bed. And in the bed under a colorful quilt, my Bonita slept, safe and sound. I dropped to my knees beside her. I hated to wake her, but there was no help for it.

"Bonita, M'hija," I whispered. "It's time to go."

She opened her eyes, had a moment of confusion, then threw her arms around my neck. " Tía. Mamá," she cried.

Cat knelt beside us, and the three of us joined hands.

I looked up at Octavio. "My lips cannot express the thanks in my heart," I said.

"We must be on our way." He smiled as he spoke.

I looked at Cat with a smile of my own, then turned to my daughter. "Come, my sweet one, my Bonita. We're going home now."